REAWAKENING

REAWAKENING

RISE OF MAGIC BOOK 2

CM RAYMOND   LE BARBANT   MICHAEL ANDERLE

LMBPN

DISRUPTIVE IMAGINATION

MAP

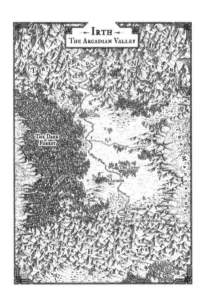

PROLOGUE

Sparks flew around the factory floor like a meteor shower on a clear winter night. The task called for perfect productivity, and if there was one thing that the Chancellor's personal assistant Doyle knew, it was how to get shit done *fast*.

Groups of exhausted workers in dirty clothes rushed in every direction; their number grew every day. The structure of the machine took form before his eyes. He could almost see its destructive potential.

The thought gave him chills.

"Everything is proceeding as planned." Elon, the Chief Engineer had appeared out of nowhere, and his presence made Doyle jump.

Elon was under pressure from the Chancellor to build the machine quickly; it was worse since the heretic and his Unlawful apprentice had taken out a group of their best Hunters only a month earlier. Chancellor Adrien was feeling pressure, and he passed that pressure right on down the line.

"Good. The Chancellor will be pleased," Doyle said, trying his best to imitate his boss's demeanor. "The additional labor is speeding up the process nicely. Any problems on the floor?"

Doyle glanced at the man, whose neat steel-gray cloak matched the bifocals sitting on his nose.

Elon never looked relaxed, but the tension in his jaw had only increased since he had been made Chief Engineer after the untimely death of his predecessor. The job was a significant promotion, but few wanted it due to its occupational hazards. "No problems, sir. Let the Chancellor know that we are on pace to meet his timeline, as long as everything goes as planned."

"As planned?" Doyle asked.

"Yes, well," Elon hesitated, "the workers are men with mouths to feed at home, and are therefore easy to control. They are obedient. But the magicians on the machine, they aren't exactly used to this kind of work. I mean, it is a bit like herding spoiled cats."

Doyle's face tightened. "You better shepherd them *bloody* well then, Elon. You don't want to give another engineer a shot at your position, do you?"

"No, sir." But the engineer's voice lacked confidence.

"That's good to hear," Doyle sneered. In the presence of the Chancellor, Doyle felt like an ant waiting to be stamped out of existence. But overlooking the factory floor filled with desperate men and foolhardy magicians, it was easy to feel the power of the gods.

If he could only keep his seat at the table, he would one day rule at the right hand of a self-made god on Irth.

CHAPTER ONE

Her back to the tree, Hannah felt sweat drip off her forehead.

She wasn't sure if it was pure terror that caused the perspiration, or the heat from the fifteen-foot-tall molten metal monster that was hunting her through the forest. She had never seen anything like the damned creature before. It was like something born of hell and given energy by every Master Magician who had ever walked Irth.

Victory was unlikely, which pissed her off beyond belief.

As the monster advanced, she could feel the ground shake under the weight of its steps. The coolness from the trees' shade disappeared, and she felt as if she were in the baker's oven just off the edge of the market.

Peeking around the tree, she watched the hell-beast advancing.

Twenty feet.

You've got this, bitch, she thought.

Ten feet.

Focus.

Taking just enough time to breathe away the fear and self-doubt, she dove out from behind the trunk and hit the ground in a roll, ending with one knee in the dirt and her arms facing the fiery metal beast. Sub-zero daggers of ice formed in her hand, then launched, landing dead center on the monster's face.

It screamed in anger and pain as it stumbled backward into a large maple.

Hannah tried to capture the advantage. While the creature was temporarily blinded, she placed both of her hands on the ground. She felt the power of the forest flowing through her hands, and she recited a silent prayer to nature.

The tree responded immediately.

Its branches reached down, wrapping around the fire monster.

Hannah smiled, amazed that the old tree had reacted to her and that she actually had this giant thing against the ropes. She decided to finish it off.

She marched forward, working her ice spell again, but this time, as the ice began to appear, she pulled her hands apart. The dagger turned into a spear, and she ran toward the bound creature, ready to plunge the spear into its chest.

But as she neared her target, the molten monster roared in rage. The heat from its fires began to burn the old tree. Its branches loosened, and the monster broke free. Jagged wooden splinters rained down on Hannah, cutting her skin.

She had to shield her eyes from flying shards, which blinded her to the monster's attack as a giant fist swung down at her. She quickly raised her spear in defense, but her spell was no match for the its strength. Its fiery hand smashed her spear and knocked her to the ground.

Still roaring with rage, the hell-monster stepped closer to its prey, slamming its arms into its chest.

"Oh, shit, I think I made it mad," Hannah muttered under her breath.

She tried to crawl backward as the giant advanced. Looking

up, Hannah saw it on almost top of her, fiery fists raised to the sky, ready to end the melee and her life.

"*Ah, hell!*" she screamed.

It was over.

The monster dropped a molten ball of metal in her direction, but just as it was about to send Hannah to meet her mother in the world beyond, it and the monster disappeared in a puff of smoke.

The sound of battle quickly faded into nothingness.

A dry voice echoed among the trees, breaking the silence once again.

"Damn it, Hannah. You need to *focus*," Ezekiel, her mentor, scolded as he walked toward his fallen pupil.

Hannah's heart continued to race. Even though she knew the monster was only a figment of her imagination—a mental spell cast by Ezekiel—it was a damned good one, giving her not only the visual image but also the feeling of scalding flesh and the smell of burning hair.

"I *was* focused. Didn't you see all that magical shit I pulled?"

"Had this been a real fight, that *shit* would have gotten you killed," Ezekiel argued, his face filled with scorn.

It had been a month since the event in Arcadia which forced her to flee the city for good. A group of asshole Hunters had set a trap for her. They had killed her father and tortured her brother to death, expecting her to come along willingly with them in the aftermath. But Hannah was no meek child.

Rage had welled up inside of her, and she had unleashed a passion-fueled magical shitstorm on them. She had destroyed both the Hunters and her home in the process.

It had caused quite a commotion.

Ezekiel had hardly gotten her and her best friend Parker out of the city before the Governor's Guard filled Queen's Boulevard. And teleporting the three of them had nearly wiped the exhausted magician off the face of Irth, but the old man was stronger than he looked, and his well of magic ran deep.

She had been training every day since then, preparing to exact justice from the person responsible for her brother's death. The Hunters she killed were just pawns. Adrien, the Chancellor of Arcadia's magical academy, was her true target. And she was getting better—a fact Ezekiel seemed not to notice.

"Come on, admit it. I did good against that thing." Hannah smiled up at her teacher.

"It's 'did *well.*' And no, you didn't." The old magician cracked the faintest smile. "I mean, that was pretty smart, adapting the ice spell I taught you to make that spear. But seriously, trying to capture a fiery monster in the tangles of a tree, which is, well, *wood*? What were you thinking? The nature magic flowed well, but it's the damned application, Hannah.

"No matter how strong the magic is, you have to mix it with wisdom—or at least some common sense—or it is for naught. You wasted energy and asked the forest to put itself in needless danger. I've told you a million times that nature magic is a relationship. Proving you're worthy of respect matters more than you can imagine. The same will be true when you lead others someday." As he said this, he reached out a hand and pulled Hannah to her feet.

Hannah stood as tall as she could, but her knees were weak. Not from her teacher's chastisement—she was certainly used to that by now—but from the amount of power she had used casting the spells. He was right, and she knew it, even if she'd never concede to Ezekiel. She had to learn how to fight, not only with strength and cunning, but also with wit and insight.

"Well, hopefully I won't be leading people against something like that monster. What the hell was that anyway? Are there really creatures like that in the world?"

Ezekiel smiled. "Not to my knowledge, not in our world anyway. I'm not sure where that particular image came from. Maybe I read it in a book when I was younger."

Hannah brushed dirt off her. "It's kind of hard to take any of this bullshit seriously when I know it is just child's play," she quipped.

"If you can't handle child's play, young one, you won't stand a chance against a minion of the Chancellor, let alone Adrien himself."

"Trust me, if I ever see the Chancellor, I won't miss. In the meantime, why don't you give me something real to fight?" she asked. "There has to be a better use of my magic than fighting your childhood demons."

Ezekiel grinned and planted his staff in the dirt. "Don't wish danger on yourself, Hannah. It will come soon enough. As it just so happens, you'll get your wish. It is time for stage two of your training: an infinitely harder and more dangerous type of magic."

Hannah's eyes widened. She hungered for the challenge. "What are you going to teach me?"

Ezekiel looked down at her. "Infiltration. But this time, *I* won't teach you anything. It's time for you to meet the mystics."

CHAPTER TWO

The house had been reduced to rubble, but Parker still pictured it the way it had been the night Hannah had unleashed the power of the universe on a group of Hunters. She had exacted pure and unadulterated vengeance, and it had been as effective as it was terrifying.

Walking past the ruins of his best friend's house, he was reminded how much he missed her. Hannah had been his partner on the streets for years, hustling for coins anyplace they could find them.

But all that had changed when the Founder returned.

The Founder was an Arcadian legend, or so Parker used to think. The great man of the gods had beaten back the Age of Madness that had laid waste to the old world. Then the Founder had brought magic to Irth, and helped found both the Academy and Arcadia itself. And the way Parker had always heard the story, the Founder had instituted rules dictating who could use magic and who could not.

It was prophesied that one day the Founder would return, rid the world of the Unlawfuls, those who used magic without the Academy's permission, and lead Arcadia into a new era of peace and prosperity in the name of Matriarch and the Patriarch, Irth's gods of old.

Hannah and Parker had thought it was all a scam until the Founder actually *did* show up and made Hannah his student. It wasn't until she had gone with the Founder that Parker started to imagine that she was something more than just the best wingman a street kid could have.

She was his best friend.

This burnt-out shell of a house brought these thoughts to the surface. And then, like every other day, it made Parker think of William.

Parker had always known that the Hunters were some of the most inhumane assholes in Arcadia. They extorted anything they could get from the commoners, and took every opportunity to kill Unlawfuls on sight, even if the official policy was to bring them in breathing—if possible. But the men who had tortured William and Hannah's father for information showed that the city's leadership was more despicable than Parker had ever imagined.

Those men had received their just desserts from the newly minted rogue magician—the Founder had taught her well. Parker pictured the Hunters' bodies torn to pieces by Hannah's magic, and couldn't help but grin. It might take some time, but justice seemed to have a way of catching up with the corrupt. He imagined that it might sweep through the land with the hand of gods.

It gave him hope.

Through the Founder—Ezekiel, he liked to be called—Parker learned that the Matriarch and the Patriarch were real. And that the magic that Ezekiel had brought to Irth in Their name was meant for the good of everyone, not just a special few who lived in the Capitol. Once Hannah completed her training, she and Ezekiel would lead the charge, making real changes in the lives of those who lived on Queen's Boulevard.

Queen Bitch Boulevard, as the locals named it, was the

quarter where the poorest of the poor lived. As Parker walked its rough-hewn streets, it was abuzz with life despite the early hour. This was, for most in Arcadia, the most pronounced change since Hannah had blown up the Hunters. The Governor's Guard and the Chancellor's Hunters marched everywhere looking for Hannah and any other Unlawfuls, and generally making their presence felt.

Parker cursed them all in his mind, but kept his mouth shut. He was trying to keep a low profile. People in the quarter knew he and Hannah had been close, and he was just waiting for the day when someone dropped his name to the Guard for a few coins and a pint of brew. They would do almost anything to catch Hannah and Ezekiel, the top public enemies.

Hannah had begged Parker to stay at the tower in the woods that night, to join her and the Founder, to join the fight. But things weren't that easy.

Her family was dead, all attachments gone, but Parker still had responsibilities. Without him, his mother would fall into squalor and be forced to sell her soul for the sake of survival. In Queen's Boulevard, a son didn't let his mother sell those kinds of goods; not if he could help it.

Parker slowed as he turned the corner by Hannah's house. The Prophet Jedidiah was already on the scene. Since Hannah's blazing display of energy, the old man had moved his pulpit from the Capitol lawn to the ruins of her home.

Old Jed's voice rang out over the crowd.

"Take a good look, brethren. This is the result of magic used unlawfully. Nothing good can come from casting outside of the law. As the Matriarch said, 'My boundaries lie in delightful places.' Do you not know what that means? It means that only ill can come from the unrestrained and unlicensed use of magic. Go on, go on, cast the spells born in your dark back rooms of deceit, and it will be a pox upon your house. On all of your houses."

The crowd murmured. Parker waited for hecklers to shout

the man down, but nothing came. While most of Arcadia used to laugh at the Prophet, the old man had taken on new importance in recent weeks. He had only grown in popularity since Hannah's attack. There was nothing like a crisis to foster solidarity for charlatans and deceivers.

Old Jed continued, "For years, dear followers, I have tried to teach you. The message I brought was one of passivity. I prayed, and I preached, and I asked that all of you use magic according to the boundaries laid out by the great Father and Mother, that those who were not accepted by the Academy would suppress their evil urges. But now I know this is not enough. Passivity will be our ruin in the end. It is time for us for all of us to rise up against the Unlawfuls. To quell the use of the magical arts in their perverse forms, to stop the use of magic in ways that go against the norms of the universe."

The crowd cheered, and Old Jed beamed.

His time had come, and he knew it.

He lowered his voice. "Brothers and sisters, the fight that is before us is not an easy one, nor is it safe. I pause to even consider asking of it of you today. But it is one that is necessary. Now is the time for us to stand against the unauthorized use of magic. Too long have we left the job of justice to the Chancellor's men alone.

"We need to take up the mantle as citizens. No, as lovers of our sweet, sweet Arcadia. Now is the time for us to be true sons and daughters of the Matriarch and Patriarch. They have ordained the Chancellor as their head in Irth, and he shall not be cast asunder. As the Chancellor decrees, so do the gods!"

A shout went up from the crowd. Parker's blood boiled with a vengeance for truth. They all responded so easily to the old man's lies.

"An assault against the Chancellor and his men is an assault against the Matriarch and Patriarch who put him in his position."

Old Jed's arms lifted in the air, and the applause seemed to carry him into the heavens. Something was different, and Parker knew it. Only weeks ago, the man was a farce with a few whacked-out followers, but his infamy had turned to validity overnight. It was as if a switch had flipped.

Parker crept away from the masses who had gathered to hear the false prophet. Parker knew the truth, even if no one else believed, but Hannah would set them all straight soon enough.

Parker headed through the crowd toward Ivan's Square, the only public park in Queen's Boulevard. Usually it was filled with drunks sleeping off a bender or mothers trying to find a spot of grass for their kids to play. But this morning the park was empty save for Eponine, a child well known in the quarter, and the four older Arcadians who surrounded her.

They all wore robes of white and circled Eponine like wild animals ready to pounce on their prey. The little girl, not older than ten, looked scared to death. Her face was white as a sheet.

"We know what you are," a woman named Jez yelled at the girl. "We know you're an Unlawful, just like that witch Hannah." Jez was only a few years older than Parker, and they had grown up together in the quarter. He never would have expected she could be caught up in the Prophet's madness, but these days anything could happen. "Now we just need to know if we should report you or take care of you ourselves. Hunters have enough on their hands these days."

The girl stood speechless in the center of the circle. For a moment, logic told Parker to keep walking. Minding his own business would keep him out of trouble, and that would ultimately serve the greater good. But conscience trumped instinct, and he cut toward the disciples and the young girl.

"What the hell is going on here?" he shouted at the group.

Jez looked at Parker, her eyes as wild as a drunk's on a Saturday night. "Mind your own business, you little twat. We're just doing the work of true Arcadians. Unlawfuls like her need to be taken care of."

Parker glanced over at Eponine and gave her a nod. He wanted her to know it was going to be ok, even if he hardly believed it himself. "Get your damned head out of your ass, Jez. She's a kid. You want to hunt Unlawfuls, that's your business, but this girl isn't one of them. She's just trying to survive in QBB, just like we did when we were her age. You're only making things worse."

The disciples looked at each other, then at Parker, and back at Jezebel. The woman knew she ran the show, and she searched for words. "Of course, you would try to divert our good works, Parker. You and that witch bitch are thicker than thieves. We should bring *you* in."

His eyes sparkled in the face of the threat. "Try it. I dare you."

Word had spread about Parker's toughness since his victory in the Pit. He had taken down Wildman Hank, the most violent fighter Arcadia had seen for some time. Jez didn't want to tempt fate, and he knew it. The disciples backed away and eventually turned to leave.

"Bastards," Parker muttered as they left the park.

Eponine looked up at him, on the verge of tears. "Thank you," she squeaked out.

"You don't need to thank me, kid. It's the least we can do for each other. Shame what those idiots have come to. Since I can remember, people of the Boulevard have had each other's backs, but this is a new day. Didn't think it could get any worse." He grabbed her arm and gave it a squeeze, a mild attempt at comforting the girl. "Where's Randy, anyway?"

The girl looked down. She and her brother, who was half a decade older, were inseparable. If you lived in the quarter, you never saw one of them without the other.

"Working, I guess," she said. "Got a new job in the factories. Trying to go honest, and they were hiring, so he cast his lot and got picked. I haven't seen him for weeks, but coins keep coming to our house by messenger, so I guess he's doing all right."

CM RAYMOND

Parker had heard rumors like this. Apparently, the industrial district was working on something big and they were willing to pay for work, even hiring people from the Boulevard.

The whole thing seemed too good to be true, but Parker had no reason to tell this girl that. Instead, he mussed her hair in big-brother fashion.

"Ok, kid. Keep your eyes open and your head on a swivel. If you need anything while your brother's gone, come find me right away."

The little girl blinked her big doe eyes and ran off into the bustle of the quarter. Parker couldn't help but wonder about her brother's new employment. The factories never hired from the Boulevard, even to do the most menial work. Something was happening—something big, and he was going to find out what it was.

Karl climbed the final steps to Craigston, a small mining town nestled in the Heights. He had cursed the mystics all the way up, as he always did. They had built the winding mountain staircase decades earlier, and they hadn't considered their altitude-challenged brethren when they spaced the steps and set the pitch. Maybe their magic helped them, but Karl had no such assistance.

Just north of five feet tall, the rearick had expended extra energy climbing into the clouds. His trip to Arcadia had been uneventful, as were most of them. Rearick transporting crystals and precious metals to Arcadia hired him to protect them and their cargo from robbers and other nefarious creatures on the road, and most of his trips were a walk in the park.

The pay was good, and, with the state of the mines recently, it was probably safer playing guard than chiseling out glimmering bits of metal to be sold.

Karl's first stop after arriving at Craigston was the mining

14

office, to collect his wages. Walt, a one-eyed man, slid a pile of coins across the table. He was taller than most rearick, but shorter than most of the lowlanders he'd seen on his journeys around Irth. Karl was sure Walt was some sort of bastard son born of rearick and lowlander, but he couldn't be certain.

Karl pushed the coins around on the sticky counter and nodded. His pay was a few coins shy of the agreed sum, but he shoved them into his purse regardless. Everyone knew the mining company shortchanged people wherever they could, and the rearick had all but gotten used to it.

He was one of the most sought-after guards, and it wasn't just for what he could do with his hammer. Karl was smart and easy to do business with. The money was good, and the work was generally easy, but he had been away from the Heights far too much for his liking. He was looking forward to some time off, settling down, putting his feet up, and maybe even getting underground for a few days.

"*Danke*, Walt," he said. "How long till the next run?"

The man behind the counter pushed a finger under his eye patch and scratched the empty hole. Walt hissed a little when he talked. "As a matter of fact, the time is now, rearick. If you're ready, you'll leave in the morning."

"*Scheisse*, so soon?"

"Yeah, Arcadia is pushing us hard for metals and amphoralds. They are paying more than ever, so they had us increase production. The sun is shining, my little friend. It's time to make hay."

Karl nodded at the mention of amphoralds. For years, the things were pushed aside as the rearick dug for precious gems that adorned the houses of the nobles. But a few years ago, orders shifted. The Arcadians had learned to store magical power inside of the once-worthless gem. Now, all anybody ever wanted were amphoralds.

"Ain't no rest for the righteous, eh? That's how the gods will it. The Queen Bitch'll have me working the road for the rest of me days, I guess."

"Listen," the words slithered out of Walt's mouth, "there are plenty of other young rearick who'd be happy to leave the mines permanently. Get an easy job like yours, swinging your war hammer. Just say the word and I'll hand your load off to the next generation. I could probably pay them half as much to do what you do."

"Bull," Karl snapped. "Ain't nobody can do what I do with this." He patted the weapon leaning against his shoulder. The cold steel of his war hammer had spilled its fair share of blood. "But I'll take the job. It's either work or drink meself into an early grave."

Walt grinned. "Early grave, my ass. By my counting, you're already long overdue. We come from the dirt, and the dirt will take us all eventually. No one's strong enough to shake it. Not even someone like you, Karl."

Karl smiled. "When the dirt is ready to take me, I'll welcome her with open arms. But it's not me time yet. I do, however, need the night to rest. Just the thought of climbin' down them stairs again has given me quite a thirst."

Walt nodded. "That's my little man."

"So, the boss is openin' another mine?"

Walt cocked his head to the side. "No. Why?"

Karl laughed. "I've been in that latest hole too much to keep me in the dark, Walt. That line is pretty much spent. Go much wider or deeper, and things might get a bit dicey down there."

Walt shook his head. "Can't start a fresh one, not with these orders coming in. Finding and tapping a new hole takes too much time. The bigwigs in Arcadia are offering premiums if we can get the resources to them fast. The mine, she'll hold. We've done deeper and broader before."

"Sure," the rearick said, narrowing his eyes, "but we've also lost good rearick in mines that were shallower and narrower.

The boss don't know what he's screwing with, Walt. Drop a mine, and no premium from the lowlanders will make up for that time or loss of labor, let alone them fathers and sons."

"Anything else, Karl?" Walt's good eye told him the conversation was over.

"Nah, that's all." He turned to leave, then looked back over his broad shoulder. "Walt, if somethin' happens, it's on ya and yer boss. Make sure ya can live with that."

"You just keep 'em safe on the road, Karl. Leave the digging to me."

Easy to dig when ya keep yer ass aboveground, Karl thought, but he left without another word spoken.

CHAPTER THREE

"Get the hell out of there, Sal," Hannah barked at her dragon. Sal had rolled up into a ball and tried to squeeze himself into her leather bag.

The problem was, the damned lizard wouldn't stop growing.

He had started as a tiny common lizard. Now he was nearly the weight of one of the goats the farmers brought in from outside the city walls, and his wings were getting too big for comfort. When spread, they spanned nearly ten feet.

It was a good thing Sal had learned to fold them neatly over his back. The changes still shocked the poor, awkward bastard. Hannah had tried to assure him it was natural, but both of them knew *that* was a lie. Like a schoolboy in puberty, he'd just have to get through the gawky stage.

Sal hopped off the bed and Hannah continued to stuff her few belongings into the bag. She hadn't brought much when they moved into their little broken-down tower—what used to be called a skyscraper. They had been safe here; apparently Ezekiel had cast some kind of mental magic over their home, a ward that kept it invisible to the eye of a passing traveler.

Or worse, a Hunter.

It had been over two months since Ezekiel, Master Magician and the one Arcadians called the Founder, had noticed her. That day had been both dreadful and fateful. It was the afternoon that she was nearly killed in the streets of Arcadia by the Hunters, with a little rape thrown in to increase the torture before her flame was extinguished.

Hunters were commissioned by the Governor and the Chancellor to find and capture or kill anyone using magic without authorization within the city walls, termed 'Unlawfuls.' Magic could only be used by those licensed through Chancellor Adrien's Academy, and he kept a very close eye on just how many students were allowed through the doors.

At the time, she had thought their accusation that she had used magic was preposterous. Hannah, a girl who had grown up in poverty in Queen's Boulevard—the slum of Arcadia, knew nothing of the magical arts or their use.

Although she hadn't known it, she *had* used magic—or at least it had escaped her control—and that magic had resulted in the temporary healing of her brother's seizures. As a side bonus, it had also transformed Sal, setting him on the path to dragonhood.

The Hunters saw it happen. They had pursued and tagged her, and just as they were about to have their way with the girl, Ezekiel shown up out of nowhere to kick ass—he didn't give a shit about their names.

Except for the one who became "Stump."

Ezekiel would have saved the girl regardless of her innate power. He had returned to Arcadia to find that the city had fallen into despair due to his old student's leadership. Ezekiel trained Adrien himself and had thought of him as a son, but in Ezekiel's forty-year absence, Chancellor Adrien had distorted Ezekiel's legacy and used the gift of magic for his own devices and power.

This was a situation that Ezekiel vowed to set right.

But to do that, he needed to help Hannah realize her potential. At least, that's what he kept saying every day as they trained.

Hannah knew that he was right, although she didn't quite know how far his teaching could take her.

But if the things Ezekiel said were even half true, she was on the road to becoming one of the most powerful magic users Irth had ever produced, and Sal was the proof. Ezekiel had told her that he had never seen anything like her, and the Founder was freaking ancient.

Well, at least to her he was. When she thought about it, anyone twice her age was almost decrepit, so he was close to collapsing, right?

She smirked.

However, if Sal was unique and Hannah was the only person who could cast that kind of magic, then the potential of her rise was also unknown.

But that didn't mean that developing those abilities wouldn't take time. And patience was no longer one of Hannah's strengths —not since her brother had died.

When she was just a beginner on the road to learning magic, her brother had somehow called out to her psychically, and she had felt his pain. Hannah still remembered her fear as she raced back to the city, only to find that she was too late.

Her father was dead, and her brother died in her arms in their home on Queen's Boulevard. Their deaths devastated her, and she took out that devastation on the men who had committed the atrocious act.

After she had lost control, killing her family's murderers and blowing up her house in the process, she and Ezekiel had become the most wanted people in Arcadia, perhaps in all of Irth.

Ezekiel had transported her out of the city, but Hannah barely remembered it. She had stayed in bed for two days afterward. Rage had taken her over, and she wanted nothing more than to raze the city of Arcadia. With the passion that boiled beneath her skin and fueled her access to magic, she might actually have been able to do so.

For the better part of a month, Ezekiel had set her to do nothing but meditate, working to control her anger. He said it would not be wasted—that her meditation would transform her rage into a precision weapon.

Needing to stay and care for his mother, Parker had gone back to the city. He could serve as their eyes and ears on the inside.

The decrepit tower in the woods had hidden them for the time being, but now it was time to move. Ezekiel's plan led them away from this place of safety, and Hannah welcomed the danger. The old magician always had something up his sleeve, though he kept his cards close to his vest. Hannah knew that they were heading to the Heights; she just didn't know why.

With her bag slung over her shoulder and Sal at her heels, she went through the staircase door that had previously remained locked for the entire time she'd lived in the tower.

She had never asked the old magician why parts of the tower were off-limits. As she climbed, the narrow staircase with its winding steps certainly gave no indication.

Perhaps it was only out of convenience, or to keep the girl close.

Six floors up from ground level, Hannah figured it out. The roof was missing from the tower, and the steps simply ended. Hannah pushed through the door and found Ezekiel standing in the middle of an open space that was exposed to the air.

"This is pretty damned cool," she said, looking at the forest. She had never been this high off the ground in her life.

Sal peeked over the edge, but kept his wings tucked in by his side.

"Yes. A shame we need to leave it behind, but I doubt it's the last we will see of the tower—if all goes according to plan. And it looks like we're leaving just in time." The old man stretched a cloaked arm out, pointing to the woods around the tower. Men with the Hunter blaze on their chests walked the land nearby in pairs. "My mental magic could keep a few of them from running into the building, but I can't control them all. Once we leave, the tower will reappear, and they'll have quite the surprise. I imagine they will be rather pleased with themselves until they find the place empty."

Hannah smiled.

Her mentor was powerful, and she couldn't imagine herself doing that kind of magic. But if what he said were true, someday she *would* be able to do it and much, much more. "So, what's this plan of yours have to do with a trip to the Heights?"

The old man's eyes glinted. "It's a surprise, but you need to know this: I can't teleport the three of us all the way there. I'll take care of me and Sal, but you will have to use your own power, with me as your guide."

She glanced off into the distance, toward the mountain range known as the Heights. The trip seemed impossible. She cocked her head to the side. "Forgetting something? You haven't taught me how to do that teleporting thing yet."

"Well, there's no time like the present. Consider this your first lesson. Tell me, do children still ride sleds in the winter?"

"Sure! Although, we have to sneak into the noblemen's district at night to do it. Wealthy Arcadians don't appreciate Boulevard kids like me in their backyards."

Ezekiel shook his head. "Child, there is so much wrong with this world. I pray to the Matriarch you can help me put it right. But enough of that. First, we need to get moving. Teleporting is a little like sledding. Picture yourself sitting on a sled at the top of a giant hill. I'll give you the push. The rest is up to you."

Hannah nodded, but was more than a little freaked out. She wondered if it was possible for her to screw things up so badly that she could end up reappearing on the sun or in the middle of a swamp, but she had come to trust Ezekiel's magic even more than she trusted her own abilities.

She knew that he needed her. The old man wouldn't intentionally put her in the middle of something she couldn't handle, at least not yet.

"Concentrate, Hannah," Ezekiel said, grabbing her arm. "You ready?"

She clenched her teeth and nodded. She felt the wind grabbing her hair at first. Then Ezekiel's grip tightened, dragging her forward.

Then, just as she was about to fall, they disappeared.

Adrien pulled the blood-red hood of his cloak over his head and marched toward the edge of the market quarter. The evening air held a chill, but the cloak also shielded his face to maintain his privacy. He didn't leave the Academy often, and he cursed the need to leave the comfort and solitude of his office tonight.

Adrien resented the filth of the common folks, even if it was his own political machinations that kept them precisely where they were. He was glad of the fact that curfew was near. Most of the people were off the streets already out of fear of the Hunters and the Guard. Thankfully, he wouldn't have to look any of them in the eyes. To Adrien, the people of Queen's Boulevard, and even many who lived on the edges of the market square, were less than human.

They were scum.

But even insects could cause problems. Adrien wanted nothing more than to get the current situation under control so he could focus on the bigger picture.

His machine was almost finished, and it was time to turn his gaze beyond Arcadia. Lack of control of Arcadia could ruin everything. Ezekiel knew how to recruit, especially from the poor and needy, and Adrien was intimately aware of the old man's tactics. As a young boy, need drove Adrien into Ezekiel's arms.

Ezekiel.

Just thinking his old mentor's name sent a chill down his spine. Adrien's power had grown tenfold in the old man's absence; he was nearly invincible. And once his machine was complete, Irth would bow down before him. The old magician was the only one in Irth who might be able to stand in his way.

Ezekiel had been incredibly strong when he left the city forty years prior, and he had come back with powers such as Adrien had never seen, and didn't quite understand.

While the Chancellor had grown in influence and some magical ability, his teacher had clearly focused on becoming the best damn magician he could.

Adrien was tempted to brush it off at first. Even if Ezekiel were powerful, he was just one man, and Adrien had an army. But Ezekiel had proven capable of finding help of his own. That little bitch was powerful, more powerful than Adrien would have given anyone from the Boulevard credit for. Adrien knew that he had to take care of them quickly, or else the old man might be able to build an army of his own.

Adrien was no fool, and he realized that must be Ezekiel's plan.

The Chancellor's policy of restricting admittance to the Academy worked. It had given him unilateral control over the city's wealthiest and most influential. It also left plenty of powerful people out in the general population. That had been fine, since fear kept them from practicing their magic. Death at the hands of his Hunters was a helpful external motivation to keep unlawful magic at bay.

At least it had been, until the return of the Founder.

Adrien assumed that Ezekiel would be searching the back alleys of Queen's Boulevard, looking for the Unlawfuls who might be courageous, desperate, or crazy enough to join his little band of rebels.

But since the day that girl had blown the roof off her house, no one had seen any sign of them. If Ezekiel was preparing for war, he was moving slowly, and that gave Adrien plenty of time to prepare. He immediately set into motion the plan that would weed out Unlawfuls and make all citizens scared enough to keep the power that ran through their bodies untapped no matter *what* Ezekiel promised them.

Twisting through the Nobles' Quarter, Adrien finally arrived at the house he was looking for. He smiled as he remembered it being built so many years before. It had been Saul's house—his partner in building Arcadia. As the city grew, he and Saul had divided the leadership. Adrien, as Chancellor, oversaw construction of the Academy—the best way to train magicians.

Saul took the Governor's seat, and, as soon as the mansion connected to the Capitol had been built, Saul had moved out of this house in the Nobles' Quarter.

His friend's tenure as Governor didn't last long. Saul disapproved of Adrien's strategy of training only the sons and daughters of the wealthy. He couldn't see that by keeping the number of magicians few and connected to noble houses, he ensured that only those who were loyal to Arcadia gained the power of magic.

Over time, their disagreement boiled over into a straight-out feud—one that had ended in Saul's death. While the two had argued heatedly and publicly over the direction of the city, no one ever found any evidence connecting Adrien to the untimely death of his friend.

And no evidence would ever be found. Adrien was careful and powerful.

Once Saul was gone, Adrien had seated a series of Governors who did *his* bidding. Each of them had lasted less than five years. Power corrupts, and there wasn't enough room in Arcadia for two powerful men. Adrien considered doing away with the governorship altogether, but having someone under his thumb to manage things left Adrien plenty of time to handle other problems. Like the one that currently took him out into the streets of Arcadia.

Adrien banged his fist against the door, reconsidering whether or not he should have left the Academy in the first place. Perhaps it would have been easier to have the man to whom he was paying a visit to come to him, but he had decided that was an impossibility; the risks were too great. They couldn't be connected.

If the man were spotted paying a visit to the Chancellor, their ruse would unravel.

"What is it?" a voice said from behind a crack in the door.

"It's me, open up," the Chancellor said.

The door swung all the way open, and a man nearly the Chancellor's age stood with wide eyes. His hunched shoulders straightened. "Sir, I heard you might—"

"Shut up and let me in quickly, before anyone sees me."

The man stepped aside as the Chancellor stormed into the nobleman's home. Carefully decorated with works by some of the best artisans in Arcadia and beyond, the living room looked more like a museum than a family residence. Adrien even spotted a piece from before the Age of Madness. He nodded in delight, figuring that the piece would be his soon enough.

"I need to see him," Adrien spat at the servant, still ogling the city's most celebrated collection.

"The Master is away for three fortnights, which—"

"Not him, you fool. I need to see his guest."

The man's eyes cut around the room as if looking for someone to help him. Finally, he said, "I'm sorry, but it is his hour of meditation. He cannot be disturbed. Very strict rules."

Adrien cursed the man in his head; then his eyes turned as black as onyx. "He will see me *now*!"

The servant's legs visibly shook. He knew that death soon followed when the Chancellor used magic. "Yes… Yes, of course, sir. Right this way."

The servant led Adrien through the twists and turns of the house until they reached the staircase to the basement. Walking through the house brought memories of Saul. He marveled at how the long-forgotten memories of his long-dead friend came rushing back.

A shame, Adrien thought. *We could have been a great team if he had only listened to reason. If he had only listened to me.*

When he stopped at the bottom of the stairs, the shaking servant's face was sheet-white. "I can go no farther, sir. You understand."

Adrien nodded. "Yes, good man. I'm glad you understand who you ultimately serve in Arcadia."

Without a word, the terrified man ran back up to the ground floor.

Adrien tried the knob of the only closed door on the basement floor. It was locked, but he could hear faint voices and what he thought might be laughter from behind it.

Moving back toward the wall, he raised a hand and twisted and turned his fingers. In a heartbeat, a blast escaped his body and blew the doors off its hinges. The sound of splintering wood was mixed with female screams.

Stepping through the door, Adrien saw two women, probably the most expensive hookers working within the walls of Arcadia, scramble for sheets and scraps of clothing. Failing to cover themselves even moderately, they huddled around the man who shared the bed with them for protection.

But no one could save them from the Chancellor's wrath, not even someone as esteemed as the Prophet Jedidiah.

CHAPTER FOUR

A wind, cold and sharp, smacked Hannah in the face when she completed the final jump. They had spent the day hopping from place to place, with Ezekiel guiding her as she learned to trust her magic. It was like falling, but forward instead of down. All it took was a willingness to focus. And a fair amount of magical energy.

This last jump nearly brought her to her knees.

As her stomach straightened itself out, she took in the world around her. She was surrounded by trees and mountains, and suddenly realized that Ezekiel was nowhere in sight. She nearly panicked, thinking she might have jumped too far, but as she looked around she heard voices echoing. Instinct took over and she hit the ground. Peering out over a rock, she saw a group of rearick dressed for the mines walking single-file on a mountain path.

"*Shit*," she thought. "*Where the hell am I?*"

Then she heard Ezekiel's voice in her mind. *Sorry, Hannah. You'll have to make the rest of the trip on your own. Take the path to your left. One's first trip to the temple must be walked. The mystics are a people of long tradition.*

"What's that?" Hannah asked aloud, trusting the old man could hear her. "A tradition of being asshats?"

Just start your climb. Even with just his voice in her mind, she could picture her mentor smiling.

Turning left, she found a course of rough stairs winding up the mountain. She watched them twist and turn until they were finally lost in the clouds.

"Ah...*Bloody hell*," she sighed and began the ascent.

Hannah stripped away her outer cloak before she had even made it to the clouds. Her body had been shaped by the physical training she had undertaken to accompany the magical mentoring.

A magician was a powerful entity, but her intention was to become a battlemage, able to level a man with the power that dwelt beneath her skin, be it magic, muscles, or some combination of the two.

But despite her athletic frame, this climb was no joke.

After climbing for what seemed like forever through the clouds, even her well-defined legs burned—like the fireball she planned on casting at Ezekiel for putting her through this. After an hour, she broke through the clouds and gasped. From this spot, she could practically see the entire Heights. It was like nothing she had ever witnessed.

Range after range spread out, each taller than the last. Hannah had seen artists' renderings of the mountains, but in real life, the scenery was more astonishing than in any painter's execution. Her gaze swept the closest range and found an enormous, ornately-designed building. Its towers and arches were an engineering masterpiece, and the whole thing transitioned into the mountainside as if it had grown there organically.

She immediately knew it was her destination: the temple of the mystics.

She gritted her teeth and finished the journey. As she took the last stair, she found herself looking at what must be the front doors of this mountain monastery. She started toward the doors but then hesitated, suddenly realizing she was well out of her depth. There was no telling what threats lay behind those doors.

But she didn't come here to be safe. She came to learn techniques to kick Adrien's ass.

She lifted the heavy iron knocker and pounded on the wood. The deep sound bounced away into the mountains, but no one responded. She waited for a minute, then knocked again.

"Come on, Zeke," she said, hoping he would answer. But she continued to stand in the shadow of the temple surrounded by total silence.

Focusing her concentration, she tried to reach out to him through her mind. *Ezekiel, you bastard, let me in. I've played enough games.* Still nothing. She thought the communication spell worked, but she was still pretty new at it. She could have made a mistake.

Or maybe Ezekiel couldn't answer. Again, the threat of this place tugged on her mind.

When it was clear that she wasn't going to receive a warm welcome, she turned the knob of the giant oak door and made her way into the monastery.

The entryway was pitch-black, and a tingle of nerves ran down her spine.

Taking several steps forward, she wondered what the hell she had walked into. Hannah spun her arms across her chest and produced two fireballs. It was one of the first spells Ezekiel had taught her, and was still her most reliable.

The fireballs lit the room and she readied them for attack, just in case she would need them.

If the outside of the monastery was impressive, the inside was downright breathtaking, clearly designed to provoke thoughtfulness and contemplation. The tension from the climb and lack of welcome vanished as her eyes followed the supporting columns upward toward a mural on the ceiling.

She had to increase the intensity of her fireballs to bring the art into view. It was a picture of a breathtaking woman with jet black hair and a perfect body.

But her most stunning feature was her eyes.

They were blood red.

Hannah returned to scanning the room. She took in its design as she stepped out of the grand hall and down a dark corridor that led into a small, darkened room. She lifted her fireballs, but they did little to fill the space despite the energy she was channeling into them. It was as if some curse had swallowed the light in the place.

Just as she was trying to increase her illumination, the lights flashed on and nearly blinded her. Shouts rose from the people who were all around her. Instinctively, Hannah spun and launched the fireballs at her attackers.

Just as she released them, she recognized Ezekiel's familiar face. Then she realized that the battle cries were actually a single word: "Surprise!"

A group of robed men and women hit the ground, ducking for cover, but Ezekiel held his ground. He spun his staff, smashing Hannah's fireballs out of the air. Small tongues of flame harmlessly rained down everywhere like sparks from a late-summer bon fire.

The strange group of people looked up from where they cowered and laughed uncontrollably.

"Welcome to the temple of the mystics, young Hannah," a man, not too much older than herself, said as he rose to his feet. "We will be sure *never* to surprise you again."

Hannah turned her gaze from the young man to stare daggers at Ezekiel, whose hands were raised in defense. "You son of a bitch!" Hannah shouted.

He smirked. "Don't blame me! My friends here are particular about the way they welcome people. I warned them about your anger issues."

Her brow knot tightly, Hannah spat, "I don't have—"

"Of course you don't," Ezekiel interrupted. "On the bright side," he shrugged motioning to the onlookers, "this *does* means you're a friend now."

Hannah's anger dwindled, and she cracked a smile—the closest thing she could produce—to join the laughter. "With friends like these," she waved to the crowd around Ezekiel, "who needs the Chancellor?"

The mystics laughed, pleased with her joke, then moved together down the hallway. Ezekiel, a wide grin on his face, gave Hannah a tiny bow and then turned to follow the group. But the young man remained behind.

He stepped forward, still smiling like a child. "It is good to have you here. Any friend of Ezekiel's is a friend of ours. I'm Hadley." He reached out a hand, and Hannah shook it.

On closer inspection, Hannah guessed he was in his mid-thirties. And even in his bulky robes, Hannah could tell he was fit. He had an angular jaw, and his eyes were soft, either because of years of meditation or the pint glass in his free hand. "I imagine you're exhausted. I can show you to your quarters and answer any questions you might have."

"Thank you," Hannah said. "No more tricks today?"

"No more *today*." He smiled and looked at her sideways. "Tomorrow? No promises."

As the mystic led Hannah to the left up a winding grand staircase, she asked him, "So what's the deal with the hazing ritual? Did that have some purpose, or are all mystics just a bunch of pricks?"

Hadley laughed. "Well, I'll let you decide whether or not we're pricks, but our little welcome does serve a purpose—an important one, actually." They reached the top of the stairs and Hadley turned to his right. "First, mental magic is different than what you lowlanders study. Physical magic has its own difficulties, but ours has a way of trying both your mind and body at the same time. The steps are a simple way of seeing what a person is capable of. If you can't make the trip without losing your spirits, you will have a very hard time making it as a student of the mystic arts."

Hannah cringed, wondering if she had shown a little *too* much spirit. But they were on their way to her room, so she assumed she hadn't completely failed the test. "And the second?"

"The look on your face! It was *freaking* priceless. Mental magic is hard. Walking around inside people's inner thoughts is sometimes the most devastating thing a person can do. And we take our magic seriously, I assure you. But rest is just as important as work.

"When we're not meditating and practicing, we're drinking and laughing. And pranks are an awesome way to unwind—to take our minds off things, so to speak. Hell, I haven't laughed that hard for weeks." Hadley laughed and shook his head. "Fireballs! That was priceless. But the old man called it. Ezekiel *knew* you'd come in with fireballs blazing."

Hannah could feel her face flush, and while she was always good for a chuckle, being the object of their laughter didn't feel great.

Just as she thought this, Hadley turned and placed a hand on her shoulder. "No, please don't take it the wrong way. We weren't laughing *at* you. Well, at least not in any sort of mean-spirited way. And once you start practicing with us, you'll understand just how much we all need it to survive, and join in."

She nodded. "Yeah. I get it. So, you've been swimming in my mind since I got here?"

Hadley's eyes narrowed. "Ezekiel said you were clever, but was I really that obvious?"

Hannah shrugged. "Suspicion comes easily for me."

Hadley nodded. "That might come in handy. But yeah, I have been peeking—bad habit, I'm afraid. I, and probably everyone else here too, but don't worry, you'll learn ways to keep us out, or at least choose what we can and can't read. Come on, let's get you to your room. Tomorrow your training starts in earnest. You're going to need your rest."

He opened the door to a room beautifully furnished with handmade furniture. Sal was curled up on the bed awaiting her arrival. Hannah gasped as she stepped in. It was by far the nicest place she had ever stayed in her entire life.

"Holy shit! This room is for me?" she asked, looking into Hadley's green eyes.

He sipped from his pint glass and gave her one last smile. "Yup." He turned to leave, then spun back at the last minute. "Oh, and Hannah, one more thing..."

"What's that?"

"No, I *don't* have a girlfriend—since you were wondering."

He winked and left her alone.

"Quite the meditation practice, Jed." Adrien sneered at the Prophet. "But I have to say, this image makes for a very unholy trinity."

Old Jed laughed, not making any attempt to cover his large naked body. "Ah, I guess my secret is out of the bag, if you will. Even a holy man has passions, and they must be quenched so I can continue my preaching and teaching." Jedidiah grabbed a sheet and gave it a tug, exposing one of the two frightened prostitutes to Adrien's gaze. "These *disciples* of mine have been quite helpful. I'm sure they'd be happy to attend your school. They could straighten out your curriculum, if you know what I mean." The fat man raised his brows and smiled. He squeezed the girl's thigh, and she shrieked in nervous laughter.

The fool, Adrien thought. His anger almost overpowered him. *He should have kept his mouth shut.*

But despite the rage boiling within him, Adrien maintained a calm demeanor. "Ladies, you will have to excuse us," Adrien said, without taking his eyes off Jed. "We have some business to attend to."

The girls grabbed their clothes in their arms and headed for another door at the side of the room.

Jedidiah finally pulled a sheet between his legs, covering the ugly stump that hung there, drooping. He lifted a glass from the bedside table and took a pull before grabbing a small glass pipe. Leaning off the bed, he pulled a brand from the small fireplace and lit the pipe. The burning odor of the imported weed filled the room, and Adrien smirked at the extent of the man's hedonism.

"Care to join me?" Jed asked, holding the pipe out.

To the people of Arcadia, the Prophet was a holy man. A wandering ascetic, fully devoted to the message of the gods. But to Adrien, the man was nothing more than a trained pig.

One who would soon be led to slaughter if he didn't tread carefully.

"I have serious work on my plate," Adrien said. "That shit will only fry your brain."

"Does wonders for my knees, though, Adrien." The man laughed, blowing a plume of blueish smoke into the air over the Chancellor's head. "Now, to what do I owe the privilege? What is so important that it requires you to interrupt my prayers?" Jed coughed, his belly rolling with each exhalation.

The man the people of Arcadia called the Prophet disgusted Adrien, but that was no matter. He was valuable, and Adrien was smart enough not to let his personal opinions about people cloud his judgment.

But that value had its limits.

"You're a damn fool, Jedidiah. I—"

"Well," Jed interrupted, "lucky for me, I'm a helpful fool at the moment. So I will enjoy my time, and trust that the Matriarch and Patriarch will guide me once my luck runs out."

CM RAYMOND

"It's not your luck that has spared you, but my mercy. And it is *my* guidance you should be following." Adrien's voice was level. He didn't need to shout to strike fear into most people. "The only reason I've allowed a parasite like you to live here, the only reason I pulled you out of that shithole you used to call a home and gave you a place in Arcadia, was so that you could keep my people content with the way things are here. You were supposed to remind people that the gods want it this way."

Jed sucked on his pipe, then pushed a perfect stream of blue smoke out between his lips. "And I have," the old man said through a wheeze. "It took a long time, but after the explosion in Queen Bitch Boulevard they're eating out of my dirty little hand. They can't get enough of the shit I'm feeding them, I tell you. I'm doing exactly as I promised, and more."

"But the girl?"

Jed laughed. "Oh, come on. No medicine cures one hundred percent of diseases. There's always going to be one or two that slip past my charms. *You'd* be the damned fool if you didn't recognize that. I'm just one prong of your little plan, and, if you ask me, my prong is working quite fine." Jed glanced at his crotch and raised his eyebrows.

"Well, the one that slipped through your charms has the potential to unravel everything."

"If you ask me, Adrien, the little witch bitch is your fault, not mine. You told me to make up stories about the Founder. You never told me he was real! That girl wasn't a problem until he showed up. How was I supposed to prepare for something like that?

"You and your Hunters should have taken care of both of them long before she became my problem, but you know what? I've made a diamond out of your shitstorm. Since she nearly blew herself and half the Boulevard up, my ministry has only grown. My message is evolving. Instead of a hero, I've painted her as the proof of evil we've needed all along. And the damned people are buying it. They've started policing their own."

Adrien's eyes bore a hole through Old Jed, but ignoring the stare, the Prophet continued, "Pretty soon you'll have no need for your precious Hunters because my angels in white will be ripping people to shreds—neighbors, friends, and even family. If you ask me, you aren't paying me enough, you stuck-up *motherfucker*. Now, if you will excuse me, I have to get back to the Lord's work. Girls!" Jed yelled.

Giggling filled the room as the Prophet's whores ran in as naked as the day they were born. Jumping into the bed, the girls cuddled with Jed, one under each of his big disgusting arms.

Adrien's heart pounded and rage built behind his eyes. It was time for Adrien to let it out. He raised two fingers, and an iron fire poker levitated out of the box of tools by the hearth. The magician slowly twisted his wrist, and the poker spun and pointed toward the bed. Jed leaned in to kiss one of the girls just as the iron poker impaled itself in her throat. Blood spurted from her mouth, covering the old preacher.

The other "disciple" started to scream. Adrien silenced her with a twist of his hand, snapping her neck like a dry twig. She fell lifeless in the pool of her colleague's blood.

"What the fuck?" the Prophet sputtered. His eyes darted around like a cornered rabbit's.

"It's as you said. I'm trying to find a diamond within the shit-storm that is your pathetic life." Adrien's speech remained calm, but his eyes grew as dark as night.

Jed continued to babble. Shock kept his words from making any sense. "But...but...why?"

"No one can know of our arrangement, Jed. *No one*. I figured even a worm like you could understand that. As I see it, their blood is on your hands. Literally. Now, I didn't leave my tower to listen to your excuses or hear your meaningless assurances. You have failed your one purpose, to keep the Unlawfuls in check. But fear not; I am merciful. I have a new plan, one that even someone as incompetent as you can't mess up. Not if you follow my commands to the letter, understand? Otherwise, I'll send you to work in the factory. I know a woman there who would just love to meet you."

Jed swallowed hard. His survival instinct finally caught up with him. "Yeah. I get it. What do you need?"

Adrien smiled. "I need you to make a very public, and very brutal, example of one of the Unlawfuls. Something people can't ignore and won't soon forget. Make them realize just how easy they had it under my Hunters."

"But… The Unlawfuls, they're all in hiding. My angels have been looking, but the fear campaign is working. I couldn't find one if my life depended on it."

Adrien sneered and looked at the dead bodies surrounding the Prophet. "Let's just say your life does depend on it, Jedidiah, but don't be so naive. I don't give a shit about whether they have used magic or not. I just care that you get the job done. It's all in the presentation. The medium is the message, my friend. Got it?"

"Loud and clear," Jed agreed.

Adrien nodded. "Good. And don't fail me again, old man, or it's your body I will be using to send a message."

CHAPTER FIVE

Ezekiel swirled the elixir around the bottom of the crystal goblet. He couldn't have wiped the smile off his face if he needed to.

Lilith, the Oracle, had taught him much about magic, and he'd learned a thing or two on his own since he had seen her last. But sitting in the small den of the monastery, it would have been hard to convince him that the mystics' brew wasn't the most impressive damned magic in all of Irth.

The taste was perfect, and it gave anyone who drank it the best buzz of their lives, but then it went no further. Getting drunk on the drink wasn't possible, and Ezekiel was happy for that fact since he'd been drinking it for hours. Not to mention, he knew that when he awoke in the morning, he would feel refreshed and ready for the day.

Mystics knew nothing of the hangovers that pints of ale in the most respectable of pubs would mete out if one went even a bit too far.

"It's good, right?" Hadley asked from his seat just a few feet away.

Ezekiel looked up and grinned. "Like you even need to ask."

Hadley hosted them, and as far as Ezekiel could tell, was at the helm of the temple while Julianne was away. The last time Ezekiel had visited the monastery, a group of Guardsmen had visited, sent from Arcadia on what seemed to be a diplomatic mission.

Unfortunately, they hadn't gotten a chance to ask anyone anything, because before much diplomacy could proceed, a Guard with an itchy trigger finger had blasted a young mystic from their side of the welcome mat. Ezekiel still wondered if the affair could have been avoided, but he knew it hadn't been what he wanted then, and was still not what he wished he had done now.

He was happy he had been there to take the Guard down.

Ezekiel had been present on his own diplomatic mission. Angry about the state of Arcadia as he found it under Adrien's regime, Ezekiel had teleported to the Heights to ask the mystics for their help. It surprised him to find the mental magicians led by a young, beautiful woman named Julianne, who had taken up the mantle of leadership after the death of Ezekiel's former student Selah.

It was no surprise that the mystics were skeptical about helping Ezekiel with his mission to take back Arcadia. Although wise in all things, the mystics were a peaceful group who preferred the taste of their elixir to the taste of bloodshed.

But after the fighting had stopped and one of the Arcadian Guard lay dead at Ezekiel's feet, Julianne realized that their deed required something from her to keep the Chancellor from bringing war to her doorstep.

The mystic, a true Master, had done what Ezekiel thought was all but impossible. Her power allowed her to look exactly like the dead Guard, down to the number of hairs on his head. It was an impressive use of the mystical arts, and she immediately put it to good use.

She left her peaceful studies in the temple and led the remaining guard back to Arcadia, with a slight modification to his memories. She'd been in the city for weeks, playing the bad guy and spying for Ezekiel.

"How is she?" Ezekiel asked.

Hadley looked up from his own cup. "Julianne? She's fine. Strongest damn mystic I've ever seen."

"Yeah." Ezekiel sighed. "And so young."

Hadley smiled. "Years can be misleading. You of all people should know that. How old are you now?"

Ezekiel smiled. This young mystic was certainly curious. Ezekiel trusted him, but he wasn't yet ready to tell him about Lilith's other powers. "Trade secret, I'm afraid."

Hadley took a large drink from his cup. "I'll try not to pry...much. But I learned it from Julianne. We trained together. Selah had taken a few of us to learn directly from him. We were young—I hardly remember life in the lowlands before Selah found me. I immediately knew that he had called us for a purpose, that he wanted someone to take his place."

He laughed and shook his head. "Sven and I knew it wasn't going to be us, no matter how much we trained. Julianne. She's a natural. Kind of like *your* young student."

Ezekiel stared into his mug and nodded. "Hannah's the most naturally gifted magic user I've ever seen. Her emotions don't hinder her like they do most magic users. They lift her up instead. I'm curious to see how her abilities will develop, especially now that you are helping. It is a shame that Julianne couldn't take part in the training. I taught Selah the arts, and he taught Julianne, but she can use them in a way I never could. You mystics have come a long way in my absence. That magic she's working in Arcadia right now... That's something special."

Ezekiel sipped his drink, letting the smooth liquor play in his mouth. The hundredth taste was as good as the first.

"I have been in contact with her," Hadley said. "Julianne was hoping that she would have seen you back in the city by now."

"Well, actually, that's why I'm here. My plan is to do just that:

get back into the city, but Hannah needs more training. I need you to teach her the ways of the mystics."

The young man laughed. "You downplay your own abilities, Ezekiel, but I'm not fooled. Selah told us stories of the Founder, after all. Why don't you train her yourself?"

"The mystic arts, they're more than just ability. They are an attitude, one that can only develop in a community like this. And, I fear that…" His buzzed mind wandered to Adrien, his student, and all that he had taught him as a boy. "Guess I'm afraid that if I'm her only teacher, I might leave traces. You know, something Adrien might be able to recognize, pick up on. I can't risk something going afoul." He paused a moment, allowing his concerns to coalesce. "The danger is too great."

The two men looked at the fire for a bit, basking in the warmth provided by it and the drinks.

Finally, Ezekiel spoke again. "But there's another reason I brought her here. I need to go away for a while. A few days, maybe a week."

He laughed, but wasn't sure why. "Hell, I have no idea how long. But Julianne inspired me, and I think I've come up with the perfect plan to get Hannah and me back into Arcadia. But first, there's someone I need to find, and I can't take Hannah with me, not on this quest. And leaving her alone so close to the city… It didn't go so well the last time."

Hadley grinned. "We're happy to have her here, of course, but it doesn't seem like she needs a babysitter. She's already *quite* the young woman."

"Hands off my girl, Hadley." Ezekiel winked. "She's more than you can handle."

The host put his hands in the air. "Ah, so you're playing the role of teacher and protective father, huh? Have no fear. She's safe here. I'll teach her what I can in the time that I have. But Ezekiel…"

There was a long pause, and then finally the old magician asked, "What is it, Hadley?"

"Julianne is important to us. She did what she needed to, to protect the Heights. But don't tarry. She is the best mental magician in Irth, but that doesn't mean someone won't sniff her out. Let's not leave her in the lion's den alone for too long."

Ezekiel finished his glass and gently placed it on the table. He considered pouring another, but decided it was time for sleep. The journey would be long and difficult. "I will do my best, Hadley. I ask you to do the same. But there's no guarantee we won't all be thrown into the lion's den before this is over."

———

The smell of eggs and bacon hit Parker in the face as he left his bedroom and headed for the kitchen. Breakfast with his mother in the morning had been a tradition for as long as he could remember, and while their rations had been cut in half due to his dwindling income, he was glad for what little they had.

Although Parker had been hustling in the streets for most of his life, he had been able to keep his mom in the dark as to his actual occupation. But after he beat the odds in the Pit—and a giant of a man named Wildman Hank—Parker's true income source became known. Since then, Eleanor, Parker's mom, had refused to let him try any new cons, but that cut down on their income significantly.

Between her pestering him to become an honest man and the increased presence of the Governor's men in the market, Parker decided it was time to try to move into the legitimate workforce. He had dragged his feet, but necessity had finally caught up with him.

"Factory is hiring," she said as she shoveled more than half the eggs and bacon onto her son's plate. "Mitsy's son just got hired on. He's working all the time, I guess. You should apply."

"Yeah. Thinking about it. Probably go and check it out today." Parker smiled, but the prospect didn't excite him.

While he knew that a lot of the men from the Boulevard had accepted these new factory jobs lately, his con artistry afforded him maximum freedom. For very little work, he could procure the same kind of wages that Hewitt, Mitsy's son, likely made in a full day working a mindless job on the line.

But taking care of his mother held priority. And if he got made by the Guard? Well, it was likely that things would go badly with him, especially with the city still on high alert since Hannah decided to avenge her brother's death and took out almost a city block in the process.

"Really, Parker, a smart boy like you shouldn't be out stealing from people. You should be putting your mind to work." She tapped her finger on his temple and smiled.

"Thanks, Mother, but you know working in the factory is nothing more than being a monkey for the Capitol. I just want to—"

"Oh, you would move up fast. In a few short months, you could be a manager or something. Now *that* would make your poor father proud."

Parker watched his mother's eyes turn glassy; he had hoped he could get out of the house without another round of tears.

His father had gone out to find his fortune years ago. And like so many of the Arcadians who left the city walls for glory or riches, he had never returned. Parker knew he was long gone, either by the hand of another or of his own choosing. Regardless, trying to convince his mother of this never ended well.

She would take the hope of her husband's return to her grave. Everyone in Queen's Boulevard had their own way of getting through the day in their dismal existence, and he couldn't blame her for it.

"I'll go check it out today. I promise."

"Good," she said, smiling up at her son. "Now eat your breakfast. I swear you are nothing but skin and bones."

By the time Parker made it to the market, the place was jam-packed. With the curfew still in effect, people couldn't wait to get back out on the street after a long night holed up under the watch of the Guard.

"How's it hanging, Parker?"

"A little to the left," he said with a grin to the man selling cheese from a cart in his normal spot in the square.

Arcadia welcomed the farmers from outside the walls into the market each day, although they required a significant cut for the space. Stan, a short and stout farmer with a beard that creeped dangerously close to his eyes, could have almost been confused for a rearick, one of the sturdy miners from the Heights. But he'd been in the lowlands so long that everyone just assumed he was from a short lineage.

Parker leaned against the cart and took in the crowd. "How're sales today?"

"Un-freaking-believable."

"Really?" Parker was surprised. Everything seemed tighter since Hannah's run-in with the Guard. He had thought everyone was suffering, but maybe it was just him. "What's up with that?"

Stan looked over his right shoulder, then his left. In whispered tones, he said, "Dunno if it's true or not, but there's a lot of talk. Shit, you haven't heard it?"

"Heard what?"

"People are getting scared. With the curfew and increased security, folks are nervous something big might be on the horizon. Had some old broad, a noble, come up to me yesterday—bought all the cheese I had. Asked me to roll the whole damn cart right down the lane to her precious little mansion. People are legitimately freaking out. Well, not out loud, but they're sure acting like a storm is coming."

Parker looked around the square. The cheese-seller wasn't wrong.

"Those kinds of rumors aren't bad for you, though, are they?" Parker asked.

"Hell, no." Stan laughed. "Charged that old cat three times what I'd charge one of our people."

Parker smiled. "She can afford it."

"Damn straight."

As Parker opened his mouth to ask if Stan had any work for him, a commotion rose across the square. Parker craned his neck to try to see what was going on.

"I'll catch you later, Stan."

The man nodded as Parker made his way across the broad, crowded square. As he pushed through the throng, he heard people saying all kinds of things.

"Serves 'em right. They've been warned."

"What the hell has this damned place come to?"

"About time someone took justice into their own hands."

Parker waded through the crowd, pushing toward the featured attraction. A sick fear gripped his chest as he broke through the final row; what stood before him made his stomach turn. An old woman, was tied to a pole held up straight by a pile of rocks. Her lifeless head hung limp. Around her neck hung a sign, scrawled in foul, jagged letters: **Unlawful**.

Across from her stood a group of the Prophet's disciples, satisfied looks on their faces like they had just seen a miracle. It wasn't hard for Parker to figure out what happened. The Prophet had been preaching for weeks that Unlawfuls needed to be wiped from the city.

His disciples had decided to take him at his word.

"This is the will of the Founder," one of the disciples yelled.

"The will of the Matriarch and the Patriarch. Their wrath will punish all Unlawfuls."

Rage churned in Parker's gut. The fact that they could do something so sick, and in the name of Ezekiel? It made him wish he had Hannah's power.

He would show *them* the Founder's wrath.

But as he turned back to the martyr on the pole, Parker realized it was Miranda, the tiny healer from the Boulevard. The woman probably had no real magic to speak of, but she worked with herbs and medicines in order to help others. Parker had known her his whole life, but seeing her like this, she was almost unrecognizable.

Parker convinced himself that anger must wait. For now, justice required a different approach.

He loosened the cloak from around his neck and stepped boldly out from the crowd. People began to whisper as he climbed the pile of rocks and draped his cloak over her, covering the woman's broken body.

The murmurs from the crowd turned to shouts as they realized what he was doing; their voices blended into an inaudible cacophony. His mind raced. He knew it was risky, that this could be the act that got him taken to the cells.

But he didn't care. Something had to be done, and if no one else would do it, he would be the one, whatever the cost.

As he untied the woman's arms, he was joined by another citizen, someone familiar from the streets of Queen's Boulevard, and then another.

They helped him take her down from the stake. As gentle as a new father, Parker gathered Miranda's body in his arms. He walked through the crowd with his burden, in a daze. A man stepped into the path the others had cleared and spat in his face, screaming, "Unlawful." But Parker pushed through without a glance behind him.

Once back on the Boulevard, he lowered her body to the ground and slumped down beside her.

Looking up, he found a group of people of all ages staring down at him. He waited for the stoning, but instead they all nodded their approval, tears glistening in their eyes.

Miranda's brutal murder was the single greatest act of hatred that Parker had ever witnessed. The fact that most of the city stood by and did nothing filled him with a pain he had never before experienced.

But this small group of people in front of him, they knew that evil had been done here today. Hints of goodness still existed in Arcadia. Parker knew he would find them. And when Hannah returned, they would stand by her side as she purged the true unworthy from Irth.

CHAPTER SIX

Hannah's dream was cut short by the hissing of dragon's breath —*literal* dragon's breath.

She waved a hand in front of her nose.

Opening her eyes, she pushed Sal away. "Just a bit longer," she begged her beast, but Sal wouldn't stop clawing at her blankets. Hannah finally relented. "Ok, ok."

As Hannah rolled over to dislodge the dragon, she found a young mystic girl standing over her bed.

"Oh, hey. Yeah, not creepy at all. You do this with all your guests?" she asked, trying to rub the sleep out of her eyes.

The girl's eyes cut to the dragon and back to Hannah.

"Don't worry," Hannah remarked. "This guy's harmless." She pushed Sal off the bed and swung her legs over the edge. "What's up?"

"I'm sorry to wake you, but that thing was going to attack me."

Hannah laughed. "No problem, and really, he's kind of a scared little douche with wings."

The girl knitted her brow in confusion.

"Don't worry about it."

She nodded. "Ok. I drew a bath for you," she said, pointing to the bathroom the next room over. "And set out some clean robes for you to train in."

"Perfect," Hannah declared. "I haven't had a bath since… What year is it?"

The girl laughed, scrunched her nose, and left.

Hannah stared at the door as it closed behind the girl. *I should lock that thing,* Hannah thought.

Although the young mystic girl didn't seem like much of a threat, Hannah was concerned that anyone could sneak up on her while she was sleeping. She climbed out of bed and found that its lock was missing. Instead, she grabbed a chair and propped it underneath the handle. "That should work," she said confidently to herself.

Turning around, she looked down at Sal, who had curled up in the warm spot on the bed she had just vacated. "Traitor," she said, but the large lizard didn't open his eyes or seem to care.

Walking past the bed and her sleeping pet, she entered the large bathroom that adjoined her room. There was a floor-to-ceiling mirror, and Hannah took herself in. She *was* a mess.

Bathing wasn't a high priority on the Boulevard, and she had been so focused on her training ever since she left that cleanliness and hair care really hadn't been a priority. But as she looked at the large stone tub full of steaming water, she thought, *Maybe I've been missing something.*

Hannah stepped out of her dingy clothes and into the bath. The water was nearly scalding, and all joking aside, she literally couldn't remember the last time she took a hot bath in a real tub. She slid her body down into the water and let the bubbles tickle her nose before she eased her entire head beneath the water. The heat stung for a moment, but then the simple pleasure of warm water soothed her tired body.

Apparently, the Heights were going to be the oasis she needed in the midst of her desert existence. All that was missing was a glass of the mystics' elixir, though she wasn't sure if it was their custom to partake before the sun was fully up.

She laid in the tub for an eternity and didn't even consider getting out until the water started to turn from hot to tepid, but she could only escape from life for so long before getting bored.

It was time to go to training.

She stood and let the water drip from her skin. The cool air in the room made her shiver, goosebumps danced on her bare arms, and she reached for a towel. But there were none, nor was there a robe. "Shit," she said gently, still smiling from the soothing bath.

Being careful not to slip, she stepped out onto the cold stone floor and looked around the bathroom. Still nothing. Even her old clothes were gone.

Thinking she might have left them by the bed, she walked out of the bathroom, but instead of her clothes, she found Hadley standing right in front of her.

"*What the hell*, you perv?" Hannah stepped back in shock and tried to cover all of her most private parts with her arms.

Hadley stared at her as if Hannah were the only thing in Irth. His eyes were completely clouded over in a white haze. "Good morning, Hannah. Just so you know, while there isn't a strict dress code here at the temple, we do recommend not running around naked like a drowned rabbit." A smile cut across his face.

"Screw you. Where the hell are my clothes?"

"You need *my* help to get dressed? Ezekiel told us you were a powerful magic user."

Hannah's face burned, more from anger than embarrassment. She looked over at Sal, who was still sleeping. *Strange that he would hiss at that little girl, and yet let Hadley come in without so much as a peep.* Turning back to the mystic, she said, "I haven't learned your mental shit yet, douche nugget. Now, give me a towel or something before I wipe that twisted smile off your damn peeping-Tom face."

Hadley crossed his arms, but his smile never wavered. "Tsk, tsk. Idle threats will do you no good in the Heights, my dear."

Hannah dropped her hands, no longer concerned with modesty. Instead, she turned her palms toward the ceiling, drawing two small fireballs from the Etheric. "Trust me; there's nothing idle about me. I don't make threats, only promises."

Hadley nodded, his smile widening. "Good. You *are* a magician. And now that you have magic on the brain, let's get to work. Physical magic is a powerful ally, but don't let it be your crutch. You won't always be able to blast shit and walk away with a smile on your face."

"It's worked for me so far. Want me to prove it?"

Hadley laughed and shook his head. "Is violence all you know? Lowlanders are so damned crude."

"Me? You're the one sneaking peeks at naked strangers."

Ignoring her, Hadley said, "Try this." He closed his eyes and spoke a few words in a strange tongue. His simple white cloak turned to a suit of leather armor.

Hannah let the fireballs extinguish. She would have more than enough time for retribution once she was dressed. She focused inward and tried to mimic the words of the mystic. Nothing happened.

"The hell?" she yelled, as she looked down at her still-bare skin.

"Don't just copy me," Hadley said. "Make it your own."

She closed her eyes and tried again, pushing any inkling of the man looking at her naked body out of her thoughts. A short phrase sprung to her mind, and she let it out. It was similar to the mystic's, but not quite the same.

Her eyes opened, flashing red, and she looked down to find herself covered by a dark brown robe. She ran her hands over it; the fabric was coarse to the touch. Even though she knew it was an illusion, simply a product of mental manipulation, the magic was so good that she had even convinced herself that she could feel it.

"Yes!" she shouted. "Take that, you jerk." But when she looked up, Hadley was gone. She looked around, ready for some other trick, but the room was empty. That's when she noticed the chair had remained in place, blocking the door.

Hannah quickly moved to it and threw it aside. Before exiting, she yelled back at Sal, "What good is having a dragon for a pet if he won't even protect me from peeping Toms?" The lizard opened his eyes, cocked his head to the side as if she were acting like a lunatic, and then went back to sleep.

Deciding to deal with her useless dragon later, she left her room to hunt down her perverted host.

She had some anger that needed a target.

The second jump landed Ezekiel at the border between a forest and an open field. He leaned on his staff as he took in the landscape. It would do for a camp that night, not that he had much choice in the matter. The place he was heading, or at least thought he was heading, was too far to make in another a jump or two.

Already two days away from the Heights, he thought that perhaps this would be his last place to camp. He didn't like being away from Hannah for long, although he trusted that she couldn't get into too much trouble with the mystics.

Gods, he hoped not. She could be surprising in all of the best —and the worst—ways.

Closing his eyes, he focused on his surroundings. As far as his magic could tell, there were no humans in the area. Although the art of the mystics wasn't his strongest, he could still connect with humans over significant distances. He then held his staff high and spoke with nature.

The nearby wildlife all seemed friendly, save a black bear wandering a hundred yards off. Ezekiel connected to the bear and suggested it keep its distance. With that, he leaned his staff against a giant white pine which was surrounded by saplings, and readied the camp for the night.

Sweeping his hand back and forth in front of him, he gathered a pile of dead branches as if he were wielding an invisible rake.

The dry pine would serve him well. The branches would give off little smoke to draw attention, and the smell was a delight. Not to mention, they were easy to light—not that setting things on fire had ever been an issue for Ezekiel.

With a twist of his hand, he made a small fireball which he dropped into the pile of sticks, instantly setting it ablaze. He dragged a few larger branches over by hand, because it still felt right to do some of the physical labor in camping, then cut each one to size using magic.

His stomach growled. He would need food soon enough, but first he wanted to sit and enjoy the campfire. Reaching into his leather bag, he pulled out the wineskin given to him by Hadley. Uncorking it, he tilted the vessel and drank some elixir.

With the sun setting to the west, the fire crackling, and the mystics' drink warming his belly, Ezekiel wondered why he didn't camp more often just for the hell of it. He was sure it was because camping had always been connected to utility for him and his family, and often enough to terror.

Camping was a way of life when Ezekiel was a child. He had been born in the Age of Madness, a time when chaos had reigned throughout Irth. By luck, chance, or providence, both of his parents had survived the early days.

But the cities of the old world were falling fast to the disease that had spread throughout Irth. At first the humans had gathered into cities, believing it would be the best defense to be among other healthy people to help ward off the zombies as they turned from normal to ravenous. But in those days, the cities had contained their own dangers.

One of which was a hate for all things paranormal.

The alien technology that had spawned the Age of Madness also gave Ezekiel, and the ones that came after him, access to magic. But those living during that dark time had no way to fathom the power running through their own blood. And when Ezekiel started manifesting his paranormal attributes, Plimstown, the little community he had been born in, freaked out.

Red eyes tended to frighten most people, after all. His parents had no choice but to flee. It was either that or let their young child die at the hands of the paranoid neighbors surrounding them.

The trek had been fierce and long. A few friends and family had left with them, willing to risk their lives to protect young Ezekiel. Many of them proved their love with their blood. None of them knew exactly where they were going, but every day they stumbled toward a mythical place that they hoped and prayed would be real.

Ezekiel's parents were hunting for Archangelsk.

The little group spent many nights sleeping in the woods or hiding out in abandoned houses in the countryside. It was a quest of its own, and one that they all knew perfectly well might end in naught. But they followed the legend, meeting both friend and foe along the way, and finally found the city they had heard about for most of their lives.

Out in the far reaches of Siberia, they settled into a community they thought was a myth, complete with creatures from fairy tales.

Ezekiel was raised among Weres and other creatures that most folks during the Age of Madness didn't believe existed. He never questioned these creatures, and he grew up counting them as friends.

But the most fantastic of all was the Oracle, Lilith.

It took a long time for Ezekiel to understand the Oracle, and if he were honest with himself, he still didn't comprehend her completely. She would dance in his mind throughout the days of play, and once he was nearing his preteen years, she started to teach him magic, and about the Matriarch and the Patriarch.

Leaning back against the trees, he let the buzz wash over his body and pretended he was there, sitting by the fire with his father and mother once again.

Hannah sprinted down the winding staircase and past a few rooms filled with meditating mystics. They were all sitting in weird poses or chanting strange phrases, but she paid them little mind. Finally, she turned a corner and found Hadley standing by a giant fountain in a room surrounded by glass. The ranges of the Heights were visible, illuminated in reds and yellows by the rising sun.

She ignored the view and stormed toward him.

"Impressive," he said. "You figured it out faster than I—"

Hannah landed an open-handed slap on the side of his face before he could finish his words. The snap of skin on skin echoed around the room. "How dare you teleport into my room when I'm naked? Ezekiel told me you were good people, but you're a sick freak."

A red mark spread on his face, but his smile remained. "I'm a mystic, Hannah. Teleportation is a gift of physical magic. I don't know how to do it."

"But you were there, then gone, and my room was still locked. I saw you there."

He laughed. "That was only an apparition—a casting of my mind. You only thought I was there. Sure, we could interact and talk; you could have even reached out and touched me, if my work in your mind was good enough. Just like you can feel that robe on your skin right now. But that is all. You didn't really see me, and I didn't really see you."

"You mean you couldn't see my..." Hannah left her question hanging in the air.

"Couldn't? No, I could have," Hadley responded. "But I didn't. Hannah, I came to the temple to study the mystical arts. My training has taught me to question the cosmos, to unravel the known universe and create it anew, to travel the stars with my mind. I didn't come here to sneak a peek at naked young ladies, beautiful, though you are."

Hannah took a breath. Her heartbeat regained its normal rhythm. "Then why the hell did you freak me out like that? I'm getting pretty damn sick of your hazing rituals."

Hadley laughed. "I assure you, this was no game, certainly not one at your expense. Your mentor told me that we don't have much time. He also said that you are more than a little pigheaded, so I thought you needed something to jump-start your training. Seems it worked."

"A short cut," Hannah mumbled and looked aside, a little red showing in her own cheeks.

"Precisely. And you performed splendidly, although I do hope you don't hit me again. It *does* seem that you could have made something a bit more comfortable than that burlap thing." Hadley nodded toward her robe.

"It just happened like this." Hannah looked down at it. "This is crazy. Looks and feels real, but I guess it's only an illusion."

Hadley shrugged. "It's all in how you look at it. You're right that it's not real in the usual sense, but perception is a powerful thing. People's senses tell them what is real and what isn't, so if you can feel it, see it, and if it does the job it was intended for, then what's the difference?"

Hannah smiled. "Well, for one, I'm freezing my tits off. This imaginary robe doesn't do much to keep the mountain draft out."

Hadley laughed. "Yes, there's that."

"Wait. You're all just walking around here naked all the time?" She glanced over at a set of mystics standing in front of the enormous window that overlooked the mountain range.

"Of course, not, but you wouldn't know if we were." He raised his eyebrows at her. "There are real clothes waiting for you back in your room. Go get dressed. After breakfast, we'll continue your training."

"Ok, but no more tricks," she grumped and turned around.

"Hannah, tricks are what whores—"

"I know, I know," Hannah sighed, calling over her shoulder, "tricks are what whores turn for money. Ezekiel loves that line, too."

───────────

Nearing the bottom of the wineskin, Ezekiel decided he should save some for the supper that the growling in his gut told him was long overdue. The sun had set, leaving only his fire to light the camp.

The magician cupped his hands and moved them as if he were feeling the surface of an invisible ball. His eyes glowed red, and between his hands a perfectly round blue orb lit. It glowed with a faint light only he could see. He tossed the orb in the air and nodded as it levitated precisely where he wanted it.

With adequate light, he went about seeking his dinner.

At the edge of his camp, where the light from the fire met the darkness, he sat cross-legged and began to meditate. He placed his hands on the ground, and the connection to the surrounding natural world flooded over him.

He could sense every living thing in the proximity. His thoughts became a prayer, and within minutes, a rabbit hopped out of the darkness and scrambled into his lap. Ezekiel petted its head and sensed its heartbeat, which was many times faster than his own.

It is said that many of the druids, the Masters of nature magic, had become vegetarian decades ago. Even this was difficult for some, as the connection to flora was just as strong with that of fauna.

But most of the forest dwellers realized that death violated no bond. There was a certain balance between them and the animals who also acknowledged the relationship, including the roles each played.

The druids certainly gave to the creatures, and the creatures gave back, even while realizing that some of them would offer their bodies as food for the magicians.

"Thank you," Ezekiel said to the rabbit, "for offering your life as a sacrifice to sustain mine. I will not soon forget you."

The little creature sniffed the magician's hand and then rolled over onto its back, offering the wizard its neck. With a swift twist, Ezekiel ended its life and then set to work preparing its meat for his dinner.

With a full stomach and a thankful heart, Ezekiel extinguished the fire for the night. He swiped his staff in the direction of the smaller pines in his camping area and they did his bidding, each bough weaving into the others to create a roof of branches and needles that would keep out even a heavy rain. Unfolding his blanket and camp pad under the newly constructed shelter, he settled in for a night's sleep.

Tonight was peaceful; tomorrow night would not be. The next jump would take him close to his final destination, and he was going to need all the rest he could get for the fight that was waiting for him.

CHAPTER SEVEN

The jump to the northernmost reaches of the Arcadian Valley required less energy than Ezekiel expected. Nevertheless, he took the morning to rest on the lip of a grassy hill, looking down on a small castle surrounded by lush green farmland.

Sitting just outside of the city of Cella, the castle was built to resemble the country manor of some long-dead duke who had ruled the region in the days before the Age of Madness. At least, that's what people said.

But its perfect lines and the fact that the place was still standing were a testimony to the fact that its resident had erected the castle within the past four decades—and proved that the person who had commissioned the building was a very rich man.

From his vantage point Ezekiel could see people walking about, tending the rows of crops. There were servants in the yard surrounding the mighty home, likely hanging the wash and performing other outdoor chores. It was an idyllic scene, but Ezekiel knew that the peaceful demeanor only went skin-deep. There was evil here, and Ezekiel had come to rectify that.

Feeling his strength returning, Ezekiel stood and headed down the hill toward the manor.

The castle workers glanced quickly up at him and then back down at their tasks. Ezekiel risked a wave, but received no reply. It was as if they were afraid of him. As he passed the laborers, everyone looked worn out. A few appeared to be at death's door.

Their master was a cruel man, and his neglect was obvious. They were malnourished and overworked.

"Excuse me," Ezekiel asked a young man pushing a wheel-barrow full of produce. "Could I—" The young man passed him without a second glance. Ezekiel approached a few other labor-ers, but they all responded like skittish cats. "Will no one speak to me?" Ezekiel finally shouted in frustration.

In response, a stout woman with a face that had seen plenty of trouble stood up from her spot tending a garden and approached. She wiped her hands on her apron and bowed low to greet him.

"You'll have to forgive the others, sir. We don't get many strangers here. The Lord of the house doesn't allow it, but he's away for the day in Cella. Is there something I might help you with?" she asked, forcing a smile.

Ezekiel returned the expression. He knew that if this woman were talking to him against her Master's orders, then proffering her hospitality was quite a risk. "Thank you, ma'am. But that's an unusual expression, 'the Lord of the house.' Funny, where I am from, Lord has a very different meaning."

The woman's sharp eyes narrowed, her brow knit. "How do you mean, sir?"

"The only Lords I have ever known are the Matriarch and the Patriarch, but I am from a long way from here. Perhaps you've never heard of them?"

A look of pride filled the woman's eyes. She stood just a bit taller. "We know of the Mother and Father here, sir. All blessings come from Them—and all *true* justice."

Ezekiel nodded, his smile softening. "Truer words have never been spoken. But since you are familiar with them, you'll under-stand my confusion. They have clearly blessed this land," Ezekiel swung his arms wide, pointing to the prosperous farm, "and yet all of you look ill-fed and uncared for. How someone could dare call themselves a Lord, compare themselves to the Matriarch and Patriarch, and yet treat their workers like this? It is beyond comprehension."

The woman's eyes squinted in suspicion. She looked Ezekiel over, assessing the strange man who had wandered into her life. "You really must be a stranger to these parts, sir. This is the way it has always been. The powerful eat plenty, and the rest of us are forced to make do. But we're tough. And we've put up with far worse than a little hunger." Her eyes turned cold as they looked off into the distance, remembering some pain or trauma.

Finally, she snapped back to attention. "But forgive me, sir. It isn't right to talk about one's Lord… I mean, one's Master, that way."

"But why?" Ezekiel asked. "Why put up with these conditions? You could leave, find work elsewhere. Find someone else to serve."

She looked up, anger now replacing suspicion on her face. "It's been tried. Those who run and are caught are beaten, sometimes even killed." She shook her head. "Not worth the chance. And if someone did run and made it to freedom, the rest of us would pay. No one wants anyone else's blood on their hands. Liberty is a fiction in this part of Irth."

"Not for long it isn't," Ezekiel said through his teeth. He nodded good day to the lady and walked with haste back up the hill away from the manor. A dark storm cloud began to form overhead as he worked out his plan.

He would show this place the Matriarch's justice.

Adrien stood at the bottom of the steps outside the Academy's main building. His tower stretched into the heavens behind him.

The beginning of the new semester was only days away, and he could already feel the energy, both magical and mundane, buzzing around the campus.

Each fresh semester was invigorating for the Chancellor, and the initial days, when the first-years were invited to arrive early, were especially exciting. He would keep his eyes open, scouting those that would be future Hunters, teachers, and engineers. They were all pieces in his game, to use at his will.

With the development of his weapon ramping up, he and Doyle had agreed to admit the largest class the Academy had seen in decades. Although apprehensive about opening the doors so wide, Adrien knew they would need the workforce since more and more young magicians were burning out in the lower levels of the Academy.

And he was confident that he could keep even this large a group under his control.

One such first-year saw the Chancellor standing there and stumbled up to his side. "Hello, sir…um…Chancellor. It's good to be here. You're thankful that I decided to take a chance on you…" Adrien raised an eyebrow, and the kid flushed. "I mean, you took a chance on me…you know."

Adrien nodded. The new students could be so pitiful, and he wondered if this one should have been admitted, even if he did enjoy the fact that the kid was clearly afraid of him. There was something familiar about the boy that Adrien couldn't quite place.

"You're here on your merits," Adrien said with a thin smile. "And if your potential doesn't manifest, you will be out as quickly as you entered."

"Yes, of course, sir."

"Run along. You should be at orientation."

Adrien watched the kid scramble up the stairs and into the main building. It took only a second to realize why the new student was so familiar. His name was Gregory, and he was the son of Elon, Adrien's new Chief Engineer. Adrien was glad that Elon's son had been admitted. He would keep the kid close. If the Chief Engineer failed him, Gregory would be a useful tool for applying some pressure—or punishment—to the man.

But so far, Elon had accomplished everything Adrien set him to, and his final project was less than a month away from completion. If the boy, Gregory, was even half as talented as his father, Adrien could find some use for him.

As the quad quieted, Adrien turned back into the building that housed his office and his home. Walking the pristine marble floors in the long hall of the academic wing comforted the man.

With the shitstorm that was going on in and around Queen's Boulevard, he found solace in his ivory tower, as if the world outside had never existed.

Intent on making his way back to his office in the tower, he almost forgot his true reason for coming down in the first place. He changed his course and headed for the Dean's office. He'd put off the meeting too long, and with the new recruits now filling the residence halls and classrooms, it was high time to have the talk.

"Come in," the Dean's familiar voice called after Adrien had rapped on her door.

Adrien stepped in and stood quietly as the Dean held up a finger indicating that the visitor should wait. She was reading a large book, completely engrossed by its words. Turning a page, she looked up and jumped in surprise, seeing the Chancellor and regretting the fact that he had been kept waiting.

When Adrien had accepted Amelia to the faculty, she was a bit of a token hire. He knew that appearances were seventy-five percent of the battle. A woman on the faculty looked good—made him seem inclusive—which would help him silence some of the grumblings he heard from the other nobles.

But her good looks weren't just representative. There were

plenty of attractive women in Arcadia, but Amelia stood above most.

She was in her forties, though she looked a decade younger. With shocking blue eyes, blond hair, and her height—she was taller than most of the men on the faculty—she looked like she was from the land to the north, beyond the borders of the Arcadian Valley, if the stories about the northern people were true.

Although she had been hired as the token female in their ranks, her gifts extended beyond her gender. She was whip-smart, a fast learner, and a better teacher than Ezekiel himself. Due to all of this, and the fact that Adrien trusted her as far as he trusted anyone, Amelia had quickly climbed the academic ladder and now ran the school's day-to-day operations as Dean.

It took her out of the classroom, which was a loss, but he had bigger plans for her.

"Shit. Sorry, Chancellor, I didn't know it was you. Please sit."

Adrien lowered himself into the soft leather chair across the desk from Amelia. She waited for him to settle in before she returned to her seat.

"Thank you, Amelia. And now that you are Dean, we are colleagues. It's time for you to call me Adrien." He smiled, which smoothed out the rough edges of his face.

"Only if you'd like, Chanc…Adrien." She flushed. He was attractive, not just because of his position and power. Adrien was the most powerful magician she had ever met.

The man was on the level she hoped to someday achieve. The Dean position would be challenging, but it should also allow a bit more time for magical scholarship, something the overworked faculty rarely had time to enjoy. "They're all here. Biggest class since I started at the Academy."

"Yes," Adrien said, still smiling. "It is always my favorite time of the year. Reminds me of myself when I met the Founder so many years ago. I, too, was filled with hope and vigor."

Amelia nodded. "I will never forget my first day. Probably

shouldn't have been here. If it weren't for Reston taking me in after my parents died, who knows where I would be? Out there on a farm with a hundred kids." She paused, for a moment, lost in memory. "Not to mention Uncle Saul pushing me toward you and the Academy."

Feeling a twinge in his stomach at hearing his old friend's name, Adrien inspected the Dean's face. Virtually no one knew that it was Adrien who removed her uncle from the Governor's seat—and from the face of Irth for that matter—and he intended to keep it that way. But her expression showed no hint of accusation.

He cast his eyes into his lap. "Dear Saul. I wish he could see us now. You know that Arcadia was as much his dream as it was mine." He chuckled, shaking his head. "I don't think he would be able to believe how much we've accomplished since his passing. Really is quite amazing."

She smiled in response, and the two chatted for a few more minutes, exchanging pleasantries about the start of a new term and the nervous first-years. But as the conversation began to wane, Amelia was impatient for the other shoe to drop. Adrien wasn't known for social calls.

"Can I help you with something today, Chanc…Adrien?" His first name felt foreign and almost mechanical passing her lips.

"Oh, right, that." His smile was all teeth. "Well, I *am* here for something. This year, as you know, our enrollment has grown. Which is a good thing, but also brings with it some, shall we say, challenges. The classroom has always been my primary concern in the Academy, and I am hoping to maintain the integrity of instruction."

She nodded. "That's refreshing to hear. I was worried that my faculty would suffer from the new ratios."

"Yes. That's why I hired you. You're their voice." He paused and looked at the painting hanging over her desk. It was as ancient as the magic they studied. In it there were men standing, talking, and even lounging to study.

The focus was a younger man and an older one. In their robes, they looked like ancient sorcerers. The younger pointed to the ground, the older toward the heavens. Adrien couldn't help but wonder if it was an original. Art from before the Age of Madness was difficult to find, but with the right magician, it was relatively easy to replicate.

He continued. "I've actually been missing teaching myself, and I think I've figured out a way to do it again without ruining your system. My plan is to start a special program for the students who show a strong proclivity for the arts. An honors college of sorts, with me at the helm. They will work on magic, but also assist me on a special project. I think this could be a key element of advancing, not only the best of our students, but also Arcadia itself."

Amelia said, "Shouldn't be a problem. How soon do you want the group to form?"

Adrien thought back to Doyle's timeline and the needs of the Chief Engineer. "We have some time. Let the first-years settle in, then start to assemble the group."

"Of course. I'll start making a file of upperclassmen today."

Adrien rose from his chair, pleased with her response. "Excellent, Amelia. But I expected nothing less from you." He reached out his hand, his toothy grin still plastered on his face.

She rose from her desk, hesitated a moment, then grabbed his hand. Before letting go, she asked, "Adrien, what exactly is this project?"

His smile faded, and a hungry look crossed his eyes. "Amelia, there's something you should know about me. When I am vague, it is *always* intentional. But I can tell you this, those chosen to work with me will help change Arcadia. Help change the *world*."

Parker kicked a loose rock down the street leading toward Queen's Boulevard. He'd spent days trying to find work outside of the factory, and he hadn't had much luck. Sure, he'd probably be able to land a job building some shit for the Governor and the Chancellor, but he'd prefer not to be a part of whatever they were working on. Parker knew full well that they were not above-board, and he considered working for the two of them as contributing to the unjust systems of Arcadia that kept he and his neighbors in the Boulevard.

All he wanted now was a bath and something to eat. By the end of the day, he had finally found some work mucking out the horse stables just outside of the gate. It was the place where the Capitol kept their horses for the Guard who went out on missions, and where the nobles kept their damned show animals.

A day's worth of shoveling shit, with shit for pay, was enough to send him home with only a few coins in his belt.

What took him half the day to earn in the horse stalls, he and Hannah would have earned in a few moments of serious hustling in the market square. But he did what he had to do, and with security on high alert and the Prophet's freak-show disciples running everywhere, he couldn't risk getting pinched.

Parker's mother needed him, and even a month in the clink could lead to her being forced to do some very unsavory things. He'd seen too many women in that position working the streets.

"Pay up, maggot." A weaselly voice broke through Parker's musings.

The man sitting on the stool at the toll that led into Queen's Boulevard was completely unfamiliar to Parker. On the night Hannah nearly burned the place down, he had gotten into an altercation with Monte, the previous goon to collect coins for Horace, the Boulevard's manager.

It took Monte weeks to get out of the infirmary from their run-in, and Parker had heard he'd lost his cushy job in the meantime.

"Not today, friend. Only got a few, and it was through honest work." Parker grinned, hoping he could charm the newbie.

"Not on my watch, dipshit. Nobody enters Queen Bitch Boulevard without dropping coin in the offering box." The man kicked the wooden container. All the residents cursed the toll as an entirely unfair system. "Don't make me ask again."

A grin spread across the guy's greasy face, and Parker wanted nothing more than to knock it off. But he knew this was the way it goes in Arcadia—not for the nobles with their horses, but for people like him just trying to get by each miserable day.

Justice needed to come calling, and it needed to come fast. He only prayed that Ezekiel and Hannah were already orchestrating its arrival.

"Sure. Here you go." Parker poured his purse into his hand and dropped in three of his ten coins.

"The toll is half, numbnuts. I might be new on this stool, but I wasn't born yesterday."

Parker's face burned, and he considered messing with the guy, but he knew that Ezekiel and Hannah might just need someone still standing on the inside. And for that, the government would receive his obedience, but never his loyalty. He dropped two more coins in.

"Horace thanks you for your support. Have a nice day," the bouncer said with a shit-eating grin on his face.

Stuffing his hands in his pockets, Parker turned his back on the man and continued into the Boulevard.

He walked toward home, imagining exactly what would have happened if he had sucker-punched the man. Of course, as it played out in his mind, everything went according to plan. He grinned as he pictured straddling the oaf's chest and throwing punches onto his fat, greasy head. Just as he was getting to the good part, a sound dragged him from his fiction.

Sobbing. Loud sobbing.

It was coming from an alley. Compassion for the people of the

CM RAYMOND

Boulevard flared, and Parker turned down the dirty alley toward the sound of misery.

A tiny body under a green cloak heaved between sobs. Parker quickly moved forward to help the poor person.

"Hey, kid," Parker said. "You ok?"

The little girl glanced up at him, then away. She was unfamiliar, but so were many in the Boulevard. It was a transient place and foreigners would often end up there after coming to Arcadia for the chance at a better life.

"I'm looking for someone, and I can't find them." She stuttered out the words between her chokes of sadness.

"Who are you looking for?"

Without warning, the girl stood and pulled back the emerald-green cloak. As she rose, Parker realized that his estimation was all wrong. Not a girl, but a young woman, a little older than him, stood in front of him.

Her name was Jez, and Parker knew she wasn't messing around. She wore a white cloak under the green one; an eye, completely black, was burned onto the front of it. It was the symbol of the Prophet, and of his fanatics.

"I'm looking for you, you Unlawful-loving scumbag." She sneered with distaste as two men in white emerged from the shadows, each of them holding clubs stained with dried crimson.

"Ah, shit," Parker said. He raised his hands and took a step backward. "Really, I'm not an Unlawful. You guys need to do better research."

One of the men spoke up. "We know who you are, and what you did with the old witch. I watched you pull her body down myself. If you help them, you're one of them. And the Prophet has called on us to do the work of the Matriarch and the Patriarch, which includes scourging the Unlawfuls from this city."

70

Parker laughed, slapping his thigh with his broad palm. "Ah, now I get it. You guys think because I pulled that old bag of bones off the stick, I'm friends with those apostates." His eyes darted around to each of the Disciples. "You're not really that stupid, are you?"

Parker could read confusion all over Jez's face.

He continued. "Come on, guys. It's all about presentation. We need to make sure that we don't freak people out with the barbarian bullshit. Now, the Prophet, he knows better. He's able to do his work without getting his hands dirty, draw people in without scaring the hell out of them."

"Wait, you're—"

"Hell, yes I am." Parker really didn't know who or what she thought he was, and he didn't care. He had to get the hell out of there, and hoped it wouldn't come to blows. Those clubs looked like they could do some damage. "Listen, I admire your passion— I really do—but like I tried to tell you the other day, you can't just accost anybody you think might be a little off. It's not going to work like that."

A bead of sweat ran down his temple, and he hoped that the Disciples didn't see that his nerves were on edge. Although his stomach was churning, Parker looked, for the most part, cool on the outside.

"Prove it," the woman said.

"Excuse me?"

"Prove you're a true follower."

He laughed. "If I had to spend all of my damned time showing you freaks that I actually work for the Prophet, I'd get nothing done. But if you insist, let me grab my credentials."

Swinging his leather bag off his back, he reached inside. His fingers worked their way past the red juggling balls, played the lock-pick set that he always had ready, and finally found what he was looking for. The glass bottle was cold to the touch, something to do with the contents, which he didn't quite understand.

Hannah had gotten the potion from Miranda, but if anyone knew he carried this kind of thing, he'd be in deep shit.

The fluid came in handy when he was doing sleight-of-hand in the market. A few sprinkles of the liquid would create sparks and puffs of smoke. The dear old woman had given it to them with a long list of precautions, and he was about to ignore all of them. Considering the circumstances, though, he thought she would have approved.

"Ah, here it is," he said.

Pulling the bottle out, he wasted no time whipping it toward the ground. It smashed at the feet of the club-bearing men at the same time Parker shielded his eyes with the edge of his cloak. A thundering crash filled the alley, and smoke overflowed the narrow corridor, giving Parker plenty of time to escape.

"You son of a bitch," he heard Jez yell behind him. "We'll get you and your Unlawful scum friends, in the name of the Matriarch."

As he pushed his legs to go faster, he thought of Hannah and Ezekiel. It was better for them that they were outside of the city walls. Now he just had to keep himself in one piece until they were ready to return.

CHAPTER EIGHT

He had only been back in the Heights for a week, but Karl had already started to feel like himself again. Being among his people brought life back to his weary soul. Far better to be in the Heights than doing mindless work in the lowlands.

He finished his pint of ale and motioned for Morgan, the barkeep, to slide him another round. A good beer-buzz was just what he needed to end the day's work. The alehouse was nearly empty. With the increased demand on the mines to get as many resources to Arcadia as possible, most of the rearick were pulling double shifts.

The company was paying a premium for overtime, so miners were happy to go underground, tired and hungry as they had become. Karl was glad that his last several guard runs had given him plenty of cash; he was not seduced by offers from the company. Nevertheless, he feared for his bearded brothers who were working long hours digging out the mines to precarious depths.

Garrett, a youngster by rearick standards, walked up to the bar and took the empty spot next to Karl. The kid had a stupid grin on his face, and as he motioned for Morgan to bring him an ale, Karl knew it was about to get a lot worse.

"Bring another for Karl, too, on me!" Garrett shouted.

"Why, that's awful kind of ya, Garrett," Karl said. "But what the hell is the occasion?"

The kid beamed with pride. "Yer looking at the newest guard fer the company."

Karl looked him up and down. He had been swinging his hammer long enough to know when someone was prepared to fight and when they weren't. And Garrett was greener than a newly mined gemstone.

"Is that right? Well, good for ya, but I'd hold off on the beer. Yer better off spending yer money on some better equipment. That armor is dog shite. I could piss through that thin leather brigandine if I squirted hard enough." Karl smacked Garrett's chest with the back of his hand. "It ain't pretty out there in the lowlands. There's evil lurking behind every damn bush, and yer more than likely to get yer ass handed to ya. And dead men drink no beer, kid."

Garrett took a long slug of his ale and wiped his mouth with the back of his hand. "I ain't worried."

"That right? Then yer even dumber than ya look. Either that, or you've got something ya ain't telling me."

"I've been assigned to travel with ya." The kid looked up at the older rearick, his stupid grin getting more pronounced by the minute. "And around here, yer a freaking legend. I've been listening to stories about ya since I was an ankle biter."

Karl grunted and turned back to his cup. "Ah, don't be so swift to count yerself safe, kid. Half of them stories ain't nothing but shite."

"And the other half?" Garrett asked.

"Just damned lies." Karl laughed to try to lighten the mood. Overall, he was happy to have Garrett along for the ride on his next trip. The journeys were long and often hard, and he liked the kid, though Karl knew his confidence could end up being a liability.

And Karl had seen enough dead men on his watch to know how ugly the world really was.

"Morgan," Karl called to the barkeep, "two more. One fer me and the other fer me new boss here."

The kid perked up next to him. "Thanks, Karl that's—"

But Garrett's words were cut short as the bar started to vibrate. Ripples formed on the surfaces of their ales, and a mighty grinding sound, like a hundred rearick beating their war hammers against the ground, followed.

The room shook like hell.

"The mine!" Karl yelled, as he jumped to his feet.

He *knew* the damned company men were making a huge mistake, continuing to push the current shafts past their limits. They should have opened a new hole, and now lives were on the line.

The world really could be an ugly place. "Beat feet, kid! They're gonna need us if there's anybody alive down there."

Hannah slumped on the couch in the drawing room.

Her head was spinning, and she wasn't sure if it was sheer exhaustion from the training that Hadley had run her through or from the elixir she had pounded back throughout the day.

Being raised with a drunk as a father, she had never touched the firewater down in the lowlands. In her view, it created assholes and miscreants—not to mention that it tasted like piss and ate you from the inside out.

But the mystics' elixir was nothing like the swill they served in Arcadia, even the best of it. It opened her mind instead of clouding it, and besides, she needed it to soothe the emotional exhaustion of their training.

Sal immediately flew over to her. He landed in her lap with a thud, and she groaned at his weight. The mountain air seemed to be doing him some good; he'd probably gained twenty pounds since they arrived. "Geez, Sal, you're going to be carrying me before long." The dragon nuzzled his head under her hand until she began to pet him, and she wondered if what she said was the truth.

The magic that had created Sal was brand new. Neither Ezekiel nor Hadley had any idea how it worked. For all Hannah knew, Sal would never stop growing.

Maybe one day her pet would get so hungry he'd swallow the whole world.

She shook that image from her mind and looked down at the not-so-little guy who had already fallen asleep on her lap. *Maybe not*, she thought.

He was far too lazy for that.

As Sal started to snore, Hannah turned her mind back toward the last three days of training. This meditation always ended the day. Hadley had convinced her that one of the major problems in modern education was that it always looked forward, while the mystics were convinced that by looking backward, they could fix the things they learned more deeply in their bones.

The first day had been a breeze. Hadley had led her to a spot on the edge of a cliff overlooking the valley. Their session was much like her earliest days with Ezekiel; he had initiated some meditative exercises on how to empty herself of the concerns of the world. She had already become good at this on her own, but a few more tricks in the toolbox would come in handy, especially if she needed them on the fly.

She thought the second day would be more of the same. Hadley again began by taking her to the edge of a cliff. They sat and meditated for most of the day. Hannah didn't mind much. The scenery was beautiful, although she was still getting used to life in the Heights, having spent all her days in Arcadia.

Just as she had emptied her mind of all its concerns, Hadley filled it back up again. He stood, took three steps, and leapt from the edge of the cliff into nothingness.

"What the *hell*?" Hannah screamed and scrambled toward the edge. She could hear the screams of the lunatic as he sailed toward the valley floor hundreds of feet below. "Hadley!" she screamed after him, knowing it would do no good.

"Pretty cool, right?"

She spun to face her new teacher. "You *douche nugget*. You gave me a damned heart attack."

Hadley laughed. "Yep. That's the power of persuasion. Just imagine how much you can do with that sort of influence on someone else's mind. Amazing, right?"

Hannah's heart was still beating out of her chest. "I think I hate you, you know that? You and your damn tricks."

Her scorn only made him laugh even harder. "You don't have to read minds to see that's a lie. But magic like that is more than a trick, Hannah. Julianne has told me what you are up against. And power like this, power to control your opponent's mind, could be the difference between life and death."

Hannah nodded. She had already seen how effective Ezekiel's illusions were in a fight.

"Change your mind, change the world. I got it. It's like the little nudist trick when I first got here?"

"Yeah, exactly," Hadley said. "But this time, the magic will affect other people, not just your own perception."

Hannah flushed as the implications of Hadley's statement dawned on her. "Wait a second. You could…"

The man winked and turned back toward the monastery. It was an act of godlike patience for her not to throw him off the cliff for real just then.

Hadley was far from normal, but she couldn't doubt the effectiveness of his methods. By the end of the second day, she had learned to cast simple images of things that weren't in the room.

They weren't perfect—Hadley also taught her how to see the flaws in the false images—but they would serve in a pinch.

Hannah could also suggest to others that she wasn't in the room, making her all but invisible. Again, someone trained in the mystic arts could see around the trick, but it would work on most of the idiots in Arcadia.

When she first arrived at the temple, she had thought the mystic stuff was mostly a waste of time; nothing compared to creating spears of ice or communing with the forest. But Hadley's lessons made the mystic arts seem damn useful.

And the best part of it all was that she was having a blast. Something about Hadley made the lessons easy to understand, and he had a direct nature that would all but baffle Ezekiel.

The more time she spent with him, the more she liked him. And, the more she liked him, the more she thought about Parker and wondered if he were safe. Thoughts of the two men troubled her, made her feel like some damn rich girl from the Noble Quarter.

As much as she enjoyed her time in the Heights, she couldn't wait to be back in Arcadia, kicking ass and raining down the fire-balls of the Matriarch's justice.

Still, her time in the Heights had been rejuvenating. It showed her a life she had never known was possible.

But it also had its dangers. Hannah had to work like hell to keep the mystics out of her head, though she had the sinking suspicion that her attempts were for naught.

"You rested yet? We've got more work to do," Hadley asked, sticking his head into her room and interrupting her meditation.

"What gives? I thought we were done for the day." Despite her exhaustion, Hannah didn't really mean it. She was ready to take whatever new hell Hadley wanted to dish out. "What do you want me to learn now? How to paint rainbows in the sky?"

Hadley grinned. "Better. Time to crawl around in people's brains."

Hannah sat up so fast she almost dropped her cup. This was something she had been waiting for since she learned the mystics could do it.

"For real?" she asked. "I don't know if I'm up to seeing your perverted thoughts. I'm scarred enough already."

He shook his head. "Unfortunately, my mind is too good for you. As are the minds of most of the other mystics. Would have to be a freaking baby mystic for someone as immature and unfocused as you to get in, and I bet the infant would still win. If anybody that lives up here wants to keep you out of their brain, they will, although most of us let our guards down. It's part of our community. The mystics are open, with each other at least, unlike you lowlanders, who do all you can to deceive."

Hadley raised his brows, and Hannah wondered if he'd been in her mind this whole time.

"Not the whole time," he said, answering her thoughts. "But long enough. No offense, Hannah, it's just something we do. Takes work for us *not* to step inside."

"But that's not who I'm going to be training on?" Hannah asked. "Why not?"

"Well," Hadley replied. "You aren't exactly going to war against us. And since you are only getting the rushed version of my training, I figured it made sense to start a little closer to home."

"We're going back to Arcadia?" Hannah's heart began to beat a little faster, and she noticed a sad look in Hadley's eyes, but she brushed it off.

"I said a *little* closer to home. We're only going down the hill to Craigston. I'm starving, and they've got a great little breakfast joint. But the rearick are even easier to read than you Arcadians, although it depends on how much they've been drinking. Just the place for my pervert-in-training to cut her teeth."

The walk down the long winding staircase was a joy compared to climbing them. Gravity did most of the work. All Hannah needed to do was keep her eyes on the rocky steps. They passed a group of mystics on their way back up to the monastery as they descended.

Hadley greeted them with a smile as they passed. She could only assume that they spoke in ways she couldn't hear, and she wondered if the subject was her. Nodding to each of them, she continued down the stairs, doing all she could to close her mind to the man three steps ahead.

As they neared Craigston, the sound of the bustling village rose to meet them. The hamlet had been established during the Age of Madness. Uniquely situated in the Heights, it remained safe from most of that damage caused by the Mad.

But over the years, the population had begun to adapt to their new surroundings. They became the rearick, a group of hard-working men and women perfectly suited for their mountain homes.

Hannah had asked Ezekiel about them once—how the rearick could change so quickly. They were practically another race. Ezekiel said that it had to do with the Kurtherian nanocytes, the alien tech running through everyone's blood.

But that alien stuff still didn't make much sense to her.

She knew that the nanocytes empowered the Matriarch and the Patriarch all those years ago. Then somehow, a distorted version of the tech had spread to all of mankind, creating the Age of Madness. But once Ezekiel had cured the zombies, the alien tech opened the world to magic, at least for the Arcadians.

The rearick, on the other hand, never learned magic and didn't quite trust it. Instead, the Kurtherian nanocytes shaped them into short, stout, strong people.

And that came in handy. The rearick were legendary fighters, and their strength and size made them perfect miners as well. And because of their access to the wealth that lay within the ground, the rearick developed into the backbone of Irth's commerce network.

For years, gold nuggets and beautiful gems held their attention. They were becoming more and more valuable as the world rebuilt itself after the shitstorm of the zombie apocalypse. But over the past few years, the rearick had found something more valuable to mine than a pound of gold or a shit-ton of diamonds.

They had discovered amphoralds.

Arcadian engineers, under the supervision of Chancellor Adrien, had hypothesized how to use these strange crystals to channel energy. A skilled magic user would be able to transfer power directly into the crystal. After years of research and design, an engineer built the first magitech. It was simple, a magic-powered flashlight, but it was only the precursor of the technology that would follow. Machines for transport and mass production, then armor, and, of course, weapons.

Hannah had seen firsthand the danger of magitech weapons.

But it just so happened that the only place the gem had been discovered in abundance was in the Heights. More specifically, right there in Craigston.

Once the crafty rearick learned about Arcadia's obsession with magitech, they realized just how valuable this gem, which they used to toss over the cliffs with the rest of the rubble, had become. And ever since then, the rearick had dug as deep and as quickly as possible to mine the crystals.

Hannah and Hadley finally finished their descent and entered the town. People rushed back and forth, their minds focused on work. Hannah could see a line of them moving in and out of a mine on the opposite end of town.

"Here we are," Hadley said, nodding to a short building with a sign that read **Ophelia's**.

They ducked through the low doorway. Hannah looked up to find a dozen sets of eyes staring back at her. The eyes were about the only thing she could make out through their thick hair and beards. Each rearick had a hammer or an ax at his feet, as well as a plate piled high with various kinds of hot meats with a large beer to match.

They nodded at the lowlanders—an expression not entirely accurate seeing as the mystics lived higher in the Heights than they did—and returned to filling their bellies before their shifts underground would begin.

Hadley grabbed a table in the corner and Hannah slid in across from him, facing the room. "Nice place," she said.

"Eh, it's kind of a shithole, actually, but the food is *really* good." He nodded at Ophelia behind the counter, and raised two fingers.

"Did you just order?" Hannah asked.

"Yep."

"What the hell are we getting?"

Hadley laughed. "Whatever she's cooking. The rearick aren't quite as refined or as picky as the mystics. You should taste their damned ale. Our elixir is good, but theirs will put hair on your chest."

"Not a major goal of mine," Hannah said with a smile.

"I hope not." Hadley gave her half a grin. "I find it refreshing to come down here and connect with people whose brains aren't always in the sky."

"Guess theirs are mostly underground."

Hannah scanned the room for Karl, the rearick who had saved her from the boar her first day at the tower, but her search came up empty. She knew he was from a mining community, but was unsure if Craigston was the one.

Then her mind turned back to the mystics. "Those mystics we passed, they looked like they'd been gone for a while."

"Yeah," Hadley said. "That group has actually been gone for a little over a month. It's a pretty common practice. We leave for a lot of reasons. We have groups that carry our elixir to Arcadia and a few other places with people rich enough to afford it. The rearick here help us along the way. Some mystics travel to visit family they've left behind, and we also have a long tradition of pilgrimage."

"Pilgrimage?"

Hadley nodded. "Too long on the mountain doing nothing but going through the cycle of meditating to sharpen your mind, practicing mental magic, and then drinking like a fish to numb yourself can take its toll. Pilgrimage is meant to get us out of our routine, push us to connect with lowlanders who think differently, and for some of the mystics, just to dry out a bit."

Hannah laughed. "That makes sense. It's amazing up there, but I'm not sure if I could do it forever."

"Nah, most can't. That's why we go. It helps a lot, and it gives us new experiences, which only fuel our creativity and our magic. I'll be leaving to go on walkabout one of these days."

"Where will you go?" Hannah asked. "Someplace where the women don't know you well enough to hate you?"

She meant it as a joke, but a sad look passed over Hadley's face. Hannah was about to apologize when he took a long swig of the ale Ophelia had just placed in front of him. He shrugged off whatever he was thinking about.

"Who knows?" he said. "Maybe you could show me around the Boulevard. But enough about me; let's focus on you. If you're going to be sneaking around dangerous waters, it's helpful to know what your enemy is thinking. And for that, mental magic is the best tool you could ask for, but it takes work to try to get into somebody's mind—even minds like theirs."

Hannah scowled at her teacher. "Better keep your voice down before any of these guys hear you calling them dummies. You might just end up with a war hammer up your ass sideways."

Hadley laughed. "The rearick aren't dumb, just unsuspecting. Most of these guys don't really give a shit if you get into their heads; not much to hide. They're simple folk, but honest. And damn good at what they do. Not to mention, the rearick are known for being the most loyal people in all of Irth. It's why they make such good guards. If they give their word that they're going to make sure you get someplace unharmed, you'll get there or the rearick will die trying."

Hannah nodded. Given the way Hadley described them, she almost felt guilty for trying to intrude into their mind space. But Ezekiel had sent her here to learn, and learn she would. Pushing away her concern for the strangers, she urged him, "Ok, tell me what to do."

"Yeah… tough one to answer. The mystic arts are the hardest because they are difficult to explain. Ezekiel has taught you nature magic already, right?"

"Yep. I can read the mind of any tree on this side of the mountain." That wasn't exactly true, but Hannah was ok with the exaggeration.

Hadley ignored her. "Well, as I understand the art of the druids, ours isn't altogether different. It might take a bit more focus and concentration. And, the mystical arts can leave you defenseless—a mental magician is pretty much in a trance state when using their power, even if it is just for a few seconds."

"Ok, so like nature magic."

"Yeah. You'll push everything out of your mind, concentrate on emptying yourself first like we practiced by the cliffs. Then when it feels as if there is nothing, you turn your center toward another person. I guess you make them your new center. It allows you to enter them."

"Sounds dirty."

Hadley laughed. "You're not far off the mark. There is a kind of intimacy that comes with mental magic. It's why the mystics are all so close with one another."

"Your big mind-orgy in the sky?"

"Metaphorically, yes."

Hannah smiled and then closed her eyes. The smell of bacon and eggs captured her mind and her stomach. She pushed it away. Then she thought of Arcadia, her brother, and finally Parker. She imagined them walking into a house, waving on its doorstep, and then closing the door. She used the different tricks and techniques that Ezekiel, and later Hadley, had taught her, and soon, there was nothing.

She opened her eyes and they were blazing red.

Hadley cursed and glanced around the room to see if anyone was paying attention. He hadn't considered that her bright red eyes might draw stares, but everyone seemed to be involved in stuffing their faces and gossiping about the foreman and his mistress.

Hadley spoke a word under his breath and then relaxed. Hannah assumed he was masking the color of her eyes to any observer.

Hannah let her head pivot, looking for the right person. She landed on a man alone in the corner and knew he was the one. Less gruff than the rest of the crowd, she could tell that he had a certain mental hospitality that none of the others shared. She focused on him, but kept getting distracted by his physical attributes—the bald spot on the top of his head and the curly beard. Whatever focus she was supposed to achieve wasn't working, so she tried a new tactic. Instead of ignoring the way he looked, she began to imagine that she was him. She placed herself in his body and in his mind again and again.

And then it happened.

Just another damned day, it'll be fine.

The words crackled like smoke and fire in her mind, an experience she had never felt before. She jumped in shock and they disappeared, the sounds of the bar returning to her mind. But she wasn't ready to give up. Focusing harder, she felt her blood boil and electricity spark down her spine. Her power was strong. She could do this, and she knew it.

One more haul. Maybe two. That's all it will take. Then, time to rest these bones. Live life with me feet up. It'll all be worth it.

Hannah realized that even though she hadn't eaten, she felt like she was bursting at the seams. She was perceiving that he was full, could almost taste the food on his tongue. She was all the way in.

Damn Walt has no idea what he's asking us to do. Fucker's never been underground, after all. One more day. The shaft will hold. Has to.

A group of rearick, dirty from the night shift, started to pile into Ophelia's. The men who had just finished eating took their cue.

One more dig, the rearick thought as he downed the last of his beer and grabbed his hammer. His mind disappeared as he walked out the door.

Hannah inhaled deeply. Her heart was racing, and she sucked air deep into her lungs. "Holy shit. I did it."

"Yeah. You did. Nice work. And that poor guy, hope he gets his haul today."

Hannah furrowed her brow. "Wait. You were in there, too?"

"Sure. Wasn't going to let you go alone."

Hannah sat at the table beaming, but then a strange feeling took her over. It was sadness, but different than she had ever felt it. Like she had been holding onto it for years, decades even. Her smile faded, and with it all the warmth in the room.

She looked up at Hadley. He had a knowing expression on his face.

"I feel terrible," she said. "What the hell is happening to me?"

He slid a beer over to her. Ophelia must have brought it when she was lost in her trance.

"Here, drink this," he said. "It will help, trust me. That's one of the aftereffects of true mental magic. Thoughts and emotions are connected. You didn't just read that rearick's mind, you read his soul. And while his thoughts may be gone, his emotions can stick around for a while—at least when you're first starting out."

Hannah nodded. The sadness she felt could have only come

from someone who had lived as long as that rearick. She grabbed the beer and chugged it down.

Hadley's eyes opened wide in surprise, and several rearick cheered when she dropped the empty tankard back on the table.

"Well, damn," she said, staring down at the empty mug. "I hope you were kidding about that hair on the chest thing." She looked around before turning back to her teacher. "What's next?"

Hadley looked at her in true shock. "I... I thought you'd be too emotionally drained to try anything new."

Hannah shrugged. "Reading that guy's soul packed a wallop, but if growing up in Queen Bitch Boulevard teaches you anything, it's to not let sadness get you down. Guess you could say I'm pretty resilient. Now, where's that food?"

Hannah and Hadley talked for nearly an hour as she shoved food into her stomach as fast as she could. Each time her plate was emptied, Ophelia brought another round with a nod and a smile. Hannah finally held up her hands in defeat. "No more!"

Her mystic friend laughed. "I should say so! You keep eating at that rate and you'll grow faster than your dragon."

Hannah washed down the last of her meal with beer, then let out a belch that echoed around the restaurant, which brought on another round of applause from rearick sitting nearby. Hannah bowed, imagining she was Parker performing on the street.

She looked back at Hadley, who had a wide smile on his face. "What the hell has come over me?" she asked. "Is this more of the aftereffects of connecting with that rearick?"

"Maybe," he replied. "Or maybe you're just a freaking pig."

"Bastard," she jeered, but there was no malice in the word. "I should turn *you* into a pig."

Hadley smiled. "Whatever it takes for you to recover, I recommend it. Mental magic takes its toll, and I know that your physical magic saps your energy, too. But if you're really on a mission to save the world, you're going to need to figure out how to keep your strength up, pace your magic, and when you can't, recover quickly."

Hannah nodded. "Yeah. Zeke hasn't gotten to that part yet."

"He will. Recovery is partially about the power inside and partially—"

But Hadley's words were cut off by what sounded like an avalanche. The room quaked, its force matching the sound. It was so powerful that it knocked Hannah off her seat. From her vantage point on the ground she could see everyone in Ophelia's jump to their feet and run toward the door.

"Let's go," Hadley shouted over the commotion. He grabbed her hand and pulled her to her feet, then pushed her toward the exit.

CHAPTER NINE

Once darkness had fallen and Ezekiel saw firelight inside the large wing of the castle, he made his way back down the hill to implement the next step in his master plan.

He once again walked past the decrepit buildings surrounding the immaculate castle, but this time the bent-over bodies toiling in the yard were nowhere to be seen. He sensed the fear that rose in this place after dark.

That was ok, though. Fewer witnesses for Ezekiel's plan.

Tapping his staff on the beautifully carved oak door, Ezekiel waited. It wasn't long before a thin man with a hooked nose and rounded shoulders answered the door.

The man looked at Ezekiel, taking in the majestic purple robe the magician wore. Of course, it was all an illusion, as was Ezekiel's now darkened hair and beard, but the man would never know. "Hello, sir. Well, we weren't expecting visitors this eve."

"Ah, is that right?" Ezekiel said. "I sent my boy out three days ago to announce my arrival." He looked back over his shoulder. "But it seems the runt has ruined things again. I am so sorry. Perhaps I could still talk with the Master of the house? I have journeyed here from Arcadia, and I have a message from the Chancellor himself that I believe Girard would be quite interested in hearing. It has something to do with his old estate and a payment that has come due."

The impish man's eyes lit up at the mention of money.

Ezekiel continued, "But of course, I could go. The discourse will wait for another time. Perhaps in the spring?"

"No," he snapped, before settling himself down. He exhaled and pressed Ezekiel. "No, of course not. We would not put out a man of your stature due to the error of a servant boy. We have our share of problems here. It takes plenty of hands to keep the house up and the Master satisfied."

Ezekiel smiled and nodded, but blood and power leapt beneath his skin. A man such as Girard would be necessary for his plan to work, but its execution would bring him great delight knowing that serving justice upon the wicked would make Irth a brighter place.

"Come in, please," the doorman said, waving Ezekiel into the foyer.

He placed his staff in the corner and hung his purple cloak on a hook. The garments beneath appeared just as noble, and a golden chain with the biggest amphorald Girard's servant had ever seen hung from his neck. The gem glowed with the power of magic.

At least, it appeared as if it did.

The servant poured him a goblet of the mystics' elixir. Sipping, Ezekiel realized it was a vintage whose barrel price could feed a village for a month in Arcadia. "Ah, a fine beverage," Ezekiel said, nodding to the servant.

"Only the best for the Master and his guests. Worth the expense." The man winked. "Make yourself comfortable."

Ezekiel wasn't an emissary from Arcadia, of course. Nor did he wander onto the property of this landowner by chance. Girard was a mark, and a carefully chosen one, famous among the nobles for making his riches in trade during the early days after the Age of Madness. Those who struck when the iron was hot had generally become successful.

For Ezekiel and his friends, success involved building the first great city in the healing world. For Girard, it was creating a business around providing cheap labor for all kinds of burgeoning industries.

He thought of himself as a middleman who vetted and provided workers, but the workers knew he was virtually engaging in the slave trade. The man paid the workers he hired so little that it was hardly a willing deal, but men and women had few choices in those days. Then he offered the desperate employees advances on future pay to help them to make it through a particularly tough week. And that is when he had them. Once indebted to him, they were stuck, as good as owned. Girard's infamy spread across the land, according to the working poor.

But Girard's reputation didn't keep people from getting snared in his web. Desperate people rarely had much choice in the options presented.

Once his empire amassed to more than the man could ever dream of spending, Girard escaped from Arcadia and used his own magicians and slaves to build the castle in which Ezekiel sat. Remote from society, the manor received few visitors, even his noble friends seldom visited.

Girard had taken a group of people to work with him on the property, most of them women and children from families inescapably indebted to Girard. The cycle was inexorable, and it always worked in his favor, which was why Ezekiel had chosen him.

"Um, hello, sir," the man's raspy voice broke into the silent room. Even the sound of his words sent shivers down Ezekiel's spine.

Ezekiel rose and sent a smile across the room. For just a

moment Girard froze, and a look, almost of recognition, flashed across his face. But Ezekiel had aged significantly in the past forty years, and he now employed just enough mental magic to alter his appearance.

"Hello, Girard. I bring greetings from Arcadia."

The man swept across the room and waved at a seat. "Please, do sit. Can I get you more of the mystics' drink?" He raised his brows. "It is a twenty-three-year-old vintage. Most nobles would agree it is the best—created after they reached the pinnacle of their brewing processes, and aged to perfection. I bought as much of the damned stuff as I could get my hands on."

"Why, I don't mind a bit."

Girard topped off Ezekiel's cup and his own. Sitting across from the magician, he said, "I'm sorry, but have we met? You seem a bit familiar, and I don't ever forget a face."

"Well, I certainly doubt that," Ezekiel said. "The name is Percival, but my close associates call me Percy."

"Percy... Percy... No, I can't place it. Huh." Girard continued to stare and for a moment, Ezekiel wished he had increased the effects of his disguise. "But you say you are from Arcadia. I don't go there much anymore. I guess it has been years—over a decade —since I went. But I knew most of the nobles in that city before I established my humble home here, and you are not, begging your pardon, a young man."

Ezekiel chuckled for the man's benefit. "No need to apologize for speaking the truth. We are not young men. But you wouldn't know me; at least, it's not likely. I'm a horse trader from the far west. Set up shop soon after the beginning of the restoration with a couple of beat-up old ponies, and now I sell a thousand head a year, sometimes more!"

"Well, that's not bad."

"Yes, well, it has made me a comfortable living." Both men laughed, as the rich often do when they downplay their situation.

"I went down to Arcadia just last year to sign a final deal with the Governor. He wanted to increase the number of horses for the Guard. Seemed rather asinine to me." Ezekiel snorted a laugh. "Who the hell would bother Arcadia, anyway? They're powerful enough to be the ruin of any invading barbarians."

"A toast to that," Girard said, lifting his glass. "What was it that kept you in the city?"

"Ah! Of course. I fell in love with the damn place. A citizenry most noble, and with the Academy there, it is the hub of Irth. And soon, all will realize that fact. Chancellor Adrien and I got quite close during my initial visit. There was a humble little place in the noble section, sits right up on a rise with nearly an acre behind it. Something that's hard to find inside a walled city. Anyway, Adrien suggested I buy the shack just for someplace to lay my head when I came in for business, and I haven't left yet."

Girard listened intently. "You are right, it is a noble place, at least part of it. But with the Bitch's Boulevard filling so quickly, I felt like the whole damned place was going to be overrun by the scum of the world. It did, however, help me to found my own business, which isn't much different than yours." Girard's eyes sparkled, as rich men's did when they were about to boast of their enterprises.

"Oh, you're in livestock as well?"

"You could say that. My stock is the kind that walks on two legs and is born in places like the Boulevard. I guess you could say I am a workers' agent of sorts."

"Is that right?" Ezekiel thought of the man's own staff and the way in which they had obviously been abused. "And it is helpful for you, since you get the pick of the litter to work your own household, like your servant who welcomed me into your home."

"Oh, you mean Bradshaw? No, no, he is my servant, but not like the others. He's a damned cousin that couldn't make it on his own. A half-wit, but he'll do anything I ask, which is, of course, a very useful thing. Keeps the rest of the scum in line. That way I only need to deal with them when I have, well, *personal* needs to attend to. If you know what I mean." The man's eyes glimmered again, and he leaned in, waiting for Ezekiel's response.

The magician wanted to confirm precisely how vicious this man was. "So, you've made an honest woman out of one of your servants? I *have* heard of such things."

"Honest?" Girard's heinous face twisted into a sneer. "Sure, I make them all honest for an hour or two, and then I send then back to sleep in the barn. Wouldn't want the livestock thinking they're part of the family."

A smile spread on Ezekiel's face. "Can't let animals think they're human, after all."

Girard drank long from the mystics' elixir. He was enjoying himself more than he had for years. It had been too long since he'd talked with someone with similar tastes. "That's *precisely* the way it is."

But that enjoyment was about to come to an end.

Ezekiel stood and simultaneously broke the mental magic that had altered his appearance. Girard's eyes grew wide as his goblet clattered to the floor. A sick fear filled the man's heart as he finally realized where he recognized his guest from. Girard stuttered out a response, "You're... You're—"

"That's right, you craven beast. I am the Founder. You would have done well to have recognized me, and better to have remembered my *wrath*."

The powerful magician felt rage run through his body, and he allowed the passion to take over. Girard instantly began weeping terrible tears that would do him no good whatsoever.

"Please," he sobbed. "I'm like you, a magic user. A noble man."

"You're no man," Ezekiel whispered. "And we can't let the animals think they're human, after all."

"How much?" Girard whimpered.

"How much?" Ezekiel cracked back, his words like thunder.

"You think you can buy me off with your money born of injustice and hate?"

The man saw murder in Ezekiel's red eyes and ran for the door, but Ezekiel was too fast. He raised his right hand and snapped his wrist like an athlete throwing a curveball. A small wooden table flew across the room. It made contact with Girard's legs, and the old man landed hard on the stone floor.

As Ezekiel walked toward his prey, he rubbed his palms over one another and a dagger of ice appeared. He stretched it out into a spear, a move he had learned from Hannah, and stabbed it through Girard's thigh, halting his pitiful attempts to crawl away.

Ezekiel knelt beside him. He wanted Girard to look into the eyes of justice one more time before leaving Irth.

"You've had your chance, *old friend*. And instead of using the power granted to you to make the world better, you became a petty tyrant. A monster in human flesh, and a terror to all beholden to you. I wasn't here to help those whose lives you destroyed, but I'm back now. And before long, I will rid the world of creatures like you."

Ezekiel snapped his fingers, and his staff flew into his hand. Spinning it, he brought it down with the force of ancient justice. Girard's face snapped to the side and back. The man still wept.

"*Please.*"

Ezekiel cracked him in the head again. Finally, taking the staff in both hands he raised it toward the ceiling and then rammed the point into the man's heart. The sound of shattering ribs filled the room, and Girard was gone.

Half an hour passed before Ezekiel rang the bell to call for the doorman, Bradshaw. When the weaselly man arrived, he saw nothing of the carnage Ezekiel had wrought upon the place. The room looked as it always had, and his cousin Girard sat comfortably in his large wooden chair. But he was alone. Their wealthy guest had disappeared.

"Master, where has our guest gone?" Bradshaw asked from the doorway.

Ezekiel, disguised as Girard, smiled. As he responded, his voice sounded gravelly, just like Girard's, and he waved his hand the way he had seen Girard gesture. "Our guest had to leave suddenly, but in the short time he was here, he helped me understand the errors of my ways."

"Errors, sir?"

"Yes. It appears we haven't taken full advantage of our status here. He has shown me a better way."

Bradshaw grinned. What was good for his cousin usually worked out well for him. "Superb. Where do we begin?"

"First I need to talk with one of our farm hands. You know the one, the stout woman who works in the garden."

"Do you mean Gwen?"

"Of course. Fetch her for me. There has been a grave injustice that needs to be fixed."

The winter chill had descended upon Cella and its surrounding regions earlier than in most years, and only a month later it was downright freezing. Lord Girard had not issued the servant's new clothes for the coming winter, so they huddled in a mass in the back corner of the barn for heat.

Gwendolyn had gotten used to the stink of the others when they were still strangers, but now, after years of servitude, those strangers were the only family she knew. Whether it was the never-ending communal toil or the common abuse they all suffered under the hand of Girard she couldn't be sure, but now, she would lay down her life for any of them as if they were brother or sister, son or daughter, and she knew that most of them would do the same for her.

As the barn door creaked open, she cursed under her breath.

Apparently, the Master was lonely, which in her world meant horny. She should have expected it, and tonight would probably be worse than normal. Today's bad omen almost guaranteed it.

She had known from the outset that she shouldn't have spoken to that strange bearded man, but Girard's slavery hadn't ruined all vestiges of the manners Gwendolyn had possessed. And despite the risks, an old-timer in need was worth helping.

But then, when she had spoken so sharply about Girard's evil, she had crossed a line that held consequences. But there was just something about him...something that spoke to her, and willed her to speak the truth. He made her feel human for the first time in years.

But now, in the dead of night, she felt nothing but fear and anger.

All of this led Gwen to a point of decision. She could either offer herself to save her family, or try to fade into the dark corner of the barn and pray that Bradshaw, that hook-nosed scumbag, would go for one of the others.

While it didn't always help, she usually chose the former, because the latter, watching another be taken instead of her, hurt far too much. The abuse had become mechanical, as much as rape could. Over the course of many years she had almost learned to close her mind and shut out the Master's attentions.

Almost.

That kind of violation could not be altogether ignored.

"Gwen, Lord Girard would like a word with you," Bradshaw hissed toward the huddled masses.

Hands gripped her shoulders and torso. It was a sign from her friends that they cared, even though they knew they couldn't stop what was about to happen.

"It's ok," she whispered to them. "At least I will be warm for a minute."

"More like fifteen seconds," a younger girl next to her quipped with a sly grin. Gwen couldn't help but laugh. Making fun of their Master was one of the few joys they had in life, an indulgence that wouldn't help her much in the castle.

She followed Bradshaw back to the house, ready to open her legs and close her mind.

"Have any strangers been on the property today?" Ezekiel, still in the form of the tyrant Girard, asked Gwen.

She stood straight and proud before him. There was only a slight shake in her hand. She knew that if she expressed any hesitation, gave him any sign of her lies, he'd turn from questioning to violence. He might anyway, even if he believed she was telling the truth.

"No. No one, my Master." Her voice was strong.

Ezekiel raised a finger along with his voice. "I will only give you one more chance, girl. Has there been a man here early today, someone around my height with white beard and hair?"

"No, sir, no one." Her shaking increased. She knew it was foolish to lie. She had no connection to that old stranger. He was nothing to her. And yet, he had treated her like a human, which was something she hadn't experienced in a while. For some reason, it was enough for her to keep her mouth shut, no matter the price.

She said a silent prayer to the Matriarch, begging Her for strength.

Over her shoulder, Bradshaw smiled with joy. While Girard liked to take servant women into his bedroom, Bradshaw enjoyed taking them to the torture chamber—although Girard only allowed that on rare occasion. Damaging the goods was bad for business, but Bradshaw knew from the tone in his cousin's voice that there was a good chance he'd get a new plaything tonight.

"Guards," Ezekiel shouted in Girard's raspy voice. Two gendarmes entered in regal uniforms.

Ezekiel had not seen the men before, but could sense them in the house. He mustered all he could not to laugh, thinking of the dead Master's hubris in his need to have this kind of protection. He glanced at Bradshaw, who bubbled over with glee. Ezekiel pointed right toward him and shouted, "Take my cousin outside and throw him in with the pigs!"

Bradshaw's smile slowly faded as confusion replaced his joy. He glanced right and left, trying to figure out who his Master was referring to. "Sir, me?"

"For too long, I have spent my days dishing out injustice, and my nights drinking in vice. My conscience can take no more."

Gwendolyn couldn't believe the words. Her captor had never shown an ounce of kindness. She wondered if her prayers had been heard.

Ezekiel rose from his chair, his raspy voice now booming.

"Tonight, I leave on pilgrimage, a great journey to see if there is any way to cleanse my soul of its wickedness. You, dearest cousin, will seek your own penance by shoveling shit. From now on, you serve at the pleasure of Gwendolyn here."

Bradshaw cowered, his eyes searching Ezekiel's face. "But—"

"But nothing. And if I hear that you have disobeyed her in the slightest, I will make sure that my greatest sin lies in the way I will disassemble your body piece by piece. And then you will become slop for the very pigs you tend. Do you understand?"

The man could hardly nod. His legs went limp as the guards grabbed his arms, dragging him outside.

After he had left the room, Ezekiel looked at the equally shocked serving woman. "Gwendolyn, you have sacrificed all to this place, though not by choice, and for that, I am sorry. I know that I have no right to ask anything of you, but these lands require more from you. I am placing you in charge, making you the head of the house in my absence. I have ruled this land poorly, but I trust that you can make things right. Do you accept?"

Gwendolyn stared at the man. It made no sense, yet she sensed no malice in him. This was no trick. She thought of the Matriarch and the stories she had heard about how well She led. Then she thought about the children sleeping the freezing barn.

She made up her mind on the spot.

"I accept," she said.

Ezekiel smiled. "Good. I have instructed the guards to obey your every command, and I trust that the rest of the servants will do so as well. In addition to my authority, you have control over all my resources to do with as you please. I may not be able to find redemption on my pilgrimage, but I know that you can begin the work of restoration here.

As her Master's words fell over her, Gwen was full of questions. "How long will you be gone?"

Ezekiel rubbed his beard, which looked shorter to the people in the room than his actual one. "That is hard to say. My sins are many. I…" Ezekiel grasped for words, then smiled as an image of Hannah floated before his mind. "I have been a douche nugget. Atonement could take some time."

The woman's face was serious. Already she was thinking of the work that the land and the people required. "I don't understand."

Ezekiel smiled. "I know. Sometimes when your eyes are opened to the truth, you're shocked at how long you did not see. And you opened my eyes, Gwendolyn."

She nodded. Her expression held no warmth—years of abuse couldn't be undone in a single night—but for the first time, she felt the tiniest glimmer of hope.

The old man had been an omen after all, she thought.

Ezekiel moved from his chair toward the door, but he looked back to offer one more piece of advice.

"While I'm away, there may be some who come asking the same questions I did, about a mysterious old man. I want you to make sure you tell them exactly what you told me. Do you understand?"

The woman nodded. "Where are you going?"

"I'm going back to Arcadia. There is more that needs to be made right."

CHAPTER TEN

"This way!" Hadley yelled, pulling on Hannah's arm.

The small dirt road that ran in front of Ophelia's was marked by bedlam. Rearick ran in every direction. The air was filled with the sound of screams and dust from a catastrophe she had not yet seen.

Holding onto the back of Hadley's shirt, Hannah made herself as thin as possible, so they could move swiftly through the shifting crowd. They reached an impasse at the end of town—a wall of men surrounding the collapsed mouth of the mining shaft.

"Let us through," Hadley yelled as he shoved his way to the pile of boulders. But as the extent of the damage became clear, his mouth hung open. "May the Matriarch and Patriarch have mercy," he said.

"Forget the Bitch and the Bastard," Hannah shouted. "What can we do?"

But Hadley had no answer.

In front of them, a group of rearick pulled at the stones with their hands, trying to clear a path into the tunnel. An older rearick led the group. His strength was incredible, and he moved boulders that likely weighed more than he did.

But despite their efforts, it was clear to Hannah that they were getting nowhere. Finally, the rearick pulled back from their labors to regroup and formulate a plan. One of them stood alone, cursing at the rocks.

"Karl?" she asked.

The rearick's eyes darted in every direction. They finally landed on her, and he recognized her immediately. "The bloody hell are ya doing here, lassie?"

Hannah looked down into the friendly eyes of the rearick who had saved her from a charging boar outside the tower. She still kept the dagger he had given her on her belt.

"Long story," she responded. "I'm training with the mystics. I can fill you in later; there's more important things…" She nodded toward the pile of rubble.

Hadley jumped in. "Karl, what can we do?"

Karl looked the young man over. "Damned if I know. Yer magic means nothin' to me. The hell can a mystic do in times like these? If we keep diggin', we might never get to them. Worst-case scenario, if we dig far enough, it might just dislodge some of them rocks on the other side. We can't keep movin' until we know if there are people trapped behind this wall, or if they have found shelter farther back."

Hannah thought of the old rearick from Ophelia's restaurant, whose mind she had just wandered through. She feared that it really had been his last day in the mine, and his last day above the ground.

Hadley grinned down at the rearick. "I guess you just told me *exactly* what a mystic can do to help in the situation."

Before Karl could respond, Hadley closed his eyes and began to hum slightly to himself. Suddenly his eyes opened, shining bright white. Hannah knew that he had left his body, projecting his consciousness into the mine.

"Damn mystics are bat-shite crazy," Karl said, shaking his head to Hannah.

The rearick and mystics had an amiable enough relationship, both in employment and as neighbors in the Heights. The rearick could offer protection, both during pilgrimages and also as they exported their elixir around the Arcadian Valley. Sales of their drink largely financed their monastic tradition, but they weren't strong enough to leave the confines of the mountains without their stout companions.

Karl, like most rearick, appreciated the greater pay they received from the mystics, not to mention they always treated their bodyguards well. Nevertheless, the rearick, at least most of them, didn't fully buy into the magic of their neighbors in the Heights.

"Trust him," Hannah said. "I've seen Hadley do some impressive things, and if he can help save your people—"

Karl snorted. "He's got five minutes, and then I'm putting me muscle to the task at hand. If they're alive in there, they won't have much time. And I won't waste it on that mind nut." He nodded at Hadley, standing stiff as a board.

With Hadley in his trance state, Karl decided to keep moving. He began shouting commands to the other rearick who had gathered in every direction around him. He called for tools, wheelbarrows, and enough medical supplies to heal the town in hopes they might be necessary.

No one questioned his commands. Rearick fled and returned, bringing exactly what he had called for. The citizens of the Heights respected Karl. He was one of the older and wiser rearick, both in the mines and above ground, and while Karl held no formal position of authority, no one doubted his leadership.

"Come on," Hannah said under her breath as she waited for Hadley to return to consciousness. She knew his power, and wondered what the hell was taking him so long.

Hadley's eyes returned to normal without warning, and he

sucked in a breath as if he had been underwater. He bent over, resting his arms on his knees. The magic had affected him, and Hannah could see the pain and fear in his eyes.

"There are at least a dozen alive in there. I instructed them to move back away from the mouth and toward a safe location, but some of them are hurt badly. One rearick," he looked at Hannah, "the old man you met at Ophelia's, is pinned under a rock near the mouth. He's in a lot of pain, and with a limited amount of air in there, they don't have much time."

"It'll take us days to dig through this shite," Karl spat.

Hadley shook his head. "Don't have days, friend. We need another way."

No one spoke for a moment as the weight of Hadley's words fell on them. The men in the mine would surely die.

Karl removed his leather helmet and cast his eyes to the ground. "Then hope is gone."

"Not yet," Hannah said. "I've got this."

―――――――

"It will be simple," Hannah said after she filled them in on her plan. She turned to Hadley. "Just keep your mind open. I might need to chat." She tried to smile, but his face held concern.

"I can't imagine you'll be able to connect with me in these conditions. You've never done it before."

She shrugged. "It's ok. I've never teleported in these conditions before either, so, I'll probably end up on the surface of the sun. Then there's nothing to worry about. Game over."

Karl stood silently next to them. Even though he didn't quite understand their magical mumbo jumbo, he was wise enough to sense both the gravity of the situation and what the young woman was putting on the line. She was beholden to no one underground. She didn't even know them, and yet she offered her help freely.

The rearick was filled with gratitude for her courage and sacrifice.

"Yer doing a brave thing, lassie."

Hannah saw the respect in Karl's eyes and nodded. "All right, enough standing around acting like a bunch of bitches," Hannah said. "Let's do this."

The men laughed, and then Hadley pulled her into a hug. He whispered into her ear, "Trust your power, Hannah. You are overflowing. Believe in yourself, and you can do this."

Hannah nodded, then began the work of centering herself. She pushed away her fear, as Ezekiel had taught her, then reached out with her mind, as Hadley had shown her. She achieved a moment of perfect calm.

Then the terror of being buried alive struck her, so she pictured the kind old rearick, wanting nothing more than to retire to a modest life, stuck beneath the surface. She stopped thrashing and embraced the emotion. She held it and nurtured it, letting it fill her. Wind began to whip around her, kicking up dust.

Then her eyes flashed red and she blinked out of sight, leaving the two men staring with open mouths.

A dozen rearick stumbled back in fear when Hannah burst out of nowhere into the small space. She appeared with a crack of thunder and a cloud of smoke. Twisting her wrist, she created an orb of light barely bigger than her fist. It lit the whole place.

"Who the hell—" a younger rearick started to say.

"It depends. If you listen to me, I can be your way out of here. Or if you act like a bunch of asshats, I might be the last person you ever see. Personally, I say we go with what's behind Door Number One, ok? Now let's get to work."

The small crowd of men and women nodded, then circled around her.

She looked around the small crowd, their faces worn with years of hard labor and pained by the more recent fear of death. The young rearick introduced himself as Garrett and waved her toward the mouth of the cave. Enormous boulders covered the entrance, with smaller rocks filling the gaps in-between. At the base, his leg trapped under a boulder, sat the old rearick. His face showed a mixture of pain and resignation.

"This is—"

Hannah cut Garrett short. "Mortimer. I know."

The old man furrowed his brow. "Do I know ya, mystic?"

She offered a grin. "Kind of, but it's a long story. And I'm not a mystic. If so, I wouldn't be standing here in the flesh."

Mortimer's eyes sparkled. "So, yer an Arcadian then? One of those physical magic users?

Hannah nodded. "You know more about magic than most of your friends here. Unfortunately, I'm only an amateur."

"Well, an amateur is better than nothin'," Mortimer said with a toothy grin. "So, ya gonna help an old rearick out, or what?"

"Damn right I am."

Hannah stepped back and surveyed the scene. She needed to figure out a way to get the mouth of the cave open, but at the same time she had to protect the man whose leg was wedged beneath the pile of rubble.

She only had so much power, and she was afraid that if she used it to free the trapped Rearick, she wouldn't have enough left to help the rest of them. She closed her eyes and concentrated on Hadley. When she opened them they glowed bright red, standing out in the darkness of the cavern. Garrett drew back in shock, but she ignored him.

Hey there, rookie. I guess you could do it after all, Hadley said in her mind.

Piece of cake, Hannah replied. *The mystical arts aren't nearly as hard as everybody said they were.*

When you get out of there, I still have a few things to teach you.

Things I could've used in here? Hannah asked.

Nope. It's something we call humility.

No time for that bullshit, Hadley, she sent. *I've got a plan, but it's not gonna be easy. Most importantly I need something from you outside. Get everybody away from the mouth of the mine shaft. If this works, shit's going to get pretty crazy out there.*

Will do, Hadley said in her mind. *Be careful.* And then she broke the connection.

Hannah looked around. "Unfortunately, my plan has nothing to do with being careful," she said to herself.

Two days until retirement at the most and this shit had to happen.

Mortimer had spent half his life underground, and he had hoped to enjoy a few years with his feet up on the back porch of his little house in the Heights, but it looked like the ground would be his beginning and the ground would be his end.

The leg which had been swallowed by the rubble had stopped hurting an hour earlier. It was as if the thing had never existed, which was probably better since he knew he would lose it in the end anyway.

He watched the young woman—girl, really—pace back and forth in the cavern. All his hope rested on this stranger, but his hope didn't amount to much. She had a fast and foul mouth as well as confidence, at least on the outside.

Mortimer doubted she could do what she claimed, but he would take anything as a last resort at this point. Most of all, he just wanted to make sure his fellow miners got out of the cave. He knew that his position, trapped at the base of the rubble, would keep them from digging quickly. If the magician could help, he'd be happy for her to give it a try, but the look on her face and her constant pacing didn't give him much trust.

Finally, she stopped. Turning to Mortimer, she announced, "I think I got it."

He laughed, which caused pain to radiate up his leg. "Not much room for error here, lassie."

"There never is, really, with magic, but I want you to trust me. If I don't take a shot at this, you're as good as dead. And most likely the others with you. I have an idea that might just save you all."

"Better than saving none of us," he offered. "*Scheisse*, I've had a good life. Make sure ya get the others out; sacrifice me if ya must. Is that a promise?"

The young woman smiled, and a dimple appeared on her right cheek. For the first time the old rearick realized just how beautiful she was, and that she would be stunning aboveground with some soap and water and sunlight.

"Don't get all self-sacrificial yet, old man. I'm planning on getting you out of here, but I need you to hold as still as possible."

Mortimer looked down at his leg, pinned by a few tons of rock. "Shouldn't be a problem."

"Hope you're ready for me, Hadley," the girl muttered under her breath.

She nodded and stepped back.

He kept his eyes trained on hers. In a few beats of his heart, her eyes turned red and glowed brightly in the dark cavern, almost brighter than the light from her glowing orb. She flicked three fingers and the orb's light vanished, her red eyes now the only things lighting his tomb.

Hannah took one last look at the pile of rubble and turned toward Mortimer. She gave him a grin and a wink, her eyes glowing even brighter red. Then she reached her hand in his direction, with two fingers extended toward him. Still clueless as to what the woman had planned, he said a little prayer to the Patriarch and Matriarch, hoping that the legendary gods of Irth truly existed.

A new light appeared in the darkness. It wasn't coming from the magician, *per se*, but it floated above him, appearing as a tiny dot at first. And then the dot spread out and wrapped in every direction around his body. He was covered in half a sphere of blue luminosity. Mortimer, for the first time, had a hunch about the magician's plan, and it scared the hell out of him.

Tilting his head to get a better view, he watched as the magician held her left hand toward him, but then raised her right hand and directed it at the pile of rock. Hannah yanked her hand back toward her side as if she were pulling on a rope in a tug-of-war. Her jaw was clenched in concentration.

She opened her hand wide and then shoved it as fast as she could in the direction of the boulders. That's when all hell broke loose. Mortimer saw the explosion around his little blue shell, but he felt it more than heard it.

Rock, dirt and dust flew in every direction, and a shower of it rained down on him. And everything from the largest boulder to the smallest mote was redirected by the magical shield the magician from Arcadia had cast around him.

He'd never seen anything like it before in all his life.

CHAPTER ELEVEN

A few coins jingled in the leather bag Parker had tied securely to his belt. He only wished there were more. It wasn't a hard decision to reach, at least that day, but he had wrestled with the idea of selling the family silver for nearly a month.

The odd jobs he could pick up around the market and Queen's Boulevard weren't going to be enough to sustain him and his mother. A few times he had even risked venturing into the noble quarter to look for any sign of work.

A woman, obviously wealthy, though not nearly as well off as some of the nobles he saw, sat on a bench at the edge of the city park. Giving a shrill whistle, she nodded in Parker's direction. "Come on over, kid," she squawked.

In hopes that she might have some manual labor to offer him, he walked toward her and stood over the woman. Her eyes sized him up.

"Looking for work?"

Parker pulled off his hat and ran his hand through his hair. "Most of us are."

"Some of you are. Most of the men of this town are already working. They hired on at the factory. It's why the place is so damn empty. Hard for a woman like me to find a man anyplace in Arcadia." She laughed. "Gets kind of lonely, if you know what I mean."

The woman was right. The streets had been desolate for weeks, and it wasn't just because of the curfew. Even the Pit, with its daily fights, had been closed due to the lack of fighters. But Parker could tell that the woman was looking for a product that he wasn't willing to sell.

"Come on, you look pretty fit for the task." She raised her eyebrows as he backed away. "I'll pay you more for an hour of time than you'd make all day out in the streets. And you just might like it. I don't bite, but I'm sure to nibble."

Parker laughed. The woman was a day's journey from ugly, but he hadn't quite gotten to the point of pimping himself out. Close, but not quite there. "Thank you for the offer, ma'am, but I think it's time I joined the rest of the men in the factory."

"Ah! There goes my last chance." She gave him a smile and nodded her head. "You must be the last virtuous guy in all of Arcadia," she said. "Not bad to have men like you around, but if your scruples change, you know where to find me."

Parker bid her good afternoon and turned toward the factory. He made a mental note not to tell Hannah about *that* conversation.

But he did wish he could ask his old friend whether he should apply at the factory. Parker was always good at coming up with cons, but Hannah, she had a much better sense about these things. He hoped it wasn't failing her now, and that Ezekiel was the real deal. The longer she was gone, the longer her talk about coming back to save Arcadia felt like a dream.

But Parker still trusted his dreams.

He knew Hannah would return.

In the meantime, he had reached his limit begging, and the money he had earned from selling their last family heirloom told him that the time was right to take his last possible means of income seriously, no matter what his gut was telling him.

He walked up the gentle rise that led from the market to the factory, which occupied the eastern side of Arcadia, stuck between the final stand of trees at the southernmost juncture of the Capitol Quarter and Queen's Boulevard. When the Chancellor and the Governor started building, they had decided that the thick band of oaks would be both a metaphorical and literal boundary between them and the common folk.

But then, when Adrien invented his magitech tools, there was no better place than that little corner of Queen's Boulevard to build the factory. He had razed several blocks of slums, which garnered criticism from the common people because the factories took their homes but didn't offer their kind jobs.

Adrien knew the outrage would fade.

It always did.

Now the factories had changed their minds about who they were willing to hire, and a line had formed out the front door of the office. Parker stood with the other men and tried to mind his own business until it was his turn to enter. They were talking about how they hoped there were still openings, and how the Chancellor and the Governor were kind enough to continue to create machines for the sake of stimulating the economy.

Parker knew better. No matter how much Arcadian propaganda machines vomited out kind words about the men in power, he would not be fooled by their manipulations.

If the Governor and the Chancellor made something happen in Arcadia, it was only for the sake of themselves, only to keep themselves in their seats of power. And, most importantly, to protect themselves from any who might want to challenge them.

"What the hell are you doing here, Parker?"

Looking up, Parker saw Duncan, an old friend of his father's. Duncan was a smart man and a hard worker. Although he lived in Queen's Boulevard, he had still been able to make a daily wage shining boots on the streets near the Capitol. Parker always thought the man's job was recession-proof, because if there was one thing that a nobleman wanted, it was a pair of boots that he could see his own face in.

"I need work, Duncan; same as the rest, I imagine. The question is, what the hell are you doing here? What happened to your cushy shoeshine gig?"

The man looked down at his own shoes, which had been polished every day for years. "They drove me off the streets, man. I had no choice."

"Who did?" Parker asked.

"The Governor's Guard," the ex-shoeshine man said. "Told me I didn't have a license to be doing business on the streets of Arcadia. Believe that? A damn license? Like anybody has ever had a license to do business in Arcadia." The man shook his head. "Things are out of control."

"Yeah, you're telling me. It's bad for everyone."

Duncan chuckled, knowing quite well the kind of work that Parker did on the city streets. "Guess they never offered licenses for your kind of work, did they, kid?"

Parker liked the man; he was always good for a laugh. Even at this moment, he drew a smile from Parker. "No, I guess they didn't. So what's up with everybody getting jobs at the factory anyway? You know anything about this?"

The man shrugged. "There's lots of talk. Some say the Governor finally decided that us folks down on the Boulevard needed a leg up. They're saying that a big project is being funded, one that will not only help the whole town but will take so much production and capital that some of that is going to trickle down to the shit in the gutter. And this piece of shit needs a little help."

"You're not the only one," Parker admitted.

He watched as the men were brought into the factory one at a time. Strangely, he didn't see anyone come out, which he guessed was good news.

Duncan had said that if you got a job, they put you to work right away. That wouldn't be so bad, and it looked like nobody was being turned away. Maybe the factory was the best thing for him and his mother after all. He knew the work would be terrible, but at least it was work. A few weeks in there and maybe he could get back out on the streets, after things settled down.

The iron door creaked open, and a man in a rough-looking brown jacket and slacks to match waved Parker in. Duncan slapped him on the back. "Good luck in there, kid. Maybe I'll see you on the floor."

Parker gave him a nod and climbed the last steps into the factory. The place was dim. The hall lacked windows, and only a few oil lamps lit his way. He stayed a few paces behind the man in the ugly brown suit. His gut was telling him this was a terrible mistake.

They walked into a room at the end of the hall, which stood empty except for a single table with two wooden chairs on either side. A small pile of parchment had a brown leather-bound volume on top of it. The man in the suit pulled the brown volume in front of him and eased into his chair. He motioned for Parker to take the other chair. The young man complied.

"You guys really know how to make a person feel welcome," Parker said as he looked around the dingy room. "It's real nice in here."

"Name?" the man said without looking up.

Apparently, there was no small-talk allowed in the factory. "Parker."

"Quarter?"

Parker laughed. "You get many nobles coming in for work? How about boys graduating from the Academy? Yeah, I guess you probably don't get many of those guys here, do you?"

The man in the brown suit narrowed his eyes, and Parker knew it wasn't the time for joking if he wanted the job. But then again, maybe he didn't.

"Quarter?" the man asked again, as if it were the first time.

Parker grinned. Seldom did he have the opportunity to rub shoulders with mid-level bureaucrats. And if this guy were any indication of what bureaucrats were like, he was glad for once to have missed the opportunity. "Queen Bitch Boulevard."

The man scribbled **Boulevard** in the leather-bound journal. "Do you have any family?"

"Just my mother. She still lives in the Boulevard."

The man nodded and scribbled again. Parker couldn't help but wonder why in the world they might need to know that.

"Her name?"

"Eleanor." Parker cracked his neck, trying to feel more comfortable. He was already suspicious of this process, and wondered what the hell was going on.

His intuition screamed at him, and having hustled on the street all his life, he liked to think his intuition was well-calibrated. But they needed the money, and he wanted to make his mom proud. "You asking me any questions about my experience?"

The bureaucrat looked up from the journal. "That won't be necessary. You'll work just fine."

As the man closed the journal, he nodded behind Parker. A screeching sound filled the room as a door to Parker's right opened. Parker turned to look just as the glowing blue light jabbed him in the ribs.

Glancing down, he saw a six-foot metal rod with a glowing blue ember on the end. He braced himself, knowing what was about to come. Kids in Queen's Boulevard called the weapon the Shocker. Parker had no idea what its actual name was, but didn't matter. He'd seen its consequences for years.

The Guard carried them, as did many of the Hunters. Fueled by magitech, the Shocker could drop a three-hundred-pound man in the blink of an eye. He knew exactly what it was about to do to him.

Pain spread throughout his body as if he had been struck by lightning. His arms and legs flailed, but only for a second. Then he lost almost all control, though he managed to somehow retain consciousness.

Grabbing him under his armpits, two of the guards pulled him to his feet and out the door. His boots dragged behind him, leaving parallel marks on the dusty floor. The door opened to a catwalk over the main floor of the factory. Parker poured his remaining energy into turning his head to take a look at his destination.

His heart rate increased as he saw his future laid out before him. Down on the floor, there were too many men to count. Hundreds. All of them looked tired and dirty, and each of them wore strange metal bands around their wrists. They were working on something unrecognizable, a machine bigger than anything he'd ever seen.

And although he couldn't identify it, he knew without a doubt that it spelled trouble.

Before dropping him into temporary confinement, the guards slapped a set of cuffs on his wrists, just like the ones worn by the men on the factory floor. The restraints turned blue and hummed as soon as they snapped into place. Then they threw him in a cell with a few dozen others; men like him who were looking for honest work.

Standing watch were a Hunter and a few of the Governor's Guard.

Whatever was going on here, the authorities were not taking any chances. Parker had weaseled his way out of many precarious situations, but none of them had involved a set of magitech cuffs and the deadliest enforcers in all of Arcadia.

The tower, the main building of the Academy, had stood tall for over thirty years. It was built not long after Ezekiel had left Arcadia, just after the workers completed the Capitol itself. The classrooms had been constructed first, as Adrien knew even then that the most important thing was to start training young magicians.

Because whoever controlled magic controlled the future.

Resourcing his young and inexperienced staff came first, but once magical education was nicely underway, he had turned attention toward the tower itself.

Soon after the first class graduated, Adrien had recruited a team of newly licensed magicians and paired them with the Master Builders who shaped many of the houses in the Noble Quarter. He tasked them with building a grand tower, one that would stretch taller than the domed roof of the Capitol building. He wanted all the people in Arcadia—all the people in the world—to know that the power resided in his house, not the Governor's.

For several years after its construction the tower was used by Adrien primarily for research. A true Master of the magical arts by the time it was erected, his first goal had been to develop new knowledge, new magic, that he could spread across the land. But that ideal, grown from the seed planted in his head by Ezekiel, did not last for long.

Whether the tower represented the desire for greatness within him, or whether it led to his own desire to stand over everyone else, Adrien was never quite certain. All he knew was that from his position in the tower, he could see the others as the insects they truly were.

Adrien mused on that thought as he sat in a leather chair in front of the broad window overlooking Arcadia. With the curfew in place and the Guard doing their job, the place was darker than a dungeon.

He preferred it that way.

He sipped an expensive wine made in the western portion of

the valley, as close to the Dark Forest as anyone dared go. Thick and sweet on his tongue, the brew left a bitter aftertaste in his mouth, a sensation only appropriate for his mood these past months.

Adrien knew that he was close. Closer than he had ever been. The machine was moving quickly, and might even meet his original timeline. Not that it mattered—he would have his victory regardless of any delays. But like a child looking forward to his birthday, Adrien could hardly wait to unwrap the present being built on the factory floor.

The list of young upperclassmen from Amelia was also coming along. The Academy's Dean was not only intelligent herself, but also able to discern potential in young magicians. He had made the right move in promoting her over others who had a longer tenure in the Academy, and that decision was about to pay off.

Soon she'd be sending him a willing supply of magical adepts, crucial to the construction of his machine.

A knock on the door interrupted his ruminations. Disturbances were unusual at this hour of the night. Doyle never worked this late, and if he did, he knew not to interrupt the Chancellor. Catching Adrien at a bad time was not a smart move, something even Doyle had been able to work out.

While Adrien's days belonged to the Academy, his nights were his own. Not that he wasn't thinking about the Academy, Arcadia, and all of Irth every night anyway, but it was good for him to know there wouldn't be any interruptions from his assistant.

"Enter!" he yelled at the closed door, ready to lay into Doyle for the intrusion.

But it wasn't Doyle who entered. Instead, a much more thrilling surprise stepped through the door.

The smell of sandalwood and wildflowers preceded Alexandra's entrance. Adrien didn't need to look to know it was her; he never did. But he nevertheless tilted his head, because any man in his right mind wouldn't miss the opportunity to take in the most beautiful woman in all of Arcadia. Adrien grinned as he scanned her body, which was carefully wrapped in a tight-fitting suit of black leather.

"Good evening, Chancellor," she said in a voice that was at once alluring and powerful. "I was hoping you would be here. I remembered that you never go anywhere after dark."

Adrien laughed, a tight, controlled snicker. "You know me too well, Alexandra. Please, sit. Need a drink?"

"Considering the shitstorm you've given me down at the factory, yeah, I pretty much always need a drink, but don't get up, darling. I'll grab it myself."

She walked over to the bar in the corner of the room, and Adrien watched every step. She was quite a few years younger than he, although the way she maintained her body made it difficult to judge her age with any precision.

"Doyle tells me that things are developing rapidly down at the factory. I assume that I have you to thank for that."

She shrugged, raised her eyebrows, and gave him a sensuous smile. "Men are easy to control. One way or the other, I get what I want from them. After all, I learned from the best, Adrien. Care to come over here and give me another lesson?" Alexandra held up her hands and her eyes went black. Sparks began to fly from her palm, and they danced from one hand to the other. "You know I have a special way with my magic."

Adrien couldn't help but grin. He rarely allowed himself the luxury of a companion, but Alexandra was a treat he indulged in from time to time. Even though their intimacies were periodic, they always proved satisfying. "Truly, Alexandra, you are proof that the Matriarch and the Patriarch are real, and They have decided to bless me with beauty such as yours."

"You're kind, Adrien. And honest. But you know better than most that I'm never swayed by flattery." She chuckled. "Force is more my style. It's power that I'm drawn to."

"Well, once you've finished your work, there will be no force greater in all the world than mine. Will you be by my side?"

Alexandra made a tsk sound with her tongue, and said, "Adrien, I've always been by your side." The woman put down her wine glass and slowly began to unbutton her top. "But maybe, for tonight, you'd prefer me to be on top."

Adrien finished his wine as he took in the woman in front of him, magical sparks still crackling from her palms. *Truly*, he thought, *when power like this comes begging at my door, there is no one in Irth who can stop me. This world will be mine.*

Hannah washed down a shot of hard liquor with the thick local ale. Karl and Hadley sat with her at the rearick bar. Each of the men had several empty tankards in front of them.

Their clothing was torn and covered with dust. It looked like the three of them had walked through the apocalypse and barely made it out the other side.

In addition to the drinks, Hannah had been given a plate of meat and vegetables, and she shoveled it into her mouth as fast as she could. Her energy had been almost completely sapped by the ordeal. It wasn't every day she had to blast her way out of a collapsed mine while also protecting others from the rocks crashing around them.

But she pulled it off.

Mortimer, the old rearick, was safe from harm and currently getting his leg bandaged by the local healers. Hannah had made it out alive, and although she could barely stand, and the rest of the miners who had been trapped underground were saved from an early grave.

"The damn rocks come flying out of the hole," said Karl, telling the bartender the story for the second time, "like the

Queen Bitch herself spat the damn rubble from her unholy mouth. I've never seen anything like it before."

Hadley laughed loudly enough for the whole bar to hear. "I guess we have a Princess Bitch among us." He elbowed Hannah and nearly knocked her off the stool.

Hannah smiled, but she couldn't match the giddiness of her two drinking buddies. She finished her ale and waved to the bartender for another. The drink was not even close to as good as the elixir they served hundreds of feet up the path at the mystics' temple, but it would do to numb her emotions. Today had taken a toll, and not just a physical one.

"Just doing my job," she replied. "And I think, in some ways, saving lives feels a little bit better than pickpocketing in the market square."

Karl threw back two shots one right after the other, then washed them down with half a pint of ale. His eyes looked lazy, but he couldn't stop smiling. "Bastards in charge are talking about why the mine collapsed, but I told 'em days ago it was gonna happen. Said, 'Yer lookin' for trouble if ya dig any farther.' Of course, they didn't listen. They never listen. All they care 'bout is how much gold they can put in them coffers at the end of the day. Lose a rearick or two, no big deal. Slow down production, all hell's gonna break loose. Arcadia ain't the only place has problems of power and leadership, believe you me."

Hadley kicked back a shot and drank ale to follow. He was still smiling, though his face was starting to look a little green. Even with his mystic palette, he couldn't keep up with the girl from Queen's Boulevard or the hard-working rearick, but he was giving it his best shot. "Way I understand it, there's not much of a difference between Arcadia and the Heights."

"What does that mean?" Hannah asked.

"Well, and my friend Karl can correct me if I'm wrong," he said while he patted the old soldier on the back, "this here little town used to be independent. It was run *by* the rearick *for* the rearick, but once you Arcadians came up with your damned magitech, they realized they were going to have to increase production. But the rearick are shrewd businessmen. They don't sell their amphoralds cheap. Now," Hadley looked around as if someone were listening in on his drunken conspiracy, "how long do you think it's gonna be before Adrien gets sick of paying for those amphoralds? You ask me, he's fixing to take this place over. He's paying now, but he'll take the whole place with his magitech army."

Karl was slumping in his chair; the more he drank, the lower he slid. "You ain't wrong, mystic. Damn Arcadians moved in and took over, at least in spirit. Now, we have this mess on our hands, and poor Mortimer probably will never walk again, but it could've been worse. If it weren't for the two of ya, a mystic and some sort of freak magician, all of them would probably be dead."

He raised his glass in the direction of Hadley and Hannah and then tilted it back, drinking faster than you could say "Rearick." "The company men will come up with some sorta shit reason why the mine collapsed. They'll blame it on us, probably. Maybe they'll say it was a structural issue with our supports, but we all know better. I just talked to the bastard in the office a few days back. He knew the dangers.

"Yeah, they'll come up with some official reason why the accident happened, but I'll tell ya the real reason. Greed. Good old-fashioned greed." Finished with his rant, the short, Karl got off his stool, then wavered and almost fell. "Looks like it's time for me to get goin', or else I'll end up sleepin' on the bar again. Thank ya again, ya two angels. The rearick owe ya something. And a rearick don't forget their debts."

Karl slapped them both on the back and headed out the door.

Hadley and Hannah left soon after Karl and started the long trek up the stairs to the monastery. She was exhausted, but it was a good kind of fatigue. The kind that told you something about yourself.

For the first time, she truly realized that the magic that she had within her came with responsibility. It could be used to make a real difference in the world. Helping to save the rearick from the accident proved that her gift was important, as was Ezekiel's judgment.

They continued up the path without speaking. She could tell that a pensive mood had also captured Hadley, a common thing for mystics, and she was happy for it. After a long day, she soaked in the silence and the beauty of the place around her.

She was beginning to see why the mystics stayed up here. Peace ruled there, in a way that the lowlands would never know.

As they crested the last run of steps leading to the monastery, Hannah's thoughts focused keenly on a bath and her bed. But she and Hadley were greeted instead by a crack of lightning and a bellow of smoke. When the smoke cleared, Ezekiel stood before them, his white beard flapping in the wind.

She looked him up and down. "Shit. Don't think I'll ever get used to that, Zeke," Hannah told him.

The man nodded. "Good to see you, too, young lady."

"You missed the excitement," Hadley said. "You'd be proud of your student. She pretty much singlehandedly saved dozens of rearick today at the mine."

Ezekiel smiled. "Glad to see some of what I taught you sunk into that thick head of yours, but now is not a time for slapping ourselves on our backs. Go pack your things. Your vacation at the temple has ended; we have to go."

"Vacation?" Hannah asked, a slight bitterness in her voice. "I've been working my ass off up here. Where the hell are we going now? What's *so* damn important?

Ezekiel's smile faded, and a grave tone replaced his humor. "It's Arcadia, Hannah. She needs us. Your lessons are over. Now comes the test."

CHAPTER TWELVE

The morning fog rose from the valley, almost reaching Hannah's position in the Heights. She felt a certain weight rush over her, the weight of leaving a place that had given solace in her dark and dreary existence.

The previous months had been both a whirlwind and a dream.

Since she had been recruited into Ezekiel's mentorship of magic, nothing had been the same. Perhaps it was the novelty of the transition, or maybe the deadening of her emotions from fatigue, but she had realized this morning that she hadn't thought of her brother William much at all over the past few weeks.

His body was buried; he had been cold for months. And as she looked out over the valley, she realized that his vengeance still awaited.

"Ready?" Ezekiel asked.

She nodded. Despite Ezekiel's desire to leave as soon as possible, they had ended up delaying almost a week. Hannah had needed time to recover from her ordeal in the mine, and Ezekiel seemed tired as well; whatever quest he had just returned from had apparently been taxing. But good food, excellent drink, and the clear mountain air had them both back to full power in little time.

It was time to put that power to good use.

She looked down and found her dragon Sal crouched by her side. She hadn't tried to alter him with her magic since his wings had appeared, but nevertheless, he just kept growing.

Since she had been in the Heights, he had grown at least six inches at the shoulders—they now rose as high as her waist. Months earlier, Ezekiel had called Sal a dragon. It had been laughable at the time, but now, poised with his wings unfurled, Hannah almost believed in him.

Hadley grabbed her by the shoulder and pulled her into a hug. She hadn't known him long, but she had grown very close to the mystic who had taught her the fundamentals of mental magic. He had shown her much, and Hannah believed that with the foundation in place, she might be able to continue learning and understanding mental magic on her own with the help of Ezekiel.

He put his mouth to her ear and whispered warm words of encouragement. "You are more powerful than you know. Remember that. Also, remember that you have a friend forever in the Heights. I will see you soon." He squeezed harder, and Hannah melted into his body. Although eager to get back to Arcadia, the place that needed her and Ezekiel so badly, part of her wanted to stay there forever in Hadley's arms.

"Thank you," she whispered, "pervert." She said it with a smile, and he nodded. Forcing a grin, Hadley turned, and went back to the monastery.

Hannah watched him walk away and wondered if she would ever see him again.

Ezekiel grabbed her arm, and she reached down and grabbed Sal's wing. "We won't go all the way," he said. "We're going to need all of your strength when we get to the city. Not that I could jump us all the way there anyway—that guy's grown a lot." He nodded at her dragon. "But with our combined power, I believe I can get us within a day's walk. If the tower's unguarded, we can stay there. Granted, it's probably covered with Adrien's men—not that they'll find anything of use. If that's the case, we can always spend the night under the stars."

"I love camping." Hannah winked at Ezekiel. "If by camping you mean passing out in the grass after too much of the mystics' elixir."

Ezekiel laughed heartily, his eyes sparkling. "Well, if our quest kills us, at least you had the chance to taste the mystics' brew before passing over to the other side. It's more than what most people in Irth can say."

And without so much as another word, they disappeared with a cloud of smoke and a crash of thunder. They left the ground shaking in their wake and more than one mystic smiled at the theatrics of Ezekiel's departure.

***

Hannah gasped as if coming up for air as they reappeared on a narrow, winding path somewhere in the lowlands. Dust swept around them, and the *boom* of their reentry faded across the empty fields on either side. She craned her head behind her as if she might be able to see the Heights looming, but they were too far off. They were in her past, and far behind.

"We walk from here," Ezekiel said.

The first few hours of the trek were walked in silence. Ezekiel led, Hannah followed, and Sal lumbered behind her. Once in a while, she looked back at him; his smooth head darted back and forth. She knew he was keeping an eye on their backtrail.

He was their watchdog, and having him with her brought a sense of comfort. Even if, more than once, he'd broken from his duties to chase down a rabbit or squirrel along the road. Hannah smiled at the dragon when he looked up, and he flicked his tongue in reply.

CM RAYMOND

Tired of the silence, Hannah asked, "So what the hell's the plan, Zeke?"

"The plan is the plan," Ezekiel said, keeping his eyes trained on the road ahead of them.

"You really are a son of a bitch, aren't you?" she remarked casually. She had forgotten how infuriating he could be sometimes.

He pursed his lips in thought. "Most of the time I am," he finally replied. "But right now, I'm being completely honest. I have a plan in mind, but it is far from clear. The most important thing I know is that you and I are powerful. If we had time to train you properly, we'd be two of the most powerful magicians in Irth. But even with our gifts, just the two of us trying to take on the forces that Adrien commands within the walls of Arcadia would be suicide. If we are to defeat my former student, we're going to need to find some allies."

Hannah scrunched her face up, confused.

They had left Hadley, a powerful mystic, and Karl, a strong and brave rearick, behind in the Heights. They seemed as if they would have been fine allies. In fact, there were many, maybe even dozens, in the Heights who would be willing to fight with them for the heart of Arcadia.

But now, they were wandering a narrow path in the middle of nowhere, and Ezekiel chattered on about trying to find allies. She was becoming more and more convinced that the man was crazy after all; either that, or he had a death wish.

As if he knew exactly what she was thinking—and maybe he did—Ezekiel responded. "If we come at Adrien from outside, like an invading army, it will confirm the fears that Adrien has preached all along. And then Arcadia itself will be our enemy.

"Arcadia's walls are high and strong. I know, since I designed them myself. The city was made for resistance warfare; for defense. Instead of striking from without, I believe the wisest course is to try and find the weakness within. If we can convince

128

the people to join us, we'll be invincible. Now, while it is tempting to take the aggressive route, I'd prefer that we first try and position ourselves as liberators."

"Liberators?" Hannah asked, then kicked a small rock toward Sal in play. It hit his side, and he eyed Hannah, who was busy looking elsewhere.

"Yes. Arcadia has become corrupt. I will not argue that," Ezekiel answered. "But there are still good people within the walls. You are one example, as were Parker, and your brother, and a hundred more you'd be able to recommend just by yourself. They only need to be shown a better way, to be reawakened to Arcadia's potential. Did you believe that you and your friends were the only good souls left in the city of Arcadia?"

"No," she said. "We were just weak."

Ezekiel laughed. "You weren't weak. You were unorganized, fractured by the very strictures and systems that Adrien had put in place. His brilliance is unmatched, and the plan that he crafted a decade before you were born worked perfectly. Even your comment about the weakness of the Boulevard confirms that you are still under his control."

Hannah opened her mouth to respond, then let it close. They walked in silence for a while as Hannah chewed on his words. She wanted to believe that he was right, that the people of Arcadia were strong and brave and true—capable of making the world better.

But she had doubts. If it were so, how had they been held so easily under the thumb of a tyrant for so long?

"And if your plan fails?" she finally asked.

Ezekiel looked over his shoulder. "Then we try again your way. We come as conquerors with flames, and ice, and swords, and the rage of the Matriarch."

Hannah smiled. She pictured the woman painted on the ceiling at the mystics' temple. *She* was a warrior. Fighting like Her; that was an image Hannah enjoyed.

As they continued their march, Hannah asked more questions about where he had been during his time away from the monastery, but Ezekiel kept talking in circles and eventually she stopped questioning him; it was like trying to squeeze water out of a stone. Instead, she fell into a quiet rhythm behind him, continuing to look back from time to time to check on her dragon, who was as happy as any creature she'd ever seen.

As they reached the top of a rise, Ezekiel froze. Hannah nearly ran into his backside.

"Shh!" he whispered as she opened her mouth to complain.

He hit the grass and pulled Hannah down beside him. They crawled together to the top of the rise and peered over, but the sounds reached her first. The sounds of steel on steel and the screams of warfare told her exactly what she would see down there.

Death and destruction.

Parker kept his head down, appearing to the world as if he were dead. The sound of steel scraping steel was the only thing that accompanied the screams of the men in the background. Parker couldn't tell if the screaming was coming from the floor or someplace farther off, but either way, it was a place he didn't want to go.

His hands dripped blood on the floor between his feet, but the small cuts on his fingers had stopped stinging days before, or at least he had become numb to the pain. His job was twisting wires the size of his pinky together and then securing them with a wooden clip.

He had no idea what his work would be used for, what it meant, or even what it amounted to. The task comprised a minute part of Adrien's grand scheme. A scheme he could only assume was nefarious. But he had been promised that his mother would receive a healthy paycheck as long as he complied.

But he hadn't seen her since the day before he started at the factory, and his gut told him the pay was a lie.

Working beside him was Jack, the man who not long before had been employed as the toll collector at the booth leading into Queen's Boulevard. Parker and Hannah had given him half their wages for years as they entered the quarter. It was a shit system, but that didn't stop them from liking Jack.

While many of the toll workers were cruel, taking advantage of their power over the citizens of the Boulevard, Jack was different. It was as if he knew their plight. He did his job with integrity, and he didn't lord his position over anyone. Most days, Jack was kind to them. Parker could only imagine that this kindness had landed Jack in this hellhole.

"What is all this?" Parker asked not taking his eyes off his work.

Jack shook his head. They all knew that they weren't supposed to talk. And every one of them had witnessed the guards walking the floor with their magitech staffs, shooting anyone who didn't work hard enough with a jolt of magic. Their means of enforcement were effective, and Jack kept his mouth shut. He had been here since before Parker arrived, and Parker had hoped he possessed information.

"It's okay, there's no one near. Tell me what we're working on," Parker insisted again.

Jack glanced up from his own work. His eyes darted back and forth then he looked back down and whispered his reply, "Not sure exactly. Sometimes they call it the machine. Sometimes they called it the weapon. Back when I was working the toll, I had a friend who worked here, not on the floor, but in one of the offices. Always tried to get him to drink too much, tell me what was going on down here, but he was usually tight-lipped about it. He didn't want to lose his job."

"But?" Parker pushed.

"But one night, he did. Well, he didn't tell us much at all, really. But after hours of drinking, we all started to talk about the machine. Started laughing his ass off. 'Machine,' he said. 'Makes it sound so nice. All kinds of machines in the world. Mostly good ones.' We kept trying to get him to talk. Eventually he stopped using the word machine or even weapon. Instead, he started talking about *the ship*, and all the fucking damage it could do. Whatever it is," Jack continued, "this thing is no joke. If it is a weapon, I certainly wouldn't want it aimed at me."

Parker kept his eyes focused on the wires in front of him. He knew Jack spoke the truth. Whatever he was being forced to make, it was part of a weapon for Adrien to use.

He prayed the Chancellor wouldn't use it against Hannah.

"Don't move," Ezekiel whispered as his eyes flashed red. His body lay motionless in the grass. Hannah had been around long enough to know he was practicing mental magic. She could only assume that he was down there scouting the area with his mind, much as Hadley had done on her first morning in the Heights.

Ezekiel's eyes glowed brighter red for moment, and then returned to normal. "It's as I feared. Remnant."

"Shit!" She put her head to the ground, then beat it twice before lifting it back up, exasperated. "Are you going to tell me that those goblins are real, too?" Hannah asked.

Her mother used to tell her stories about remnant. Warned her that if she didn't behave, remnant would sneak into their room and eat her and her brother. Even as a kid, Hannah thought the idea of the distorted half-men was silly.

"You really were quite sheltered from the outside world, weren't you? How about from now on, girl, you take everything that you thought didn't exist and assume that it might," Ezekiel barked softly. "But we have no time to talk about goblins or dragons or even lycanthropes. There's a group of rearick down there getting their asses handed to them as we speak. I think we should go even up the battle. What do you think?"

At the mention of rearick, Hannah immediately thought of Karl and jumped to her feet. She pulled his gift, the silver knife, out of her belt, ready to put it to good use.

"Let's do it," she agreed as the older man surged to his feet.

Ezekiel ran double-time down the path toward the melee, and Hannah followed. He was damn fast for an old guy.

"You flank them on the right; I'll take the left. Just be careful out there, and I'll see you in the middle." Ezekiel spoke into the wind.

"Got it. I'll get to the middle and then keep working in your direction," she said with a grin, but her throat still tightened, and her stomach turned over in the face of what could be considered her first true battle.

As they neared the fight, the dire odds against the rearick became clearer. Half a dozen men and women from the Heights were surrounded by a group of remnant easily twice in number. Most of the rearick were miners and traders, not warriors, but they swung hammers and axes as if they'd done it all their lives.

The remnant, on the other hand, were a teeming mess. Their sallow skin, darkened by dirt and blood, was poorly covered by ragtag bits of armor and clothing that had clearly been stolen from Arcadians, rearick, or other civilized people.

One male remnant was completely naked. He spun and slashed with two jagged knives, completely oblivious to the cuts and wounds he was taking in return.

What the remnant lacked in order, they more than made up for in ferocity. If Hannah had run across them a few months earlier, she would have been scared shitless.

But Hannah had developed enough ferocity of her own to welcome the fight.

The first remnant she killed never saw her coming. He was focused on a rearick woman, who kept him at bay with a long spear.

Hannah decided to save her magic and instead lowered her shoulder. She rammed hard into the remnant's back, pushing him forward onto the rearick's spear. Thick black blood splashed out of the gaping hole the spear left in his chest, but the creature kept gnashing his jagged teeth until he bled out all over the spear.

Hannah's move worked, but it drew the attention of a female remnant, huge and wielding a chipped and dented hand axe in each hand. But Hannah wasn't fooled by their poor maintenance —they still looked like they could do some nasty damage.

The remnant let out a roar, her eyes glowing bright red in the early morning light as she came at Hannah.

Hannah let out a battle cry of her own, and she swung her arms down across her chest. Two fireballs burst to life in her palms; Hannah dove into a roll and came up with the fireballs in front of her. The remnant opened her arms wide for a vicious double arc, leaving her core exposed.

Hannah slammed her fireballs into the remnant's chest. Bestial screams mingled with the smell of burnt flesh until the sound turned into a death rattle. The monster dropped, a smoking hulk, to the ground.

The fire magic sapped some of Hannah's energy, but her heart pumped faster than ever and adrenalin carried her deeper into the fray.

Hannah never noticed the remnant coming at her from behind, nor did the remnant notice the huge green lizard with wings when Sal jumped on its ass, hissing in fury as he ripped out the remnant's throat.

CHAPTER THIRTEEN

Karl's hammer took the head of a male remnant clean off, and he followed through with a spinning attack that left another of the creatures writhing on the ground with a shattered leg.

The rearick warrior had been fighting remnant for most of his life. He had lost all pity for them years ago.

But hatred toward the raiders wasn't the same thing as confidence in his own men. They knew how to hold their own in a conflict, but they weren't fighters by trade. Garrett was the only hired guard on this shipment, and he wasn't much more than a boy. Karl had tried to keep an eye on the young rearick, but the chaos of the fight overwhelmed his hopes to see Garrett through the melee.

Karl silently cursed himself as he rained down blows. The raid had come out of nowhere, but he should have seen it coming. The last couple shipments had gone off without a hitch, which had maybe made him overconfident.

But as the sickly creatures came screaming over the hill, Karl immediately knew they weren't going to make it out of this one without taking some losses—if they made it out at all.

The rearick saw fire flashing to his right, but before he could get a good look at it, a large devil of a beast jumped in front of him. The remnant was completely covered in armor, although not one piece of it matched.

Karl parried a blow from the savage's long sword and slammed his hammer into the remnant's breastplate. The force of Karl's strike caved in the armor, and his opponent toppled over backward.

But before Karl could finish off the kill, he was struck motionless by what came into view.

There in front of him was an ancient looking lowlander with a torn robe and flowing white hair. Despite his age, the old-timer twirled around like a young man, smashing a wooden staff into the remnant like he was threshing wheat.

Karl, an old campaigner who never lost focus in battle, stood awestruck by the bizarre sight. And it was just enough of a distraction for the bleeding remnant at his feet to grab him by the leg and pull him over.

The creature was on top of him in an instant, terrible breath and bloody spit falling on Karl's face. The remnant held a crooked knife, and Karl caught it just before it plunged into his eye. Karl was by no means a weak man, but the remnant had size on him and leaned all of his weight into the attack. Karl knew that if he didn't think of something quickly, the remnant's wicked blade would plunge into his skull.

But the remnant lacked patience for the kill. He smashed his forehead into Karl's nose, dazing the rearick. Then the monster straightened, raising his dagger high to finish Karl off, but before he could deliver the final blow, a silver dagger drove into the remnant's neck. The creature's red eyes faded as he fell to the side, choking on his own blood.

There, standing before Karl, stood a beautiful young lowlander holding a bloody silver blade. She smiled down at him, and it took the old rearick a moment to recognize who she was.

"Hannah? What the hell ya doing here?"

She cocked her head to the side. "Saving your ass, you ungrateful geezer." She looked left and right quickly before looking back down. "Turns out this knife you gave me works after all. Stab them in the throat... Isn't that what you told me?"

He looked over at the dead remnant that almost ended him and back toward the girl. "*Scheisse*, I'm awful glad I did."

Hannah dropped to the ground, surrounded by the blood, guts, and pieces of bodies. It was mostly remnant, but the marauders had taken their toll before she and Zeke had arrived. There were certainly more than a few dead rearick on the ground.

Others, maybe half a dozen, walked around as if in a daze. She spotted one man a head shorter than her trying to pull a blade out of his leg. Karl and Garrett, the young rearick along for the trip in order to gain some experience, stood nearby.

"Not bad for a baby," Karl said to the kid. "But don't forget to keep yer guard up. That one goblin, the one tougher than yer mother, he almost took an ear off."

Garrett had a gash across his face that almost perfectly followed the line of his beard. It dripped blood, but the young rearick didn't seem to notice. He was dancing side to side, glad to be alive and still buzzing from his first real fight. "Thanks. Killing them damn buggers is harder than I thought, really."

Karl slapped him on the side of the arm and said in his grizzled voice, "Well, it was one of the easiest fights I've seen in me life. If that's yer idea of hard, ya might be screwed after all."

The young rearick wandered off, and Karl took a seat in the grass next to his lowlander friend. "Ya've come a long way since running from that boar in the woods, haven't ya, lassie?"

Hannah was too tired to come up with a smartass response. She just nodded. "Yeah, I've learned a thing or two. Mostly thanks to him." She nodded in the direction of her mentor.

They both watched as Ezekiel moved through the casualties. As he found rearick moving on the ground, he knelt by their side, laid his hands on their chests, and with glowing red eyes, he pushed life into them.

Hannah knew exactly what this meant. Healing magic wasn't easy, and combined with the power she had seen him use during the fight, she knew that the aftermath of the raid would slow down their plans to save Arcadia even more.

Even if the city was near and dear to the old magician's heart, there was something even more important—every single life he met along the way. While some people lost their compassion to their ideals, Ezekiel's ideals only fueled his compassion. It just wasn't in him to let someone die when he could save them.

Ezekiel finally wandered up to Hannah and Karl, and she introduced the two men. Chills ran down her spine watching the two, both of whom had saved her life at different times, shaking hands after the hard-fought battle.

Ezekiel stretched his back, his eyes continuing to survey the violence that lay on the ground around them. "I don't have much patience for these remnant. I can't imagine many do. A man who does evil, whether due to lust or hatred or something else—him, I can still pity. We all do things we don't want to often enough. And sometimes we don't do things we want to. But in these goblin men, there is no rational desire outside of their hunger."

Hannah's eyes narrowed. "What are they?"

"Now? They're monsters, but they haven't always been this way. The remnant are descendants of men and women from the Age of Madness. Even though I and another magician had found a way to cure the disease and stop it from spreading, there remained a group too far gone to be cured. While the Mad were nothing but hunger, the cure helped them to regain some form of consciousness—but not completely.

"Mixed with the animal instinct to survive, many of them learned to scratch out a living by consuming the world around them. Decades later, we have these," he pointed to the carcasses across the field "remnant. They aren't quite the mindless hordes of the Age of Madness, those creatures of the night that you and your friends call zombies, but what intelligence they do have is geared toward their animal nature. Their only desire is to eat, mate, and destroy."

"What do they eat?" Hannah asked.

"Mostly human flesh," Karl said, jumping in. "The damn goblins are worthless in our world. Less than worthless. They don't build, or bake, or create anything of value. All that they have and all that they want is stolen from their victims. Them remnant live on the spoils of their wretched raiding. And like Ezekiel said, they only live to eat, screw, and screw others over."

As Hannah listened to Karl talk, it was clear that he had experienced more than his fair share of remnant.

He began to tell them about the mission, and how it had gone smoothly ever since they had left the Heights. Escorting a group of other rearick was usually the easiest task a guard like him could have. He talked about how the mystics, with their minds in the sky, were probably the hardest to watch out for; it was like babysitting a herd of toddlers who drank too much ale.

When the remnant raiding party had come out over the rise, they were ready for them. Nevertheless, they were outnumbered. The remnant never minded a fight. They had no care for their companions. Remnant only focused on the kill, and the prospect of coming away with full bags of coin. They deemed trinkets from fallen soldiers worth the risk of their fellow raiders' deaths.

The rearick looked around at his fallen comrades. "But maybe we're not much different. After all, these men died much fer the same reason."

"I'm sorry for your loss, Karl. What are you hauling?" Hannah asked.

"The usual," Karl replied. "Some gold, a few precious gems, and a shit-ton of amphoralds. For the past year, that's all Arcadia really wants. It's like they've forgotten about all the other beautiful things we pull out of Mother Irth."

It's what they use to power the magitech, Ezekiel's voice suddenly said inside her head.

Hannah suddenly pictured the Hunter who killed her brother. He wielded a magitech staff.

Does he not know what Adrien uses them for? Hannah asked back.

I'm not sure, but it's not our job to inform the rearick of the injustices he is fueling by the sweat of his brow. At least, not yet. We must keep things running the way they are. Any disruptions and Adrien will be sure to see them and suspect us. For now, keep it to yourself.

"Darkness is coming," Karl said, breaking through their thoughts. "Ya are welcome to camp here with us. There may be more remnant hiding in them hills, and there is safety in numbers. Then, in the morning, I will bury me dead."

The rearick picked up his hammer and walked off through the fallen. Hannah wondered how many more dead she would see before this was all over.

Parker looked up from his task of twisting wires to the balcony walkway overhead. The bridge above him was the perfect place for the factory's overseers to observe their progress. He saw Doyle, the Chancellor's assistant, looking down on the men. Most within the city walls thought the bookish Doyle simply helped with the day-to-day functioning of the Academy, a sort of an academic administrator.

Parker had thought so, too, before he was enslaved in this place.

Doyle had been there every day since Parker started working in the factory. The man had to be somehow involved in overseeing the machine project, beyond crunching numbers and counting tuition dollars. Which wasn't a surprise. This machine had Adrien written all over it—why wouldn't his people be involved?

The person who had joined Doyle on his perch, however, did surprise him. Parker did a double-take when he recognized the Governor of Arcadia staring down at them as well.

Shock sunk in Parker's gut.

While Adrien often made public appearances on the steps of the Academy to large crowds sitting on the lawn, the Governor was a shadow. Everybody in town knew he was simply a figurehead, that Adrien held the real power in the community. But seeing the Governor in the factory made Parker realize that the thing they were building was bigger than he had first imagined.

"I guess everybody's involved in this thing," Parker said to Jack, who had fallen silent next to him.

"Hmmm?"

Parker nodded toward the balcony. "The Governor's here. I was saying that this must be a pretty big project to bring him out of the Capitol building."

"Oh, yeah. He's always here," Jack said. "I should think he spends more time in the factory than he does at the Capitol these days. Not sure what the guy does. I mean, Doyle and the Chief Engineer run most of the logistics here—them and that woman. The Governor just comes down to throw his weight around from time to time."

Jack's comment grabbed Parker's attention. "What woman?"

Jack's face fell white—he looked more afraid than he had all day. "I don't know who she is, and I don't want to know." He quickly looked over his shoulder, as if she were right behind him.

Parker knew that prying got him nowhere when Jack got in this mood, and the two went back to their work.

Parker tried to cope with the monotony by thinking about Hannah. She had been gone for months, and he was beginning to think something might be wrong. He feared she might have been hurt, but deep down inside, he knew that his worse thoughts included her running off with the wizard, leaving them all behind.

It was possible that she might not be coming back.

Maybe that magician had convinced her to leave Arcadia behind and to go and make a new world for new people. That was what revolutionaries were about. They saw wiping slates clean and starting over as often easier than the long, hard work of restoring something broke long ago. But Arcadia was worth the work, and with or without his friend, Parker maintained his commitment to the task. Which meant he had to get out of the factory.

"Has anybody tried to leave?" Parker finally asked.

Jack laughed. "I wouldn't recommend it. Once you're here, you're here until they're done with you. It's kind of like a prison sentence, but with pay. You know François?"

Parker thought for a while, Arcadia was filled with people, and he only knew so many. But then he remembered. "Is he the guy that ran that little black market magitech ring?"

Jack flinched at Parker's words. He shushed him and looked over each shoulder. "Shouldn't say that here. You know, with all the magicians around, they can hear just about anything they want to. But yeah, that guy. François dropped out of the Academy —hell, I don't know, maybe he was kicked out. But he ended up taking what he knew and starting that little business you spoke of.

"Of course, when everything started to tighten up on the Unlawfuls, François decided the risk was too great. It was time to stop taking the chance of getting pinched selling illegal magitech. The way I understand it, the Hunters are harsher on people selling magical items than they are on those who are restricted but still practicing."

Parker thought about Miranda and the way she had been tortured and hung to die on the stake in the middle of the square. Everybody knew that Unlawfuls were often killed on the spot, but most of them weren't murdered in such a public fashion. Maybe Jack was right.

"Anyway, François, he tried to get a job here early on when they first opened the floor. It worked, but apparently, once he was in he had second thoughts—kind of like you are right now. The guy tried to break free, get loose from the factory. And it didn't go so well."

"He didn't make it out?"

Jack paused from his work and laid his hands flat on the table. He checked over his shoulders again and then talked in a hushed tone. "He didn't even make it off this floor. It's these damn cuffs. There's some sort of magical force field or something surrounding the place. You try to get out with these magitech cuffs on, it zaps you right there on the spot. You'd be a fool to even try. You hear those screams?"

Jack nodded toward a large metal door at the other end of the factory. A man's screams had been echoing out from there for days.

Parker nodded.

"Who do you think is behind that door? That's where François is now. And that's where you'll end up if you try to run. Just keep your head down, like me. They'll have to release us once this thing is done, right? And who knows, maybe the pay is real?"

Parker nodded, trying to offer Jack some comfort, but he knew the truth. You didn't handcuff paid employees to their work. And there was no way the Governor would be bold enough to show his face here if they had any chance of getting out alive.

Parker needed to find another way, one that helped him out of the cuffs.

He looked back toward the end of the factory once again. François' screams continued to echo overhead through all of the other noise.

CHAPTER FOURTEEN

Doyle could feel his legs shake as he stood outside of Adrien's office door. It wasn't like his visits to the Chancellor were uncommon—he came nearly every day—but his nerves never calmed, and the anxiety never went away. Doyle knew from experience that he lived life just one wrong word away from obliteration. It was like working for a lion.

He'd seen Adrien kill a man for bad reports, or laziness, or even just a simple error. For some reason, Doyle had been able to keep his boss happy for this long, but each time he arrived at the door, it was like he was playing a hand in a card game in the market.

Luck only lasted so long; that's why they called it luck.

Doyle took a breath, straightened his shirt, and knocked on the door. Before he got to the third knock, the familiar voice rang out from inside.

"Enter!"

Doyle walked into the room and found his boss sitting behind the massive table, as he always did. Usually he had to wait for the Chancellor to finish whatever task his hands were set to, or perhaps just wait for no reason at all. But today, anticipation for Doyle's visit demanded Adrien's attention.

"What's the report?" Adrien snapped.

Doyle swallowed hard before continuing. "The good news is that the work on the floor of the factory is going very well. The men are working their fingers to the bone, and the entire thing's taking shape. I can almost see it in its completed form. A little pushback here and there from some of the men who didn't realize the terms of their agreement, but overall, the guys are just happy to have work and pay going home to their families. And as long as we keep them…well, imprisoned at the factory, it's one less mouth to feed at home. So I guess they believe it's a win in the end."

Adrien was nodding. His face lacked expression, but Doyle could read the displeasure nonetheless. Finally, he spoke. "And what's the bad news?"

Doyle could feel his palms beginning to sweat, even as his throat ran dry. "Like I said, the physical structure is not a problem, but we don't have enough magicians working on the magitech core. There is, of course, some trial and error that goes into building a magitech machine of these proportions. I don't want to speak poorly of the men.

"I mean, the magicians are doing all they can, but you know how magic works. They're just being worn out—one can only expel so much energy until they need to rest. We need more magicians, or this thing will take forever. We'll have a beautiful steel contraption with nothing to make it run."

The Chancellor jotted some notes on a piece of parchment on his desk and then looked back up at Doyle. "Fortunately, I have that under control. I've recently initiated a new scholarship program, and Dean Amelia has been most helpful in finding me recruits. I'll have your magicians—top of the crop—and I'll have them soon. Don't you worry about that."

Adrien looked back down at the piece of parchment, then

turned it over and started scanning the page, using his finger as a guide. He glanced back up at Doyle, who was still standing at the edge of his desk. "There's something else?"

"Well, yes, sir. It's about the Prophet."

"Old Jed? What's he been up to?"

Doyle insisted on getting consistent updates from the Governor's Guard about what was going on in the streets of Arcadia. Adrien was the brain of Arcadia, Doyle its hands and feet. He had to keep this place moving. "It's just that his disciples are getting very, well, *violent*. They've begun striking out at the citizens, and many believe their attacks are indiscriminate."

The Chancellor laughed, which always made Doyle feel uncomfortable. He knew the man was probably judging him, if not considering ousting him. "Doyle, have you come so far as to believe that I'm a man who does not treasure religious freedom within the walls of Arcadia?" Adrien laughed harder, as if he had just told the best joke ever. "Don't you worry about old Jed. He and I have an understanding. If people have been attacked, then I'm sure it was the will of the gods. Everything is going to work out exactly as we planned. Is that all then?"

"The only other item is the Convocation tomorrow. Do you have your speech ready to go?"

Adrien looked up from his table and smiled. "Yes Doyle, I believe I do. I've decided to throw out the old script. That was a speech for days gone by. Tomorrow's Convocation marks the beginning of a new, brighter future for Arcadia. For all of Irth! I'm about to lead us to a place the old man never could; a place where even he can't stop us from going."

Ezekiel's sleep that night was not restful. Like most nights, it was filled with dreams that quickly turned into nightmares. It was almost always the same.

The dream began with him and Eve, not as they were now, old and weary, but when they were young, at the founding of Arcadia. In the hazy fog of nighttime images, he walked hand in hand with his love. They talked about their visions for what the city could become, and the way Arcadia might just pull humanity out of the Age of Madness and back into a civilized state.

That dream never lasted for long.

It would move quickly to the night they adopted Adrien, welcomed him into their community. But instead of the innocent teenage boy, they adopted the older man Adrien was today. All the others, enthusiastic to help Adrien, opposed Ezekiel, whose intuition told him to cast Adrien back out into the darkness, but the others won. Then his dream would fast-forward to the fall of Arcadia and the tyranny of the orphan they'd taken in.

It always ended with Adrien cackling like a madman, standing amidst the ruins of their city.

Ezekiel gasped and sat up, as he did most mornings, his eyes glowing red and his body tingling with magical energy. He slowly allowed himself to calm down. Looking around, he took his bearings.

He could make out a row of the rearick off in the distance, finishing their funeral ceremony. Their tradition was to bury the dead before the sun rose, born out of the long history of the mining people. From darkness they came, in darkness they worked, and in darkness their lifeless bodies would be returned to the ground.

The good people of the Heights buried nearly a dozen dead that morning, and the number would have been far greater had Hannah and Ezekiel not arrived when they did. Karl had mentioned how the remnant had been attacking the lowlands more and more in recent days.

They were on the move, and Ezekiel had no idea why.

Camp was broken in silence. Ezekiel, Hannah, and her pet dragon walked toward the back of the column. They respected the community of rearick on their mournful march toward Arcadia. The group caravanned together for several miles, and then Ezekiel reached over to grab Hannah by the arm, and pulled her off the path.

"We leave them now."

Karl made his way to them from the front of the pack. He removed his iron helmet and bowed his head in Hannah's direction. "We owe the two of ya our lives. I'm forever grateful. Hopefully we'll see each other again in New Arcadia. May the Matriarch and Patriarch be with ya."

Ezekiel nodded, and Hannah considered stepping forward and embracing her friend. But the rearick turned too quickly, and before she could respond, he was back at the tail end of the caravan walking with his friends toward the gates. He didn't seem much like the hugging type anyway.

"Why are we leaving them?" Hannah asked. "Aren't we all going to Arcadia?"

"Indeed, we are, but there are some things we need to do before we enter the city gates. And if our friends thought their world was a living hell fighting the remnant, the last thing they need to do is walk into Arcadia with the Founder and his Unlawful student. Their fate would be much worse than that of the brothers and sisters they left in the dirt this morning."

They stood in silence as the rearick marched away. When they were alone, Hannah asked, "I get why we can't go with them. I don't want to put anyone else in harm's way because of me. But if that's the case, how the hell are we going to get into Arcadia ourselves?"

"That, my dear Hannah, is the question." As Ezekiel said this, he turned from the main road and walked into a stand of trees off to the side. Hannah followed as he continued his speech.

"As I have said, Hannah, not everyone within the walls of Arcadia is bad. And we need to find those allies who will support us. You've been assuming that our only options lie with the poor

—those who live within Queen's Boulevard, but this isn't true, of course. While they are few and far between, there are some rich and noble people who also balk at the practices of bullies and tyrants. It's our job to find them, and wake them up to a better way."

Hannah tilted her head and narrowed her eyes. She had listened to the riddles of the magician for a long time, but she still hadn't been able to master the answers. She tried to wait him out instead. Unfortunately, her patience evaporated before Sal could look around and find something to chase.

"And how exactly are we going to do that?" Hannah asked. "I kinda don't have many friends in high places."

"You may not," Ezekiel said with a smile, "but Lord Girard does."

Hannah's eyes narrowed as she looked at the old wizard. "And who the hell is Lord Girard?"

Zeke couldn't help but laugh. "He just happens to be the man whom I visited when I was away from the Heights. Girard is a man of great wealth, honor, and position within Arcadia. He is also an insufferably cruel individual.

"Years ago, Girard moved out of the city and bought a manor in the country to the north, once he had made his money off the backs of the poor. The damn place, if sold, could pull half the Boulevard out of poverty. Instead, the nobleman lived there in a life of vice. But he's had a reawakening—a restoration of sorts—and now travels to Arcadia to seek redemption."

With a flourish, Ezekiel threw his cloak off his shoulders. Hannah watched it drop to the ground. When she raised her eyes again, Ezekiel was gone. In his place stood a taller man, with a face soft from a life of ease. His beard was shorter, and his shockingly white hair had turned dark. Marvelous crimson with golden embroidery draped over his body.

Her mouth dropped open. "Holy shit, Zeke. You're kind of

hot. I mean, still old, but not too shabby." She walked around him to check out the robe.

Ezekiel, as Girard, laughed. "Yes. They say that magic can work miracles. And now it's your turn."

Hannah's eyes dropped to the ground, and she thought of that day when she made herself a robe in the Heights to cover her naked body from Hadley's eyes. "I might be able to manage the wardrobe, but I'm just not strong enough for the total transformation."

His eyes flashed red, and Hannah was dressed in clothing like Ezekiel's. Her hair was different as well. Previously straight and dark, she now sported curls of strawberry blonde.

Sal hissed in surprise, then relaxed as he sniffed Hannah's hand.

"Son of a bitch," she said, checking herself out. "We look every bit like those rich pricks. I imagine we can pull this off."

Ezekiel nodded. "We might just be able to do it if you keep your filthy mouth shut," he said with a wink. "I've given you new clothes and new hair. The rest of you looks like you. But if you work on refining your manners, we should be able to blend in."

"Wait," Hannah said. "My face is the same?" She ran a finger down her nose and across her cheekbone.

"Yes, same old beautiful you."

"But, everybody in Arcadia is looking for me," Hannah said as if Ezekiel was an idiot.

"That's right. They're looking for a rough-and-tumble girl from Queen Bitch Boulevard. Not the person you look like now —an elegant woman of noble status. It's amazing what people will and won't see, and the rigid class lines in the city will ensure they will not see a poor person in wealthy clothes. Act like a noble and they will see you as a noble. I assume you can keep up the charade?"

She nodded, but the thought of doing this was more frightening than facing the remnant.

Hannah realized she didn't have much of a choice. The magician could only get her so far. The rest was on her. Ezekiel had made the original change, but Hannah would need to sustain it, which would take a significant amount of magical energy. This plan would have to work, or else they would have to be inseparable inside the walls of Arcadia, which wasn't an option either.

"There are few things I trust about the nobles and bureaucrats of Arcadia," Ezekiel said. "But one of the things I know will always be true is that their prejudice outweighs their reason. When they look at you, they will see the daughter of a nobleman, not the orphan daughter of a drunk. Not all education is useful, and they have been trained for a lifetime to see things within narrow categories. Their limitations will ultimately serve us well."

Ezekiel turned to walk away before Hannah reached out and grabbed his shoulder. "Uh, Zeke? Don't you think you're forgetting something?"

He looked confused for a moment, until she nodded in the direction of the dragon standing at her feet. "Don't you think I'll look a little suspicious coming into the city with a hundred-pound dragon by my side? I mean, Sal is more than a little conspicuous."

Ezekiel smiled. "Ah, yes. I almost forgot." His eyes turned red as he mumbled something under his breath. Sal began to hiss again, but within seconds, the sound was no longer coming from a lizard, but a large wolf-like creature.

Hannah smiled as she knelt to pet him. "Awww, Sal. Who's a good puppy?"

Sal looked less than pleased in his new digs.

"Unfortunately, he won't really sound like a dog," Ezekiel said. "So he'll have to try and keep his hissing to a minimum. Now, we really should be moving."

Hannah, Ezekiel, and their dragon-in-wolf's-clothing cut through the woods and found another small road heading west toward Arcadia. A carriage with two beautiful horses and a uniformed driver waited there for them.

Ezekiel walked up and ran his hand down the neck of one of the horses, whispering into its ear. He greeted the driver and stepped into the carriage, offering his hand to Hannah. It took a fair amount of effort not to trip over her elegant skirts as she entered the carriage. Sal leapt in after her.

Zeke closed the door and waved a hand once they were inside, blocking their conversation from being heard outside of the carriage.

She had never ridden in a carriage before, and the jostling on the rough road surprised her. She always imagined the rich and noble rode in complete comfort in these things. But their journey had been long, so she wasn't going to complain about a bit of jostling as long as she didn't have to walk.

Sal sat beside her, obviously enjoying the trip. He stuck his head out the window and she wondered if this felt like flying.

"Where the hell did this carriage come from?" Hannah asked. "Did you...conjure it?"

Ezekiel sighed as he looked out the window. "Did that boy, Hadley, teach you nothing? Not all illusions are magical. This carriage is real, along with the driver and horses. I own them, or at least Lord Girard does. And since no one will ever find his body, I am the real Lord Girard now."

"Damn," Hannah said, admiring the efficiency of her mentor.

"My sweet daughter," Ezekiel said, with a slightly formal clip to his speech. "What did I tell you about using that language?"

"Dear Father," Hannah replied, in a terrible fake accent. "What exactly is our plan when we reach the city? Who the hell am I?"

"Well, let's start with me," Ezekiel said. "You should learn these details by heart. I'm Lord Girard. Years ago, I took my extraordinary wealth and left Arcadia for what I thought was the rest of my life. The real Girard was a horrible person. He had no nobility whatsoever, but now he is dead. I put an end to his viciousness. Only now will he be able to offer something of value to Arcadia—to all of Irth."

"Okay, that's just a little creepy. What about me?"

"You are Girard's daughter. Noble by birth, but uneducated due to our life in the country. It recently struck me that I did not want my daughter growing up in ignorance, so we're returning to enroll you in the Academy."

Hannah's eyes opened wide, and she dropped all pretense of an accent. "I'm going to be a student at the Academy?"

Ezekiel only nodded.

"Holy shit." She shook her head. "Zeke, this is never going work."

"You're wrong." He pointed out. "It will work because it has to." Ezekiel looked out the side window of the carriage in silence for some time. Then he turned back to Hannah, who had been doing the same. "There's a trunk in the back of the carriage with enough expensive clothes to keep you outfitted. You won't have to waste energy on the illusion every day, just on your hair. They will help you fit in at the Academy, but remember, you're going in knowing next to nothing. And you certainly aren't in any way some sort of amazing magician trained by the greatest wizard alive."

"So I need to play dumb?" she confirmed.

Ezekiel laughed. "Not dumb, just inexperienced. I imagine you can handle that. Hell, I've only been working with you for a few months. Is your memory really that short?"

"As short as your sense of humor," Hannah said with a wink. "I'm sure I can play dumb enough to fool those rich asshats."

An hour passed before the carriage pulled up to the gates of Arcadia. Hannah looked out the window, happy to see her old home again. A long line of farmers, hunters, and trappers waited to enter, and Hannah spied a group of mystics with a cart full of barrels surrounded by several rearick. She strained her neck to see if she recognized anyone, but she didn't.

One of the Governor's Guard stepped around the line and pointed at the carriage. He waved them to the front. Ignoring the line was just one of the many advantages of being noble.

Ezekiel watched the process as they pulled up to the gate. Everything had changed. Just months before, the Guard at the gate did almost nothing; most of them sat lazily around, talking and laughing. But their number had doubled, and all of them focused their attention on searching the carts and wares of anyone trying to enter the city.

The travelers grumbled to each other, but little could be done but accept the increased scrutiny.

A guard came up to the carriage and poked his head in. He was a young man, dressed in well-made light armor, carrying a magitech rifle.

"What is your business in Arcadia?" the guard asked.

Ezekiel cleared his throat. "I'm Lord Girard. I have returned from the country, as it is time for my dear daughter to enter the Academy."

The Guard looked at Hannah and then back at Ezekiel. "She looks a little old to join the Academy now. Do you have any proof? Perhaps her acceptance documents?"

Ezekiel's voice turned hard as granite. "Guard, what is your name?"

The man's face flushed, and Hannah could nearly hear him swallow. "It's, um, Anthony, sir. I'm sorry," he looked over his shoulder and then back at Ezekiel, "it's just that I have to ask. We have all sorts of dangerous folks trying to enter the city these days."

Ezekiel ignored his excuse. "Anthony, is your commanding officer here?"

The man looked down at his feet. "No. Well, I'm actually the commanding officer on duty right now."

Ezekiel broke out into laughter, long enough to make the man want to melt. "I'm sorry," Ezekiel said. "Did you say that you're the *commanding* officer?"

"Yes, sir. That's right."

"Well, Anthony, I suggest you let us through. The Chancellor and I are close, always have been. Now, you can hold us up here over your half-cocked suspicions, but I imagine that the Chancellor is going to be very unhappy about your decision to delay us as soon as I inform him."

The man stood there, looking back and forth between Ezekiel and Hannah. Hannah held her breath and then ran her fingers through her curly strawberry blonde hair. The man's eyes lingered on Hannah's face. For a minute, she thought the guard had made them.

She took a chance—passing him a wink and a smile.

Finally, his eyes cut back to Ezekiel. "My apologies, sir. Welcome back to Arcadia."

"Good man," Ezekiel said. "I'll be sure to put in a good word for you when I see the Chancellor."

The man nodded and stepped down from the carriage, giving the Girard's beautiful daughter one last look.

"Oh, and one more thing," Ezekiel said in his direction. "On our way here, we saw a band of remnant raiding some traders heading toward the city. I suggest you run this up the chain of command. If we had been just a few hours earlier, it could've been us attacked by those foul creatures. Perhaps it's time that the Governor take some of your men off this Guard post and send them out to protect people like us in the countryside."

The man nodded again. "Of course, sir. Thank you, sir."

At that, the carriage started to move past the frightened Guard and into Arcadia.

CHAPTER FIFTEEN

Hannah could feel Ezekiel relax next to her on the bench seat of the carriage as they approached the gate, which was just in front of them. She was glad to have the inspection behind them. But just as they were passing through the portal, another guard stepped up to their vehicle and held his hand up to indicate that the driver should stop.

Some words were exchanged between the driver and the guard. Hannah couldn't make them out, but she knew they were not pretty.

"Another gate check? If this guy looks at me like the last one, I'm going to rip his head off and shove it right up his ass," Hannah said.

"You're really not working on this noble girl thing, are you?" Ezekiel smiled. "There will be no heads shoved up any asses today, my *darling* daughter." Ezekiel raised his eyebrows. "Make sure you behave"

"No promises," Hannah said mutinously. "I thought our noble status would allow us to come right in."

Ezekiel poked his head out the window and looked at the guard, who busied himself inspecting their luggage. "I did too, but things have changed in Arcadia since your little show of strength. I imagine they're taking extra precautions, even more than you would've imagined."

The guard, a burly man with a face not even a mother could love, stepped up to Ezekiel's side of the carriage and pulled open the door. "Need you to get out, old man."

Ezekiel tried the outraged act again. "This is preposterous. I've been away from our beautiful city for years. I come back, and this is the welcome I get? Do you know who I am, young man?"

It shocked Hannah to see just how stately Ezekiel looked sitting in his nobleman's clothes. She was impressed by his ability to be someone completely different than himself. Nervousness ran through her body, and she wondered if she would be able to pull it off.

"I don't give a shit if you're the Queen Bitch herself," the guard spat back. "Knowing you is not my job. All I know is that you're new here, even if you are old. And my number one priority is Arcadia, not worrying about offending some old rich bastard from out of town." The lines in the man's face got deeper as he scowled at them. "Now, you can get out of the carriage the hard way or the easy way. Your choice."

Hannah tried to read Ezekiel, to see how they should react. She hadn't had the chance to change into actual noble clothes, and she wasn't sure if Ezekiel's magic would hold up under scrutiny. Sal, still looking like a dog, hissed at the man. He gave the creature a weird look, but before the man could react, another, much taller guard, stormed over.

"What the hell do you think you're doing, you shit head?" The new guard towered over the other. His face was covered in indignation. "Who told you it was ok to harass the nobles? What are you, crazy or something?"

"Sir, they were being obstinate," the ugly one said, trying to keep calm. "I'm just doing my job here."

The superior balled his right hand into a fist; Hannah was

157

ready to watch the rude Guard get clocked. "Your job here," he said, "is to follow my command. Right now, I'm commanding you to head off to the stables. Maybe you'll work off some of that steam shoveling horseshit for the day. No, make that two. I don't want to see your face around here for two days, and if I do, you'll wish you were permanently on shit duty."

The ugly guard looked at his feet and then back up at his commanding officer. "Yes, sir. Forgive me, sir."

The man shuffled off, and the new guard looked into the carriage.

"Thank you, my good man," Ezekiel said to the commanding officer. "I'm just glad there's still someone in Arcadia with an ounce of reason and an eye for refinement."

"It might not be that easy, old man." The guard's eyes cut toward Hannah and inspected her face and then back at Ezekiel. "I'm still going to need you to come with me. My problem with Bruce was his means, not his end. Have your driver pull the carriage through the gate and off to the side. This won't take long, but I'm going to need you to come inside the Guard station. Make sure you bring your documentation. A lot has changed in Arcadia since you left, if you've really been gone for as long as you say. And if you truly love the city, as we do, you won't mind obliging our diligence."

The guard turned and headed for the small shack off to the side of the gate. Hannah felt sick to her stomach and started to focus the energy within her. If there was going to be a fight, she could use the nerves.

If there was one thing she had learned from her training over the past several months, it was to put away all the emotions that hampered her casting, and to channel the ones that were helpful. Fear and rage were among the most helpful.

She told Sal to stay, then climbed out of the carriage.

"We going to need to take them down?" Hannah asked Ezekiel as he joined her on the ground.

"Patience. Revolutions are won by the inch, not a mile at a time. This man will be no problem for us. I can guarantee that."

They followed the man through the narrow door into the tiny Guardhouse. Relatively empty, the room was furnished only with a desk and a few chairs. It looked like it was seldom used and smelled like stale smoke from the guards' pipes, likely just a place for them to get away from the wind in the winter and the sun in the summer.

Hannah rolled her wrists, readying them for an attack if necessary. Ezekiel closed the door behind them, and the guard closed the blinds.

"Your travels have been good to you, Ezekiel," the guard said. "You look years younger than when I last saw you."

Ezekiel smiled. "Wish I could say the same for you. You look like shit."

Hannah stared wide-eyed at her mentor, thinking he had lost his mind, but the guard's perpetually angry face softened as the large man broke into laughter. Ezekiel followed.

Hannah, on the other hand, didn't get what was so funny.

"What the hell is happening?" Hannah asked, looking from one to the other.

Ezekiel took a breath and smiled. "Didn't I tell you? I've got an old friend working here now."

She looked over at the brute of a man, and his eyes turned perfectly white. Then he was no more. Hannah couldn't tell whether it happened all at once or if time stood still and the transformation was incremental, but before she could make sense of the situation, the guard was gone and in his place stood a tall, beautiful woman about her own age.

"Holy shit!" Hannah exclaimed.

"Classy. You sure she's going to fit in?" the woman asked.

Ezekiel laughed. "She's a fast learner."

She smiled. "Good thing, because you're about out of time. At least she looks the part."

"Um… Thanks?" Hannah replied, still confused about what was happening.

"Now, Hannah," Ezekiel admonished. "Meet Julianne, the Master of the mystics."

Hannah nodded at the woman. Hadley had spoken often of his teacher, but he wouldn't tell Hannah where she was—only that she was off serving humanity.

Hannah pictured her feeding the poor or curing diseases, not masquerading as a Capitol Guard. And she had also pictured her as a shriveled old lady, not as the lovely woman in front of her.

"So what gives?" Hannah asked. "What are you doing here?"

"That's my doing, I'm afraid," Ezekiel responded. "When I traveled to the Heights over a month ago, my intention was to visit my former student Selah. Unfortunately, I was a few years late, but I was glad to find Julianne there in his stead. She is the new Master of the mystics, and it looks as if she is going to be an amazing advantage in our cause."

Julianne sat in the chair behind the desk and put her feet up on its surface. She reached into a bag on the floor and pulled out a wineskin. "This kind of meeting calls for a drink," she said with a smile. "Come and sit for a while. I mean, I am the commanding officer at the gate for another six hours. We might as well make the most of it. And the longer I keep you in here, the tougher the other Guard will think I'm being on you."

She offered the wineskin to Hannah, who grabbed mystics' elixir greedily. She tilted the skin and drank deeply. Surprisingly cold, it worked instantly to settle her nerves.

"Thank you." Hannah passed the wineskin back to their host.

"Your teacher wasn't the only person to visit us in the Heights that day," Julianne said after she took a drink. "Chancellor Adrien had sent a group of his Guard to get information from us. I guess he was a little concerned about whether or not the mystics would prove to be a problem for his plans in Arcadia. Quite frankly, we probably wouldn't have been, but things went sideways. And once the shit hit the fan, we had no other choice but to return blows with his men. Naturally, if they didn't return to Arcadia, we would've been in big trouble. And apparently, Ezekiel doesn't have the self-control of even a mystic child." She thought about that comment, then changed it. "Make that just a child."

The old man laughed. "If I hadn't killed that man he would've killed me, and come after you next. I'm not sure if all the meditation in the world would've stopped him."

A thin-lipped smile spread on Julianne's face. "You might be right, Master Magician, but I guess we'll never know. Because of Ezekiel's action, I found it necessary to take action of my own. I volunteered to masquerade as the dead man and made my way to Arcadia. Not the most enjoyable of pastimes, I can assure you."

"Wait," Hannah interjected. "I thought it was impossible for a mystic to look exactly like someone else."

"Impossible for all but those at the top," Ezekiel replied. "And Julianne is, by definition, at the top."

Julianne smiled. "I appreciate the compliment, but I'm happier still that you've come back. I've learned quite a bit since I've been here, and I have to tell you, I think things might be worse than you expected."

"Adrien's big plan," Ezekiel mused, "is to build a machine. Is that right?"

Julianne nodded. "It's all very secretive. They withhold things even from people in positions like mine, but they're building something in the factory. Something despicable enough to keep out of view. Not just a machine, but a weapon."

Ezekiel nodded, a grave look on his face. The mirth of their initial meeting had disappeared. "Yes, my old student said something about his plan for Irth. This must be it. And the amphorald shipments that are increasing—I assume those are not for the sake of making more simple magitech adorning the streets of Arcadia?"

Julianne shook her head. "The shipments come through here

at the gate. We're supposed to send them right down to the factory. The rearick are the only ones who get fast-tracked into the city. I have no real idea what they're building, but I'm sure it's not designed to promote world peace."

"If Adrien's involved," Hannah jumped in, "you can bet it's something awful."

"Well," Ezekiel said, "that'll be one of the first things we will have to find out once we enroll Hannah in the Academy. Think you can handle a bit of espionage?"

Hannah turned to Ezekiel. "Listen, don't forget I've been running the streets since I could walk. Deceiving people becomes second nature to a Boulevard kid like me. Hunger has a way of making you hustle. But now that I've got magic on my side, Adrien and his minions will *never* see me coming."

The carriage wound through the tight Arcadian streets, bucking the foot traffic. For all the problems in Arcadia, people still flocked to the city. It made Hannah wonder just how bad it was elsewhere in the world. She really had seen very little of it, despite the fact that she had traveled more than most people born in the Boulevard.

But their driver pushed on with skill, and he made his way toward the Noble Quarter without any problems. Most people moved quickly out of their way—rule number one of living in Arcadia was that it didn't pay to piss off the nobles. Being on this end of that rule was an experience altogether alien to her.

In all her days in Arcadia, she had never even expected to be treated like a person, let alone nobility. And while she had been in the noble district before, she was seeing it with new eyes.

She looked around for Parker, but he was nowhere to be seen, which wasn't much of a surprise. Hannah assumed he was off pulling the wool over someone's eyes, like the old days. The thought of Parker made her happy, but she had no time for nostalgia—she had a revolution to start. She pushed Parker out of her mind as the driver pulled up in front of a place that looked as grand as it did empty.

"This it?" Hannah wondered.

"Yes," Ezekiel confirmed. "This is our new home."

"Whose is it?" Hannah asked.

"Why, it's mine." Ezekiel laughed. "Lord Girard—the bastard —has maintained this place ever since he moved out of Arcadia, although it was completely unnecessary. It's sat like this ever since. Part of the problem here is that the nobles don't know what they have, and their greed takes away from everybody else. There are systemic problems in this city as well as magical ones. I aim to cure both, but Arcadia wasn't built in a day and it can't be rebuilt in a day. Until then, we'll use this as our headquarters."

As they approached the front door, they realized that the house wasn't quite as grand as it had looked from the outside. Distance granted it a bit of grace, but now that they were standing on the front doorstep, the entire residence looked like it'd been abandoned years before. Ezekiel tapped the end of his staff on the door and waited.

"Maybe there's no one here," Hannah said.

"There is. More than one," he muttered. "I can feel them."

He knocked again and waited a few more minutes. Then the magician took two fingers and pointed them toward the lock. He spun his wrist to the right, turning his fingers like a key. Hannah heard the lock snap open to welcome them into Girard's house.

Hannah pushed the door open. "After you, Z… Father."

Ezekiel, still looking like the nobleman, stepped across the threshold. Hannah followed. Walking through the short foyer, they stepped into the large living room. Its vaulted ceiling bounced the echoes of the two people snoring, asleep in the living room.

A woman, still clad in her sleeping gown even though it was

past the noon hour, lounged on a sofa with a plate of what looked like fine chocolates on her lap. A man in a chair across from her was dressed in the same way. A hardbound book lay open in his lap, but he wasn't reading. His head tilted back, and he was dead asleep.

"What the hell are you doing, you miserable servants?" Ezekiel boomed into the room.

The pair jumped out of their seats, eyes wide. The man, probably in his mid-forties, stammered as he stared at the Master of the house. Luckily for him, the woman was much better on her feet. "Why, my Lord, welcome back to Arcadia," she said with an artificial smile on her face. "I must say, this is quite an unexpected visit."

Ezekiel looked around the room, casting his eyes slowly around the mess. "I'd say it's a surprise for both of us! And what the hell have you two been doing in my house? Haven't I been paying you to keep this place in order?"

"Oh, right. This." The woman swept her hand across the room. "Oh… We've been, um, there's been a sickness moving through the Noble Quarter. Charles and I, we've just had it terribly. That's all. It normally looks tiptop around here."

"Tiptop," the man, who was suddenly awake, repeated.

The woman got to her feet. "But now that you're home, my Lord, I will get to work at once. Sickness or no sickness, I will make sure that you have the grandest visit you've ever had to any place in all of Irth."

"Yes, in all of Irth," Charles mumbled after her.

"There's an old saying, Margaret. You can't bullshit a bullshitter." Ezekiel narrowed his eyes at them, and Hannah could barely stifle a laugh, considering the fact that she and Ezekiel were indeed pulling some *major* bullshit right then and there.

The servants looked at one another and then back at the person they thought was Girard. They both laughed nervously.

"Of course you can't," Margaret said. "And there will be no bull-shit in this house."

"That's right, no bullshit here." The man flushed.

"Good, then we have an agreement. From the looks of this place, your sickness must be more long-term than any I have seen in all of Arcadia. You must be nearly dead, and I am afraid it may be catching. If you know what's good for you, you'll get the hell out of my house as quickly as you can. And if you don't, I'll make sure your disease becomes permanent."

The woman stammered again. "But… But… But… Lord, please have mercy on your servants. You've always been such a good man. Kind and generous and full of care. May we have another chance to—"

"You will get out of my house, and you will get out now," Ezekiel bellowed. "And you won't mention anything about this to anyone. If you do, in the name of the Matriarch, I will make sure that I bring down all the wrath I'm able to muster. I will rip your lazy tongues from your lying mouths."

The servants turned sheet-white and ran from the house.

"Well, I think that went well," Hannah said with a grin. "Very low profile. I'm sure they won't tell anybody about this little meeting."

As she spoke, Hannah moved around the room, observing the furniture. It was all highly ornate, with wooden carving and upholstered surfaces. She ran a finger across the tabletop, drawing a line in the dust.

"This sucks."

Ezekiel turned to her, brow furrowed. "Nothing a little cleaning won't fix."

Hannah rolled her eyes. "Not that. I lived in a three-room apartment with my brother and my drunk father all my life. Everybody I know lived the same way. And there are houses like these, just sitting empty. This shouldn't happen."

Ezekiel's face looked grave. "It was never supposed to be like this. We spent so much time planning and dreaming and planning some more, just to make sure that Arcadia would never be the kind of place that it has become, but we couldn't plan for Adrien's treachery. He will pay, and pay dearly."

"But it's not just him. I hate the guy, too, but it takes more than one man to keep a system like this alive. The nobles are just as bad."

"Yes," Ezekiel said. "But they have been taught that this is the way to live. The way to be. In many ways, they are children."

Hannah stuck out her bottom lip as if she were pouting. "Awww. The cute little nobles are really victims."

Ezekiel's face looked as serious as the Age of Madness. "Sort of, yes. You can't cast such an indictment in ignorance. I agree, their naiveté doesn't make them innocent, but it does give them potential. Maybe they just need a new teacher."

"Like you," Hannah said.

"Like *you*," was Ezekiel's response before he turned and walked deeper into the house, leaving Hannah's look of shock behind him.

Hannah ran after him. "What do you mean, *me*?"

"There will always be some who are richer than others, Hannah. As far as I can tell, the world has always been like that. It's kind of like magic. Some can control the Etheric as if they were gods, and some live and die without ever knowing the power within them. But the problem isn't that some have wealth or power when others don't. The problem is how they use it.

"And while the nobles may have resources, I believe it is the poor—those like yourself—who can teach them how to best utilize what they have. When the rich and the poor, when the magic users and those without, are united and not deliberately kept separate from and at odds with one another, then we will have true peace. And that's part of why we're here.

"Yes, I want you to infiltrate the noble echelon to learn about Adrien's plans, but I also think you could find us some allies here.

If we can get the Boulevard and the nobles to work together, taking down Adrien will be a piece of cake."

Ezekiel finished his speech and picked up a vase full of wilted flowers. "But in the meantime, we'll have to hire new servants."

Hannah looked at him quizzically. Their ruse could only last so long, and the house would no longer be their residence once the plan had been completed—or if it failed. "What do we need servants for?"

"Our mission," Ezekiel said. "The mystical arts can only take us so far in keeping up appearances. There are some things that we will have to do for people that are more, well, *mundane,* if you will."

"Then we'll need servants, and maybe even a driver." Hannah raised her eyebrows.

"Now you're talking like a noble." Ezekiel chuckled.

"In that case," Hannah said, "I know some people—good people—who can work for us. They're from the Boulevard, which means they can use the work, but it also means that they're trustworthy, unlike old Girard's servants."

Ezekiel looked around the house. The place was in shambles. They were going to need significant help to blend in.

Before he could respond, Sal, who had been sniffing around, leapt into the air. Two leathery wings broke through his fur coat and he began to fly around the room. The rest of the illusion broke with it, and Sal was fully dragon once again.

"Let's keep it small, for now. Why don't you give me the name of someone you can trust—and who won't freak out when they see a dragon in the house. And then, I think there's another woman I would like to have close to us. She won't be a servant, more of an attendant to the lady," Ezekiel said with a wink.

At first Hannah was confused. She wondered who this lady might be; then she realized it was her. "Naturally the lady will need an attendant."

Ezekiel laughed. "I think you're finally getting the hang of this noble thing. You're going to do just fine, but you'll need an attendant because there are preparations to be made."

"Preparations?"

"Yes," Ezekiel replied, "for your interview for admission into the Academy."

"Ohhhhh… shit!" Hannah groaned.

CHAPTER SIXTEEN

Ezekiel left Hannah at the house to rest and practice her magic. He tried to convince her that she could use her skills to clean up the place, but she refused. The girl had a long list of spells that she wanted to practice, and in Hannah's words: "I didn't learn magic so I could wash the damn windows!"

Before he left, he warned her to stay in the house. Zeke knew that Hannah was anxious to visit the Boulevard and see old friends, or at least one old friend.

But in his opinion, it was far too dangerous for her to chance going there. Her disguise would work among the upper crust, but the streetwise contingent in Arcadia would see her for who she truly was—one of them.

Not that she really was one of them anymore. The girl had flourished in the past months, despite the dangers and the grueling work. Hannah had become a woman of neither the Boulevard nor the Heights. Ezekiel doubted if she really knew it yet, but soon enough it would be clear.

Returning to Arcadia was only going to highlight just how much Hannah had changed.

Ezekiel knew that better than most.

He made his way through the Noble Quarter, whistling softly as he walked to a quaint little house on its east side. He stood on the doorstep, hesitated a moment to look around the street, and then dropped the illusion. He wanted the two ladies inside to see him without his disguise. Then he plunged ahead and knocked on the door.

The house belonged to Eve, his oldest friend. Well, oldest human friend. Lilith didn't really count. He and Eve had worked together in the early days, as the Age of Madness came to a close. She had been there in his darkest hours, when madness almost seemed preferable to the work ahead. Without Eve, there would be no Arcadia, and probably no Ezekiel either.

She had made him the man that he was.

As he waited, he once again felt like a schoolboy riddled with nerves, about to ask a girl on a date.

The door opened slowly, and Madelyn, Eve's niece, stood in the entranceway. It struck him again how much she looked like her mother. Since her mother's passing, Madelyn had come to live with her Aunt Eve, helping to take care of the place.

The girl's face lightened as she recognized him, but then, as quickly as it had filled with gladness, it transformed to concern. Nevertheless, she tried to smile. "Ezekiel, welcome back to Arcadia. You've been gone too long."

He could tell she held something she needed to tell him, and fear gripped his heart.

"Eve?" He couldn't help but ask in the simplest way he could.

The girl nodded. "Gone. A few days after your last visit. It was as if she had waited all this time for your return, and once she had spoken with you my aunt just, well, let herself pass."

Ezekiel stood there speechless. The pain in his heart transcended all words.

Finally, he fought past the pain and scraped out, "I am sorry."

"Yes. We both are." Madelyn stepped away to make room for the magician to enter. "Won't you come in?"

Ezekiel walked through the doorway and into the living room. The house still smelled like his old love—like it did when he last visited. He turned and sat on the couch, still trying to make sense of it all.

He and Eve had really only known each other for a few short years, but their feelings for each other ran deep. Whether they were fueled by the mission to build the new city or a connection from surviving the Age of Madness, he couldn't quite be sure. But he knew that the two had fallen fast and hard. Leaving her behind for all that time was the worst part of his forty-year journey.

And now she was gone.

And, though he would miss her deeply, he also knew that her death would enable him to focus single-mindedly on saving the city—*her* city. He pictured her as she had looked in her bed the night he first returned, and he felt a sense of relief that he had gotten to see her one last time. Though her body was frail, Eve's spirit had been as strong as ever.

She had never stopped believing in Arcadia.

Madelyn came back into the room and placed a tray of tea with some expensive-looking cookies on the side table next to the couch. Ezekiel lifted his cup and sipped on the hot herbal drink. "Thank you."

Madelyn nodded silently and took a seat next to the refreshments. "She went fast, Ezekiel. And you need to know that she ended her days in joy, primarily because of your visit. My aunt had lived a good life; she always took care of me and anyone else who needed her. A good woman all of her days."

Ezekiel nodded. He knew these things, but it was nevertheless nice to hear them said out loud. They sat for a while, discussing the woman they both loved, laughing and crying together.

As the hours passed, Ezekiel knew he needed to shift the conversation to the matter at hand. There was more to be done;

Eve would have wanted him to keep pushing toward the redemption of the city. "What will you do now, Madelyn?"

The young woman flushed, just a little. "Please call me Maddy. Only my aunt called me by my proper name. And as for what will happen now," she paused a moment, "I'm not sure. My resources are dwindling, and it isn't likely that I'll be able to stay in this house forever." She scanned the room, taking in all the old artifacts left behind by her aunt. "Not sure if I want to anyway. There are memories nestled in every corner, and I've been thinking that maybe it's time to set my eyes on the future."

Ezekiel smiled. "Hmmm. The future, yes. You know, I think I might just know a nobleman who's in need of someone with your talent. Any interest?"

"A nobleman?"

Ezekiel placed his teacup down on the tray and told her the entire story of what had happened since the day he last saw her—about Hannah and his plan to take back Arcadia.

"But my girl is definitely from Queen's Boulevard, not the daughter of a noble. She's going to need help, someone to show her the ropes. And I think you're just the one to do it. That is, if you think this is something worth doing? I'm not going to push you on this. Your aunt and I made our own decisions for our own lives. You need to make yours."

Maddy bit her lip and thought about the choice. Finally, she smiled and nodded. "Yes. I'm in. I do want to help—to honor my aunt's name, and to make Arcadia everything she ever wanted it to be. I'll do whatever you ask. It shouldn't be too hard to teach her the ways of the nobles."

Ezekiel snorted, almost spilling his tea as he thought about the rambunctious young woman. "You think that now, but just wait until you meet Hannah. I promise you, you're going to have your work cut out for you."

Karl had spent half the day waiting to make it through the Governor's security at the gate. He cursed Arcadia and all those who ran the place.

Normally they let in rearick carrying shipments without much hassle, but when the guard saw Karl, with his heavy armor still stained with the blood of the remnant, they decided to take their time searching their goods.

Karl didn't mind traveling the road from the Heights, helping caravans make it to the city. It was waiting in the city that bothered him. Even the occasional bloodbath in the open plains of the lowlands was better than the shit he had to put up with in Arcadia

And it was only getting worse.

Finally, after confirming that the rearick hadn't hidden an invading army in their wagon, the guard let them roll through. The wagons carrying gold and amphorald gems bumped along the dusty street and into the city.

It was far too late to start the journey back to the Heights that evening, not to mention his party would want to blow off some steam in Arcadia before they left. The head trader paid him half his wage, as they had arranged, and Karl headed for the only reasonable watering hole he knew in all of Arcadia.

Sully's Tavern was the kind of place a man would never take a date, let alone try to find one—exactly the kind of joint that Karl appreciated after a long walk in the hot sun. It was dark, usually quiet, and pretty damn cheap.

He expected he could get in, drink enough to dull his dismal spirits, and get out without much trouble at all. But a long life of experience had taught Karl that trouble tended to find him in the most unexpected places.

He waved at the bartender, who slid a pint of mead across the bar. Arcadian booze tasted just a little better than drinking piss and wasn't much colder. He was used to the elixir of the mystics, the finest drink in all Irth, and the thick beer rearick brewed in the Heights, which made this cheap Arcadian booze seem like rainwater.

When you spent your time drinking the best, nothing else was quite as satisfying. There were bars closer to the noble section where he knew he could order some of the mystics' brew, but it would cost him nearly half his earnings by the time he was comfortably numb.

It took him three pints before he stopped minding the taste, and by then Sully's was starting to fill up for the evening. The men drank fast, knowing that they would have to clear out soon enough due to the curfew. Even as the crowd grew, Karl realized it was smaller than usual—mostly just old men and town drunks.

"Where is everybody?" Karl asked the bartender, looking around at those sitting and drinking.

The bartender ran a towel across the bar in front of the rearick and said, "You haven't heard?"

"Obviously not, or I wouldn't be askin," Karl growled.

The bartender was unfazed by his tone. "They have been pulling more men in to work at the factory on the other side of Arcadia. Damn place must be pretty much filled with anybody over eighteen who can work, at least those who didn't already have a job."

Karl snorted. "But nothin' makes a man want a drink more than a long day at work. Where're they at?"

The bartender looked over his left shoulder and then his right, checking for prying ears before leaning on the bar in front of Karl. "That is a hell of a question. It's weird. Once they started working, they just stayed there. I guess it's the long hours. The Governor's Office continues to send checks home, so nobody's really questioning. Except for me, of course. I'm gonna go out of business if I don't get some of my best patrons back on their stools." The barkeep turned around, pulled another pint of mead, and turned back to slide it in front of Karl. "Speaking of which, here's another for you."

The alcohol was starting to kick in, and Karl was glad for that. "Thanks, Sully. Yer a good one."

Sully walked away and left the rearick with his drink. The room started to go a little fuzzy, and Karl knew he should probably call it a night, so he took his time with this one, settling into his stool. But just as his buzz really set in, a couple of locals standing behind him broke into an argument, shattering his peace and quiet.

The Pit, Arcadia's favorite form of violent entertainment, had been closed for months, so Karl assumed that the bar brawlers behind him just needed someplace to take out their aggression. He glanced at Sully, who shook his head and went back to pouring drinks.

Their volume increased, and Karl tried to ignore them. From the slurred speech and incoherent statements, he knew they were a little further along on the mead than he was. He glanced over his shoulder and gave them a look that told them to shut the hell up, but neither of them caught his eye. The men argued about the Prophet. One of them, apparently a recent convert, was adamant about Old Jed and his newfound religion.

He kept going on and on about the end of days.

The other kept calling Old Jed names and talking about his nickname in the Boulevard—Dirty Dick Jed. Rumors floated around Arcadia that the holy man wasn't quite so holy after all.

The shorter of the two men snickered "Dirty Dick" one more time and received a shove from his recently converted—and much larger—friend. Karl wouldn't have minded so much except for the fact that he was the unlucky obstacle that stopped the man's momentum. Half of his pint splashed on his leather overcoat, drenching his beard in the process. Karl looked down at the glass—his last one for the night—and cursed, then jumped off his stool.

Turning around, he glared at them. "You two need to chill the fuck out and let me finish me drink in peace. Ya got it?" he growled at them through clenched teeth. The ale running down his beard made it look like he was frothing at the mouth, which was actually close to how he felt.

The two full-sized humans looked down at the rearick and laughed. One of them asked, "What was that, little man? I can't hear you from up here." The other man, the one who had just shoved his friend, slapped the guy on the back. Apparently, their argument ended when they found something they both agreed on—picking on the rearick.

Karl shook his head, his eyes narrowing. "I wouldn't be makin' jokes like that if I were ya."

The taller drunk took his turn. "What's the matter? Little rearick's got his feelings hurt?"

Karl moved faster than the onlookers would've expected from the short stocky figure. In one swift move, he grabbed his stool and shattered it against the man's legs. As he dropped, Karl's fist connected with the man's chin.

"That's one down." No scream, so Karl wasn't worried about him.

The taller man, stunned by Karl's act of aggression, nevertheless had time to react. He threw a punch toward the rearick, not realizing that fighting was in Karl's blood and bones. Frankly, the rearick could see the asshole's intention for what seemed like hours before he finally threw the punch.

He grabbed the guy's wrist with both hands and spun, twisting it behind his back. The man dropped to his knees in pain, but Karl refused to let go.

He leaned in close, twisting the wrist a little farther, and whispered into the man's ear, "You know, I'd love to let ya leave here without a broken arm, but it can be hard for a *little guy* like me to be the bigger man. So, I think yer gonna hafta apologize first.

The Arcadian whimpered a response. Karl upped the pain level and leaned in closer. "I'm sorry, I couldn't hear ya from way up here. Say again?"

"I... I said I'm sorry."

"There ya go." Karl beamed, "Now, I feel all better. And you will too…in a couple of days."

"Wha—" but before the man could finish his question, Karl slammed the man's head into the bar. The unconscious drunk slid to the ground and landed on top of his friend.

Both Arcadians were breathing, which Karl considered a mercy. Years of combat had given him pretty thick skin, but he had a sore spot when it came to wasted beer and short jokes.

Sully came out from around the bar and nodded at a bouncer standing at the door, who dragged the friends out of the bar and dropped them into the dusty streets.

Sully slid another mead across the bar to Karl. "Here's one to replace the other."

Karl nodded, though he wasn't quite sure if he was thankful after taking a sip. If the bartender had done his job and stopped the bickering early, Karl wouldn't have had to get his hands dirty. But on the other hand, it felt good to get the blood flowing once in a while, and a little guilt-free bar often served as the only fun for Karl inside the walls of Arcadia. He decided to leave Sully a large tip. He finished the first half of the pint and then turned toward the new one.

"Not bad for an old-timer," a man said as he took the empty stool next to Karl.

"Well, we rearick only get better with age. I'm old enough that I'm almost perfect."

The man laughed. "Buy you another?" He nodded at Karl's mead.

"Why not? I'm stuck in this here damn place for a while, might as well do it shitfaced," Karl said.

The man sipped from his own glass and looked around the bar pensively. He couldn't have been older than forty, but the lines on his face and the calluses on his hands showed decades of experience. The hair around his temples was cut short, indicating that he was likely in some sort of service to Arcadia, and it was starting to gray. Some fading scars on his face showed he'd seen a few fights of his own.

He took a large swig of beer, then turned toward Karl.

"You know, I'm currently in need of a man with your talents," the stranger finally said. "Interested?"

Karl took his time answering, trying to read the man to his side. "Not sure. I don't usually work fer lowlanders. They can be a touch unruly."

The guy laughed again. "You ain't wrong, friend. But after what I saw you just pull, I'm guessing you can handle a little unruly. And since you're in the neighborhood anyway…"

"What are ya hiring for?" Karl asked. While he didn't love the idea of spending more time than necessary in the city, he wouldn't pass up a good gig.

"I head up security at the factory on the other side of town. Been there for seven years, but lately, we've been hiring new men hand over fist, and the place is starting to need guards of a somewhat higher caliber."

Karl raised his bushy eyebrows. "The hell do ya need guards on the factory floor fer, anyway?"

"Oh, you know. They're hiring just about anybody off the streets, and the riffraff get violent sometimes. First honest work some of these bastards ever had. Let's just say they don't like to be told what to do. Usually the guards don't have to do much of anything, but when things get heated, my men aren't experienced enough to take care of things, uh, quickly." He jerked a thumb toward the street. "Like you did with those two guys. Thought maybe if you're going to be in town for a few days you might want to make some coin."

Karl snorted. "Now yer talking me language. I might be interested, just need to see how long my party's in town fer."

The man extended his hand out toward Karl. "The name's Stratton. Stop at the factory in the morning, after you sleep those off," he said nodding at the empty pints in front of Karl. "Give you a few days, and I'll pay a bit more than you make on your shipping runs with the mystics and other rearick from the Heights. Maybe have you do some training with my men or something."

The rearick grabbed the man's hand and gave it a firm squeeze. "The name's Karl. And all right then, I'll see ya tomorrow"

A job at a factory, Karl thought to himself as he finished his drink. *What could be easier than that?*

CHAPTER SEVENTEEN

Placing her hand under the showerhead, Hannah was shocked to feel that the water was scalding hot. She laughed as she watched the fog come up from the cold floor. Personal hygiene had never included a shower, let alone one with hot water. She was suddenly both delighted and confused by noble life.

She would have to ask Ezekiel how exactly indoor plumbing worked. It was like there were a cauldron boiling the water outside and a peasant boy pumping a mechanism to get the water into the house, but she knew that that probably wasn't the case at all.

Most likely it was some sort of magitech, the basis of the best things in the noble world. That's the way of it in Arcadia. Kids like her went hungry on the streets, stealing food and conning tourists just to get by, while rich kids had unlimited luxury.

After what felt like an hour in the shower, Hannah got out feeling like a new woman—which was precisely what she aimed to become. She applied some of the fancy creams on her face, but the colors looked all wrong. She decided to come back to the makeup, and put on a beautiful day dress from their trunks.

She stood before the mirror, feeling a little exposed in the drafty outfit. Pants were more her style, but even she had to admit that she looked good in the dress.

Sal lounged lazily on the bed, bored by her fashion show. He had shed his dog illusion hours ago, but he still wasn't happy about being confined in the house, big though it was.

"Sorry, Sal, but we've all got to make sacrifices here. Just be lucky that I don't make you wear a dress!"

He cocked his head to the side as if considering that prospect.

Hannah turned back to her makeover and focused on the last element. She concentrated, letting the meditative words bubble up inside of her. Her eyes flashed red and her straight dark hair slowly transformed before her eyes, starting at the scalp and working its way to the ends. She shook her head from side to side, and strawberry blond curls bounced along with the movement.

Although an illusion, she couldn't help but giggle at how silly she looked. She was a little glad Ezekiel had told her not to go to the Boulevard. They'd laugh her right out of town.

The illusion was far from perfect. Her eyes still glowed red, a feature unique to her and Ezekiel among the users of magic, and she still didn't quite understand it. Because most magic users spent their lives working with just one type of magic, they limited their own connection to the Etheric realm, the dimension from which they drew their power. Hannah and Ezekiel had a purer, stronger connection, and the red in their eyes reflected that.

It was the same red Hannah had seen on the mural in the mystics' temple. Hadley told her that the painting was of the Queen Bitch herself. Hannah was honored that her eyes would glow the same as their God-Queen of old—if she truly existed, that is.

Then Hannah thought of the remnant. Their eyes also glowed with the same violent red.

Power has two sides, she reminded herself. Maintaining control had to remain a priority.

Hannah focused a little harder, and the red faded into a serene blue. Hannah had always had dark eyes; she figured a little touch of color wouldn't hurt.

Ezekiel sat at the dining room table reading *The Arcadian*. He looked at Hannah over the parchment and nodded as she descended the steps. She sat across from him, wondering what would happen next as the smell of bacon, bread, and eggs floated out of the kitchen.

"You making your magic cook for you now?" Hannah asked.

Ezekiel lowered the broadsheet, folded it in half, and placed it on a chair. "Not really. I've hired some new help."

On cue, Eleanor, Parker's mom walked into the dining room carrying two full plates of breakfast food. Hannah had known the woman most of her life, but she had never seen her like this before. In place of the dirty rags that most women in the Boulevard wore, a neatly pressed black and white uniform covered her frame. Even though it was the uniform of a servant, Eleanor looked almost majestic in it.

Hannah jumped to her feet, nearly knocking the chair over. Her relationship with Eleanor had always been a little shaky. She suspected that Parker's mom had always known of their means of making a buck, and like the best mothers in the Boulevard, she didn't approve.

Hannah wondered if Eleanor blamed her, which would have been unfair since their cons were usually Parker's idea.

Despite their past, seeing a familiar face caused a massive grin to explode across Hannah's face. She reached forward and wrapped her arms around the woman, nearly knocking the plates of food out of her hands. She squeezed as if Eleanor were her own mother.

Hannah looked up into her face grinning madly. "How is he?"

Eleanor tried to keep her composure, but her eyes got teary.

She broke free of Hannah's grip and put the plates down on the table, then returned to the girl for a proper hug. After a moment, she looked into Hannah's eyes. "Hannah, I barely recognized you." She turned Hannah a little left, then a little right. "You look so nice for a change." Parker's mother held her hands up, taking in the new noble woman standing before her. "I hear I have you to thank for this new job. And Parker... Parker's good."

Hannah ignored the slight. Parker's mom always slipped in backhanded insults like that, though Hannah suspected they were unintentional. All she cared about at the moment was Parker, and she could feel the tension in Eleanor's words. "I'm happy to help, Eleanor. Thanks for not assuming I'm an Unlawful, or whatever it is they're saying about me down in the Boulevard. Is Parker here?"

Hannah looked behind the woman as if Parker were about to burst out of the kitchen with that goofy grin on his face.

Eleanor blinked, and a single tear broke free from her eye and rolled down her cheekbone. "Oh, they're saying much worse than that about you, but I don't listen to nasty rumors. And no, my son is not here. He's finally working—something legitimate this time. Parker got a job at the factory, and they send his pay to me and give him free room and board."

Hannah nodded as her throat got tight. She lacked words for the woman, but she knew deep down that any work for the government couldn't be good work. Parker would have only accepted it if he were desperate. She dropped into her seat and started to eat her eggs and meat.

Eleanor placed a hand on her shoulder and squeezed. "He cares about you very much, you know?"

Hannah just nodded and took another bite.

"Thank you, Eleanor," Ezekiel said. He pointed his fork at his plate. "This is amazing. Let me know if there's anything you need as you get adjusted here."

The woman smiled, then left the room.

Once Eleanor was gone, Ezekiel spoke through a mouth full of eggs and bacon. "We start today. You know the plan, right?"

"How can I forget? You've only said it a bazillion times."

Ezekiel grinned. "Okay, smartass, so for the bazillion and one-th time, *you* walk *me* through it."

"It's easy. I become a student at the Academy. While I'm there, I try to make contact with any of the nobles' children who aren't pure evil. Shouldn't take me long, since there aren't *any*. Nothing good has ever come out of the noble district, and nothing ever will."

"That's where you're wrong," Ezekiel said. "You need to have faith, Hannah. Not everything is as it appears. There are those even among the wealthy with a deep love for Arcadia—not this Arcadia, but the true one. The Arcadia that was meant to be. Just because they are nobles it doesn't mean they don't have hearts."

"If they had hearts, they wouldn't sit on their fat asses and watch us starve to death."

Ezekiel's eyes narrowed. "You may have a point. Then again, maybe there are some among those nobles who are a bit more patient than a nineteen-year-old girl with a fresh mouth. Trust me, Hannah. There are people among the rich in Arcadia who still love the place. Many eyes have been covered and deception runs deep.

"Your job won't be easy, but it is important. You need to be patient and wait, look and listen. Find people inside who will join us in our mission. Right now, we are still very weak, but strength comes with numbers, and the more people that we have on the inside, the better. The other students in that place, their parents are among the most influential people in Arcadia.

"They might have some information, and they might serve as some of the best allies we could ever find, but you're going to have to keep a low profile at first. Play the part, make sure you don't make enemies. And be open to any new alliances that might serve us well." He paused a moment. "I did mention don't make enemies, right?"

Hannah wanted to call bullshit, to tell him that all those kids had silver spoons shoved way up their asses. He had been away from Arcadia for forty years, and it was the only home she'd ever known. And while the kids from the Boulevard and the noble kids never hung out much, she saw them enough to know that none of those stuck-up assholes were worth anything at all to their cause.

But she knew it would only make Ezekiel mad, and he was a real bore when he got upset, so she kept her mouth shut.

"Okay, also, while I'm in the Lair of All Snobbery, I'll be keeping my eyes open for any information about this machine the Chancellor is building. We'll meet up every few days and I'll pass along any information I might find. But what are you gonna be doing this whole time?"

Ezekiel raised an eyebrow. "If I can pull off another deception, yours might not be the only eyes on the inside. I—" A knock at the door interrupted him.

Hannah immediately tensed, but Ezekiel only smiled.

"Relax. I believe our new help has arrived."

Ezekiel left the room and returned with a young girl at his side. She was a dainty thing with a pretty smile, but her eyes were sad.

"Hannah, I'd like you to meet Maddy. She's aware of your...condition, and she's going to help us out."

"Condition?" Hannah asked. "What condition?"

Maddy giggled, her eyes picking up a little warmth. "Well for starters, that weird mismatch of color on your face makes you look like a clown or something."

Hannah touched her cheek. She had forgotten about the makeup. She laughed along with the girl.

"All right, doctor," Hannah said with a smile. "Fix my face! Make me beautiful, so I can dazzle the world."

"Stand up straight, dammit," Ezekiel said, keeping his eyes forward.

Maddy had coached Hannah on proper posture, but her shoulders had fallen into their usual slump as they made their way through the noble district toward the Academy.

For Hannah, turning a lizard into a dragon seemed a simple business compared to acting like a young woman from the upper class. "I am," she whispered out of the side of her mouth.

"You're about as upright as the slumlords in the Boulevard. Push your shoulders back."

Hannah giggled. "It looks like I'm trying to show off my goods." She arched her back and gave her chest a tiny shake.

"Dammit, Hannah," the old man sighed. "You need to take this seriously."

"Relax, Zeke. I've got this." But deep down, she doubted if she did. They were literally walking into the lion's den.

Ezekiel had given her strict instructions about the examination, but when it came down to it, neither of them really knew what would happen during the interview. It was obvious that she would answer some simple questions and most likely be asked to show any magical talent she had, but Hannah had already received more training than almost any of the incoming students, so it would be necessary to balance a desire to prove herself and maintain the fiction regarding who she was.

Ezekiel feared that Hannah would get hot-headed and try to show off, or worse, get passionate enough to explode. He knew it was going take a great deal of control to be able to make it through, and mouthing off to him was no way for her to be ready for the biggest test of her life.

They walked up the steps to the double doors that would usher her into a new stage of her life. Pulling up her long dress to make climbing the steps easier, she nearly tripped over the fancy shoes that felt like two boards clamped onto her feet. All she really wanted to do was strip off the dress and shoes and run barefoot through the streets with Parker.

Parker.

She thought of him as they walked through the doors and into the Academy. She could tell by Eleanor's face that even his mother knew he was not in a good place. Hannah's gut told her that Parker was in danger, but she had to trust that her friend knew what he was doing.

The fact that the factory had never hired people from the Boulevard before, and now they were sending paychecks, made her uncomfortable. Hannah figured this was some sort of social control on Adrien's part. Offer the poor enough coin, and they would rationalize anything. But the look on Eleanor's face told her the truth. She was smart enough to know that the situation was fundamentally rotten.

Maybe now that Hannah and Ezekiel had come back with enough money to buy a damn castle, she could convince Parker to quit.

But she had bigger fish to fry at the moment than her friend's employment status; she needed to get accepted at the Academy.

A young man greeted them at a desk, some sort of student worker. He had a tiny mouth and eyes spread a little too wide apart. "Lord Girard?" the boy asked as he rose from the desk.

"Correct," Ezekiel answered, smiling through his magic-altered appearance. "And this is my daughter, Deborah. She's here to be admitted to the Academy."

The boy flushed, half from embarrassment for the nobleman's presumption. It wasn't uncommon for nobles to believe their children were shoe-ins for the Academy. But everybody inside the school knew that wasn't quite the case. Only those who were good enough were actually offered the chance to enroll.

The other half of his flush was due to the fact that the girl standing before him was shockingly beautiful. He had never seen her before, but he hoped she would pass the test so that he might see her again.

"Well, yes. I have you right here in my book. To be *tested* for admissions," he said, his eyes on the girl.

Ezekiel's laughter echoed through the empty hall; in Hannah's ears sounded altogether foreign, filled with self-importance. "Well, son, I've known this place for a long time. Probably for twice as long as you've been taking up space in Arcadia. If anyone rejects admission of my daughter, they're damn fools."

The boy working at the desk stammered and pushed around the parchments in front of him, unsure of what to say. "Yes, well, of course…"

His eyes cut back to hers. Remembering Ezekiel's plan, Hannah gave him a smile. "Well, my father has more confidence in me than I have in myself," she murmured, trying on the tone Maddy had taught her. "But I do hope I get to be one of your fellow students. If I pass, will you give me my first tour?"

The kid turned beet red and looked back down at his parchments. Without looking up, he agreed, "Of course. I'd be happy to. The testing room is this way." He stood up and headed down the hall.

Zeke and Hannah followed the blushing upperclassman through the tower. This building had cast a shadow over the city her entire life, but she had never seen the inside of it. And if she didn't play things right, she might never see the outside again, either.

"Good luck," the student said as he left Hannah and Ezekiel outside a door on the second floor of the Academy.

"She doesn't need luck, child. She has magic," Ezekiel asserted.

Hannah reached out and brushed her fingertips along their guide's arm. "Thank you…"

"Matthew. It's Matthew. And I do hope you make it." The boy forced an uncomfortable smile into his red face.

Squeezing his arm, Hannah said, "Well, I hope so, too, Matthew. If only for that tour you promised me."

The boy turned and rushed away from them, glad to be out of the situation.

"What the hell was that?" Ezekiel whispered after the boy left them alone.

"What?" Hannah asked. "You told me I needed to get to know people."

"I meant you should strike up conversations, not bat your eyelashes at every boy in the school. You have the potential to be the greatest magic user who has ever lived. You're more than just a pretty face."

Hannah smiled up at the old man. It seemed like he was taking his fatherly role seriously. "Being pretty and being powerful aren't mutually exclusive, Zeke. And besides, it's like you always say: there are different kinds of magic. Growing up on the Boulevard taught me to use any angle I could find, and we're going to need every advantage if we're going to pull this off. Don't worry, *dad*, I'll be a good girl."

Ezekiel's concerned look lightened. He mumbled something she couldn't make out as he shook his head and turned to look at her. "You might just be getting the hang of this after all." He laughed. "But I'm pretty sure I'll always worry about you." He put his hand on the knob in front of them and paused. Gazing down at Hannah, he said, "This part of the plan is pivotal. Be confident and controlled in there, but whatever you do, make sure that you only use physical magic and not much of it."

Hannah smiled, exhibiting a confidence she didn't quite feel. "Piece of cake. You're not coming in? I thought you were here to see me through this."

"I trust you to figure it out. And besides, I've got more important things to do." At that, he started walking back toward the staircase.

"Like what?" Hannah called after him.

Ezekiel turned, a sparkle in his eye. "I'm going to look for a job."

CHAPTER EIGHTEEN

Parker and the other workers could talk during their brief lunch breaks, although the guards kept a close eye on the enslaved men to make sure there wasn't anything that might challenge the authority of the Capitol being talked about.

Parker grabbed his rations—they could only be loosely described as food—and eyed the lunchroom, trying to find the person he needed to talk to. Jack caught his eye and tried to wave him over, but Parker gave him a little shake of the head and kept looking until he found the young man.

"Hewitt, good to see you," Parker said approaching the table where a guy about his own age with sandy blonde hair sat.

Hewitt looked up in surprise. "Parker! What the hell, man? I didn't know you were here." He got to his feet and shook Parker's hand vigorously.

Parker sat next to Hewitt, his friend from the quarter. "Yeah, I guess I'm kind of here because of you."

Hewitt furrowed his brow. "How so?"

"Well, you know I always hustled on the street. My mother looked the other way for a long time, but once the curfew set in,

CM RAYMOND

and the Governor started to tighten down on street activity, even in the Boulevard, she pushed me pretty hard to go legitimate."

Hewitt glanced around the cafeteria at the tired men sitting like zombies in front of their plates. "You call *this* legitimate?"

Parker couldn't help but laugh. "Well, according to what your mom told mine, this is the straight and narrow. I heard it every day, 'Why can't you be more like Mitsy's boy?'"

Hewitt looked down at his lap, silent for a moment, but finally he said, "Hell, man. I'm sorry about that. I guess my mother has no idea what's going on inside the factory. Nobody does. I sure didn't. But, why the hell aren't they asking any questions?"

Parker said, "They don't know. And they're getting more coin right now than they've ever seen in their lives, although not as much as the Governor is making off us." Parker shrugged. "Maybe they *are* asking questions. Can't imagine my mother would believe that I would actually just up and disappear inside of this hellhole."

Hewitt said, "I've been here over a month. Think my mom would have wondered by now. Not to mention, she went on to your mother about how great it was to get into this place. Now we all just want to get out."

Parker's spirits lifted, if only a little, at his friend's words. "So? You've been here longer. How do we get the hell out?"

Hewitt shook his head; his sandy hair shook over his forehead. "As far as I know, there's no way out of this shit. That is, until they're done with us or until we break, and then only the Matriarch knows what they do. They're taking more guys off the floor, and it's not always pretty."

A guard walking close interrupted their conversation, and the old friends ate the rest of their meals in silence. Hewitt's resignation to a perpetual life in the factory was hard to swallow—harder than the moldy bread on Parker's plate.

But Parker wasn't so quick to hang his head. He knew he had to get out or die trying.

Parker's hands ached. The repetitive work on the assembly line tore at them, but he couldn't slow down. It had been a week, and he thought he would've moved to a different job by now, but he continued twisting and capping wires.

He worked twelve or fourteen hours a shift, maybe more. He didn't really know. Each day felt like a lifetime, and all the workers on the floor just waited for the final bell to ring. At that point they were ushered off the factory floor and back toward their rooms as others were immediately led in to take their places. Not a second was wasted on the factory floor.

For the most part Parker was able to fall into a zone, which helped him pass the brutal time a little quicker. He thought about his mom most days. It brought him satisfaction and maybe a little hope knowing that she received payment for his days of misery. It was precious little consolation, but any consolation was worth something on the factory floor.

He glanced over at Jack, the big old guard who used to work at the entrance to Queen's Boulevard. While Parker adapted well enough to the mundane tasks and brutal conditions, Jack's transition was different. The man would stop work and stare off into nothing several times a day—a risky move in the factory.

Parker started keeping an eye on him, jabbing him with an elbow when this happened, but when the factory guards caught him before Parker did, they zapped him with their magical weapons from behind.

Burns and open sores covered his body.

Jack's condition continued to decline. Parker knocked him in the ribs three times before the man looked up.

"Hmmm?"

Parker spoke without looking up from his task. "Jack, you gotta stay with it, man. I don't know what they're doing to the men they drag out of here, but I'm sure it's no good. Get back to work."

The man coughed, his chest sounded funny. "Yeah, right. Thanks, Parker."

Parker smiled. "Just paying my toll."

Jack smiled for a second, remembering the good days, then bent his head to the job at hand.

It pleased Parker that he had spared the man a little pain, and maybe a bad exit from the factory. Although he couldn't be sure what happened when the men were pulled off the factory floor, he knew it probably had something to do with the screams he could hear at night from his cell. There was something going on in the Arcadian factory, and Parker was pretty damn sure he wanted to be gone before he found out what it was.

Parker glanced around the room as the bell rang to indicate the end of his shift, then grabbed one of the stiffest wires on his bench and slid it up under his sleeve. He'd been watching the guards as they patrolled the floor for days, especially during shift changes.

For the most part, the guards were lazy—they pretty much stood around with their thumbs up their asses. They had the help of the magitech cuffs that all the laborers wore, making their jobs simple.

The power in the cuffs kept the men trapped within the factory walls. Thoughts of escape were futile, as long as Parker remained locked in the cuffs.

He kept his head down as a guard led back to his eight-by-eight cell, part of his compensation for his diligent work for the Capitol. Despite the crude room, the cell gave him his only privacy, and he needed it to plan his escape.

While pretending to sleep, he kept his ears open for any sound of the staff beyond his door. After a few hours passed, he felt secure that no one was watching him.

He drew the thick strand of wire out of his sleeve.

The shackles were composed of two iron wristbands attached by a chain long enough to allow the workers to do their jobs. Not only was the metal strong, but, Parker could hear the gentle hum of the magitech core.

He straightened the wire as best he could and inserted it into the cuff's small key slot. He wiggled it around for almost an hour, but had no luck.

Picking locks was a skill he had learned on the streets, and these metal bracelets should've been easy to open. But they weren't ordinary—in addition to keeping him trapped within the factory, the magitech design somehow made the lock impossible to pick.

Damn it, he sighed.

Finally giving up on the project, Parker laid down on his cot and closed his eyes, trying to ignore the screams beyond the cell-block. Whatever was happening was terrifying, which must have been the point. Those screams provided a stronger motivation than anything else to keep your head down and focus on your work.

Parker thought about Jack. He realized that if the large man continued his downward spiral, he would soon be in one of those cellblocks—another example for the rest of the men.

He finally fell asleep despite the screams. In the morning, they were silent, which concerned him even more. As the shift bell rang, and Parker made his way back out to his workstation, he caught the eyes of a few other men, who looked spooked by what they had heard the night before.

They would all work hard today.

The situation on the factory floor grew more difficult. Every day someone was dragged away by the guards to a room adjacent to their workstations. One day when the cries started, they got so intense that Parker had a hard time paying attention to his job. After about an hour, the screams suddenly stopped.

Parker's hands continued to bend and cap the wires, but his

eyes turned toward the doorway, watching the guards removing a lifeless body from the floor, one that he recognized from Queen's Boulevard.

Everyone could tell the man was dead. The factory nearly came to a stop as they all stared at the body—their fate if they didn't behave.

But Parker noticed something no one else was looking out for. The dead man pulled from the torture chamber wasn't wearing any cuffs.

Parker returned to his work, a grim smile on his face. At that moment he began to craft his precarious plot to get out of the factory and back to Hannah.

Having dropped Hannah off at the examination room, Ezekiel was free to make his way to another part of the Academy. He had business to attend to and hoped that it would all go as easily as planned.

Walking down the shining marble hallway, Ezekiel arrived at the spot where he had lashed out in anger and blasted the statue of the Chancellor to bits during his first visit to the Academy. He had expected that the image of Adrien would still be missing from the hall, but it had been replaced by a statue both larger and more austere than the first.

Nice to see they're using their resources and magical abilities to help the community, Ezekiel thought as he passed Adrien's carved face. Defacing the new piece of art wasn't out of the question—it still filled him with a powerful rage—but Ezekiel thought better of it. He had to keep a low profile to accomplish the next step of the mission.

Two floors up from where he'd left Hannah, Ezekiel found the administrative offices. The clerk behind a small desk pointed him toward the Dean's office. He tapped his staff on the door and entered when called by a gentle yet firm voice from inside.

The office was simple, yet refined. Shelves of books lined the walls, and a painting from the old world had been hung behind the desk. A large window overlooked the Academy quad below. Just beyond the quad, Ezekiel could see the Capitol building in all its glory, even though from the outside he knew its splendor was muted by the bigger and grander Academy.

The woman behind the desk looked up from her parchments. "Lord Girard, is it?" She stood and extended her hand in Ezekiel's direction.

He searched her face for any hint of recognition. She was middle-aged but younger than Girard, so she likely hadn't met the nobleman before. Ezekiel had to be very careful in his guise— he didn't have the skills or experience of Julianne. If the Dean had never met Lord Girard, the whole thing might be easier to pull off.

Taking her hand in his, he said, "Quite right. It's nice to meet you, Dean."

The woman laughed. "I'm still not used to that. Please, call me Amelia."

"As you wish," Ezekiel said, still holding her hand. "But when I went to the Academy, people referred to one another by their titles."

The academic grinned. "That could be the case, but you're not nineteen anymore. And Arcadia has come a long way over the past three decades. I like to think of this as the new Arcadia."

"Well, then," Ezekiel said. "To the new Arcadia." He took a seat across from her without being invited, and she followed suit. "I am here today dropping off my daughter for the examination."

"Yes. Deborah, is that correct? I've already looked at her documents. Seems she has a gift."

Ezekiel grinned. "I wouldn't be a father if I didn't think of my girl as gifted, but growing up in the country provided plenty of time and space for developing the arts away from all the distractions of the city. I couldn't keep her locked up forever, though. I do hope—or should I say expect—her to be able to find a place here at Arcadia just like her mother and father did."

The Dean flipped open a folder from the tall pile on her desk. "I assure you that we will give her a fair shake. I will tell you, though: noble or not, rich or poor, should she not make it, we will still expect her to adhere to the rules of the city. The restriction against unlicensed magic is for the good of Arcadia."

"Yes," Ezekiel said, "or at least that's what you tell the locals, isn't it?" Ezekiel winked at the Dean. "But to tell you the truth, Amelia, I am here for more than just my daughter. I was hoping that the Academy might have a place for me. I've recently retired from my business up north, and with my daughter in school I will have a fair amount of leisure. I'm thinking it's time to give back to the place that gave me so much."

"Well, that is certainly a noble gesture." The woman took off her bifocals and placed them on her desk. "But I'm sorry, Lord Girard, there are no positions open at the Academy right now. I'm sure a man of your stature can find other ways to occupy his time."

Ezekiel stood, turned, and walked over to the window. He looked down at the students crossing the quad. "That's too bad," he said. "I truly had my heart set on working here—teaching was always a dream of mine."

Amelia kept her eyes trained on Ezekiel, who looked majestic disguised as the noble from the north in his purple robe. "I can certainly keep you in mind for an opening."

Ezekiel remained facing away from her, which is why the Dean never saw his eyes flash red. "Actually," he said while reaching into her mind. "I imagine you could open up an extra section in one of your core classes, perhaps the History of Magic? I'm sure your students would love to hear the experiences of a devoted alumnus."

As the man spoke, Amelia found herself slowly persuaded—more by his mental magic than by his rhetoric, but she would never know that. "Hmm, an extra section of the History of Magic? Why yes, that is not a bad idea at all, but do you know enough about the subject?"

Ezekiel turned from the window and back to the Dean, a grin on his face. "History of Magic? Oh, I know a thing or two."

CHAPTER NINETEEN

The examination room where Ezekiel left Hannah was the biggest room she had ever been in—bigger even than the great hall in the abandoned tower where Ezekiel first trained her. Its enormity was accentuated by the fact that the place was nearly empty.

She sat at a long wooden table. Across the room, nearly thirty feet away, sat three people she had never laid eyes on before in their relatively small town. It wasn't a surprise. They were faculty members at the Academy, which made them nobles. Nearly all the nobles worked at the Academy or the Capitol, if they worked at all.

August, the chief examiner, a portly man around fifty, sat across from her. His face was friendly, and he hadn't stopped smiling since she'd walked into the room. Physical magic was his specialty, and while the others would teach the basics of the art from time to time, his job was to help third and fourth years master the craft.

Next to him sat Charlotte. She looked Hannah's age, but was nearly twice that. Compared to August, Charlotte appeared cold and withdrawn. As she introduced herself in monotone, a mole on her cheek danced around. Hannah had to stifle a smile. Specializing in theoretical studies, she taught the History of Magic, the Proper Use of Magic, and Magical Questions—some sort of magic-based philosophy course that sounded boring as hell to Hannah.

Charlotte had written the book on the History of Magic—literally. Her revisionist history texts were part of Adrien's propaganda, like stories the Prophet told in the Boulevard. This false history paired well with her Proper Use of Magic course, something Ezekiel had dreamed up as a way to teach the ethical use of the arts. Instead, Charlotte had massaged the curriculum into a brainwashing event to restrict magicians in Arcadia.

Finally, there was Nikola on the end. Legend around the Academy said that he was the one who had actually discovered how to imbue inanimate objects with magic, allowing Arcadians to make the tools termed 'magitech.'

This story danced around the quad in hushed whispers because, in the historical account written by Charlotte, Adrien had been the one to power devices with magic. If the official account was a lie, Nikola was not the man to set the record straight. He was a beanpole, his face always a sickly white. While most men in Arcadia chose to go bearded or cleanshaven, Nikola had a perfectly manicured handlebar mustache.

"Welcome, Ms…" August paused, a smile still hanging on his lips.

"Deborah. I am Deborah, daughter of Lord Girard."

"I heard that Girard had returned," Charlotte said, her voice lacking any expression whatsoever. Hannah couldn't be sure if she was thrilled or if she wanted to murder the man.

The teachers all looked at each other, eyebrows raised. Hannah knew full well that the real Girard had been a total bastard, and his death at Ezekiel's hands had made Irth a better place for the rest of its residents. But who knew, maybe the fact that Girard was a douche gave him respect in the eyes of these nobles.

Nikola put a finger in the air as if he were testing the wind. "So, our hope is to test your aptitude for magic. As you might not know, since you've grown up away from here, magic is well regulated within Arcadia. No one may use it unless they have studied at the Academy. But before we can admit you, we need to know if you have any potential. You should be able to do *something*, of course." The pasty-faced man's mustache twitched as he spoke.

Hannah bit her lip to keep from laughing. *If they only knew*, she thought.

Instead, she played their game. Clearing her throat, she said, "Naturally, my father has taught me some of the tricks—"

"Magic," Charlotte interjected.

Hannah purposefully squirmed in her chair, feigning nervousness. "Of course, sorry. My father has taught me some magic. Nothing much, but a few tricks, I guess."

Charlotte's eyebrows raised. "Kids do tricks, Deborah. We cast magic. It is a serious business, and so you must regard it to be considered for the Academy."

Hannah wanted to blast the smirk off her face, but she tucked her hands under her legs. So far, the steps she meant to accomplish were done. She had established herself as a noblewoman, admitted to some magic use, and convinced them of Deborah's ignorance about Arcadia: its magic, culture, and traditions.

August stepped in, trying to make peace in the room. "Ok. Shall we begin?" Without waiting for an answer, he pulled a coin from his purse, flipped it into the air, and with a quick turn of the hand, the coin levitated before his nose.

"Cool," Hannah cooed, trying to act as naive as possible.

August's smile spread wider, which Hannah would have thought impossible. Clearly pleased that his magic had impressed the girl, he scissored his first two fingers back and forth, making the coin danced around in front of him. Hannah squealed in delight for him.

Finally, August made a move that she herself had mastered within her first week of practicing. He cupped his hands and pulled them apart. The coin became a perfectly round metal sphere and grew until it was the size of his happy, round face. Flicking his wrists, he tossed the ball. Hitting the ground, the sound of metal on stone echoed around the big, empty room.

"Can you lift it?" he asked.

Does a rearick shit in the woods? she thought. Ezekiel had warned her to hold back. Not to do anything impressive, but to still show them that she had potential.

"That?" she asked, pointing at the ball. "Looks heavy."

Nikola leaned in. "It's all right. We all start somewhere. Give it a try." He smiled, but all Hannah could do was watch his perfect mustache.

"Ok. Let me try. You guys all use your hands, right?"

The faculty exchanged looks back and forth. She had them right where she wanted them.

Hannah contorted her hands in awkward jutting movements. At one point, she squeezed her eyes shut. At another, she pulled her brow down hard. After several minutes, she collapsed back in her chair. "Come on!" she yelled with her eyes on the ball.

She looked back up at the panel of judges. Each of them had a familiar look of disappointment. Even August's smile had evaporated.

"Can... Can you give me one more try? Maybe something else?"

The three professors scribbled on the parchments sitting in front of them. Hannah wondered how far she could take the ruse, and what she had to give them to make sure that she got into the school. She knew that admission was not easy, but Hannah also knew that, despite what they said, it was more based on who you were than what you could do.

Magic existed in all humans, after all—Ezekiel had taught her that. As long as someone could control it without exploding into a million pieces, they could learn, but unless that person were a noble, they couldn't get into the school.

Luckily for Hannah, Girard's name carried some weight.

"How about I just roll it?" Hannah asked.

August nodded, the smile came back onto his face. "That would be a good start. Don't worry; as Nikola said, we all start somewhere. Don't be nervous. Try to shut all that out."

Hannah pushed the back of her hand across her forehead and wiped away imaginary perspiration. She constructed a nervous laugh and turned back toward the ball.

This time she stood and pulled her hand as if she were trying to loosen up her wrist. They could barely see it from across the room, but the faculty members were pretty sure that the ball started to move ever so slightly. Finally, she rolled it over one full rotation.

Hannah dropped back into her chair and sighed in fake exhaustion. "I did it! See?"

The faculty leaned back and forth whispering into each other's ears. August talked quickly with his hands, and Charlotte just kept shaking her head. Hannah wondered if maybe she had taken her act a little too far.

"We will have to talk," Charlotte said. "But I'll tell you right now, young lady, I'm not exactly sure if you are cut out for the Academy. We might have some disagreements among us, but I think it's good that you know where I stand before you leave today."

Hannah put her hand over her mouth. "But this is all I ever wanted. And now you're taking that away from me? I tried so hard."

"It's not just about trying. Our job is to make sure that the right people are using magic. I'm not convinced that you're the right person to even start to study magic. I've seen dirty kids from the Boulevard do better work than that, and you spent all of your life having nothing to do but play in the woods and practice your little 'tricks.'" Charlotte made air quotes overhead, and her eyes shot with daggers.

Up until that point, Hannah had only been playing, enjoying the game. When Charlotte decided to bring up her people in Queens Boulevard, Hannah got pissed.

"Is that right? I'm just as bad as the scum?" Hannah repeated, her eyes narrowed.

Charlotte stood, her chair squeaked out behind her echoing through the empty room. "No. If you had listened closely, you would've realized that I said that you are worse than the scum from the Bitch's Boulevard." The cold woman pursed her lips and waited to see if she had broken the privileged girl sitting before her.

Hannah rose in response. Her eyes locked on the teacher. "I thought the women of the Noble Quarter were a bit more refined."

She closed her eyes so that the faculty couldn't see them flash red. Emotions had taken over, and Hannah decided it was time for her to guarantee herself access to the Academy. She had tried it Ezekiel's way; now it was her turn. With hardly a flick of her wrist, the ball shot to the ceiling and came back to the center of the room. It spun fast enough to make a humming sound.

Hannah clasped her hands together, arms extended. Without warning, she pulled her fingers apart, and as she did the ball broke into a hundred pieces—each piece spinning in thin air. The instructors all ducked or raised their hands in defense, afraid they were about to be struck by the spinning projectiles.

But before they could do any damage, Hannah took it a step further. With several twists of her hands, each little metal shard transformed into a butterfly and flew around the room.

She opened her eyes to the applause of August and Nikola.

"Splendid," the professor of physical magic said with his

hands pressed against his cheeks. "I don't know the last time I saw anything like that."

"That," Charlotte said, her voice still cold, "is because we don't use magic in such frivolous ways here, no matter how impressive the feat."

The man continued to clap, despite Charlotte's disapproval, and Hannah took a bow. "Sorry. Guess I should've done that in the first place. I just didn't want to show off. My father said the people of Arcadia don't like someone who gloats."

Charlotte spun and walked out of the room, her hard shoes tapping as she went.

"Don't worry about her. It's safe to say that you are the Academy's newest student." Nikola smiled. "If you have your things, we will find someone to escort you to a residence hall."

"Yes," Hannah said, beaming. "My father was pretty confident I would be able to pass the test, so he had me pack my things. They're just outside the room."

"Very good," August replied, sifting through some parchments. You'll be staying in Memorial Hall. Do you know where it is?"

Hannah shook her head. "No, but I can find it. Maybe I'll follow my butterflies."

Both men laughed again, shaking their heads. Hannah took a deep breath and wondered what the hell she had gotten herself into.

It wouldn't be the last time.

───────

Walking across the quad toward the residence halls, Hannah spotted a group of boys sitting cross-legged in the grass. It was unusually warm for this time of year, and the young men were taking full advantage of it. She sized them up like a warrior surveying an opposing army. Getting into the Academy was only half the battle.

She needed information, and to get information, she would need to make friends. The hell of it was, Hannah had no idea how to make friends. She had known all her friends since birth. There was Sal, of course, but she assumed rich guys might be a little harder to talk to than dragons.

As she approached, Hannah could feel their eyes on her. Fixing her gaze on the perfect green grass, she pushed on, hoping to skip any conversation. She wasn't ready to wage war just yet.

"Hey, Red," one of the boys called. It took Hannah a second to remember she was no longer a brunette.

She kept walking. Maybe it was a mistake; she couldn't be sure. She just wanted to be alone for a minute or two.

"What's the rush, sweetie?" he called again. "Come join us."

Hannah stopped, then spun to face them. A guy in the middle of the group, the one that looked more douche-y than the others, grinned and nodded. "So you *can* hear. And I thought you were just a nice pair of legs."

Hannah had experienced catcalling before; it was nothing new. What was new was that she now had magic on her side. She thought about scorching his ass with fire, but she just gave him her middle finger instead. "Screw you," she shouted, then turned and walked toward Memorial Hall.

"What the hell's your problem?" another voice asked from behind her. This one was close and female.

A young woman about Hannah's age caught up with her.

"Those asshats are my problem," Hannah responded.

The girl tilted her head toward the boys. "Ross and company? Asshats? Hey, new girl, the cutest guy in school was just trying to flirt with you. What are you, some kind of idiot? They think you're hot. Just look at you."

Hannah *did* look at herself. She had washed properly and wore an expensive gown. It was a reminder that she was no longer the dirty hustler from the Boulevard, and people were going to treat her differently now.

"Thanks," Hannah said.

The girl laughed. "Don't thank me. I'm not your friend. I'm *competition.*" The girl spun and pranced over to the circle of guys.

Shit, I hate this place, Hannah thought as she entered Memorial Hall.

Jack must have woken up on the right side of the cell, Parker thought.

The large man had been talking all morning without interruption. "I'm telling you, man, things weren't always great for me in the Boulevard either. I know that you and the girl, Hannah, thought that we all had it made—those of us that were working for Horace. But it wasn't easy, not if you had a conscience.

"That's what got me into the shit. Being nice to you guys. I think I was nice to everybody, even though I was trying to do my job. Can't be a nice guy and work for Horace, I think that's the lesson. I learned a lot of lessons like that. And here's another thing…"

Parker kept nodding as Jack revealed all his benign secrets about working for the slumlord of Queen's Boulevard. None of it mattered, and Parker couldn't care less. As long as Jack was working, Parker was happy. Didn't want any attention drawn to the two of them, not today.

Parker glanced over and watched the big man's fingers twist nuts onto the bolts of the large metal pieces that he was in charge of. After that, he'd slap a large wrench on them and tighten them down before passing them on to the next person on the assembly line. It was perfect work for the brute, and Parker was glad that he was sitting right next to him.

"You know what I mean?" Jack asked.

Parker nodded as he continued to twist the wires. "Yeah, man.

Exactly. That's exactly what I think." He had no idea what Jack had said, and it didn't matter. He wouldn't be around to finish the conversation.

His eyes kept sliding up to the catwalk over the floor. After another hour of Jack's talking and nearly one more thousand units finished, it finally happened. One of the guards, a kid not much older than Parker, came down off the balcony.

Parker heard every step of his boots on the metal steps. Knocking twice on the door that led off the floor, the young guard waited. Within a few beats, the door squeaked open, and an older guard, who stood a head taller, emerged. The two exchanged a few words, then the younger guard relinquished his post.

It was now or never if Parker's plan was going to work.

It had to.

He'd studied the pattern for countless days, every second accounted for. Once the older guard released the security door, Parker grabbed the three-foot piece of metal right out of Jack's hands. Jack said something, but like most of his words to Parker that day, they went unheard.

In three steps, Parker was on the guard. The poor guy didn't stand a chance. Things were easy on the floor. The workers were broken men.

Except for one of them—Parker the Pitiable.

The guard never saw his approach or the hunk of metal that connected with the side of his head. He dropped immediately. Parker hopped the unconscious guard, dropped the metal bar, and slid his fingers between the door and its jamb half a second before it sealed shut.

He exhaled. The plan was still in play. He slipped through the door before the sounds of men yelling behind him got too loud.

Kicking off his shoes, he moved quickly down the hall after the younger guard. Stage one had been perfectly planned. Now he was flying blind, and he would have to work with his instincts and guts. Turning a corner, Parker saw the kid in front of him, whistling an old folk tune from before the Age of Madness. Poor bastard thought his day had just gotten better.

Ten feet in front of the guard stood the door that led off the factory floor and onto the next stage of the plan. Surprise was a powerful weapon, and Parker wielded it well. He picked up his pace and closed the gap between them. Only four feet distance, he screamed at the top of his lungs. It was guttural, and not even Parker knew what words were coming out of his mouth.

Turning, the kid's eyes went wide. In that instant, Parker realized that the guard wasn't much different than himself. Probably some guy living on the edge of the market. His mother had talked him into casting his lot in with the guards. The Matriarch knew they needed all the able bodies they could get.

But wherever he came from, the guard stood between him and freedom; between him and Hannah.

That made him an enemy.

Parker didn't hesitate. Letting his momentum take him, he dove at the guard, large metal cuffs extended out in front of him. The sound of crunching bone and cartilage filled Parker's ears, and the kid dropped into an unresponsive heap on the floor. Shuffling through the guy's pockets, Parker found a set of keys.

He tried them all in rapid succession, but none of them was the right size for the cuffs shackling his arms. He cursed under his breath, then turned and ran down the hallway, praying that Jack had exaggerated when he talked about the magitech security field.

Standing before the next door, he fumbled with the keys, trying each as he went. Finally, one found purchase in the lock, and Parker heard a click—another barrier down.

The next hall was so damned dark that he had to move more slowly, but there was a light ahead, and Parker moved toward it. As he approached, he held his breath, knowing that only one wrong step could land him in the hands of the enemy.

The light leaked in from another room, and Parker stood on his tip-toes to peer through the grated window. He couldn't believe his eyes. In the middle of the room was a machine like nothing he'd ever seen before.

Tubes, beams, and levers ran in every direction. The metal monstrosity was gigantic, and his eyes followed its frame up nearly twenty feet. An enormous funnel topped off the machine.

He watched as man after man—each wearing their own cuffs —rolled carts toward the funnel from a walkway above. When they reached the edge, they dumped their loads. Within minutes, he observed hundreds of pounds of amphoralds—the gemstones from the Heights—pouring in.

It was some kind of magitech, larger than Parker had ever seen.

Brow furrowed, he muttered to himself, "What the hell is it?"

Parker's eyes scanned the machinery back to its base. There, chained to a bench, was a man in a robe. His eyes were black like the magic users', but they had dimmed somehow. His face lacked any emotion. Wires ran from his head to the machine. And every few seconds, the man's body would twitch. It took a second for Parker to put the pieces together.

Amphoralds weren't magical in and of themselves; they stored magic. The research and design wonks in the Academy had figured out a way to channel a magician's power into the gems. They were like holding tanks that could distribute the energy on command, like the power generated by windmills outside the city walls.

Clearly, they had figured out how to draw power from a magician to fuel the amphoralds. They were creating a giant power source for whatever the hell Parker, Jack, and the other workers were building.

In the few minutes he watched, he could tell that they were sucking the life out of the magician connected to the machine. They were killing him to fuel their evil. He thought of Hannah and the Founder and prayed that whatever plan they were working on would happen soon.

Whatever Adrien was up to, it was no good—and freaking *huge*. The Chancellor needed to be stopped, and Parker needed to make it happen.

Alarms sounded all around him. His escape was now public knowledge.

"Shit," he grunted as he broke for the end of the hall.

CHAPTER TWENTY

Hannah placed her hand on the metal knob. At her touch, the locks clicked open.

Cool, she thought. Magitech like this didn't exist in the Boulevard, and since the technology was invented during Ezekiel's absence, it wasn't something she had spent much time around recently either. Like everything else in her life, it took a little getting used to.

She turned the knob and stepped into her new dorm room. Small by noble standards, it still dwarfed the room she had grown up in, and it was perfectly tidy. The space was a mirror image: two of every piece of furniture sat directly across the room from its twin. Two beds. Two desks. Two chairs. Two dressers. Two of everything.

The only difference was that the left side was full of someone's personal effects. The desk on the left had parchments and pens lined neatly on its surface. Apparently, her roommate had already arrived.

Hannah turned to her right and stepped over to her bed. A note sat on the pillow:

Hey, roomy,

Welcome to Arcadia! You're going to love it here. Drop your stuff and come on over to the theater in Old Main. Convocation is today, and you don't want to miss it.

Yours,

Cassie

If Hannah didn't know how to interact with the guys on the lawn, trying to room with a rich young woman would be utterly impossible. She removed the note off her pillow and dropped it on the desk, then laid back on the bed for a few minutes. Everything was moving so quickly; she just had to think.

She wondered what Parker would do.

He'd charm the pants off these people, she thought. Her friend always knew how to read people better than she did. Where Parker flourished while grandstanding, Hannah's strengths were always in subtlety. Maybe it was no different here. *Just keep my head down,* she thought to herself. *Let the opportunity come to me.*

She began the meditation techniques that Hadley had taught her and immediately relaxed.

After collecting herself and pushing all anxiety out of her mind, Hannah got up to head to the theater. She had spent her life surviving and pretty much kicking ass wherever she went. And while the Academy presented a new kind of challenge, it was a challenge she knew she could handle.

She crossed the quad, which was now empty, and entered the theater on the other side of campus. Her heart sank as she saw that the tiny auditorium was already full. Noble students were busily talking to one another as they waited for the Convocation to begin—not that Hannah had any idea what a Convocation even was.

The only seats remaining were down at the very front, already forcing Hannah to abandon her low-profile approach.

Nothing like being the new girl doing the Walk of Shame. She took each step carefully, making sure not to trip.

At the bottom, she found an empty seat next to a guy with tight frizzy hair and thick spectacles. Even though the assembly had not yet begun, his pen already scribbled notes.

Grabbing the seat, she looked up to find a line of chairs on stage filled with prestigious-looking older folks. She recognized the faculty from her examination. August caught her eye, his smile as large as ever.

At least I have one friend here, she thought to herself.

Scanning the crowd, Hannah realized she had no clue what the hell was happening here. For all she knew, the Academy kicked off the year with a virgin sacrifice. For the first time, she was glad for that one night with Franklin a summer ago.

Deciding to grab some intel, she elbowed the guy sitting next to her in the arm. His head snapped up from his notebook, an apprehensive look on his face.

"Hey, any idea what this is all about?" she asked the frightened young man.

The kid pushed his thick glasses up the bridge of his nose and blushed, then looked back down at his notebook. Hannah glanced down at herself, remembered her fitted noblewoman's dress—and the figure inside of it—and smiled. It wasn't rare for guys to hit on her back on the Boulevard, but she had always figured they were all idiots.

Based on how the young men here were treating her today, she started to wonder if she was considered damned attractive by Academy standards. The realization couldn't help but make her happy, and she nearly laughed, thinking about Parker and what he would say if he was here now.

She decided to try it again. "Hey man, I won't bite. I'm just new here. They didn't really explain stuff at the door."

The nervous student looked up from his notes. "It's... it's Opening Convocation. To welcome the students back to school."

He turned back to his notes, and Hannah decided to leave him alone. As she waited for the assembly to begin, she listened to the voices behind her. Over and over she heard people mention some new person, and Hannah's paranoia made her assume they were talking about her.

But before she could sink lower into her seat, Ezekiel walked onto the stage. Hannah realized that he was the new person they were all referring to. *This must have been the new job he meant,* she thought.

Ezekiel, still in the guise of Lord Girard, stood out from the other faculty. His purple robes looked majestic; the amulet made of the giant amphorald hung in front of him. Hannah knew that it was only a manifestation of his mental magic, but the others in the room saw it all as real.

Amphoralds made magitech work, which made them very costly. Hanging a rock that size around your neck was showing off. If all the nobles were rich, that necklace made Girard and his daughter look obscenely wealthy.

Hannah remembered that Ezekiel wasn't just her teacher; now, in the halls of the Academy, he was her father. They had to play the part. Making sure that several of the kids around her were watching, she gave Ezekiel a wave. He nodded back. Exactly what a nobleman bloated with his own consequence would do.

But it was more than an act. At that moment, Hannah realized that Ezekiel acted as more of a father to her than anyone had ever. She smiled. It gave her comfort to know that she wasn't alone here. She had an ally who truly cared about her—one who could kick ass.

Another man followed Ezekiel onto the stage and any sense of calm Hannah possessed was shattered.

Adrien took the podium.

Hannah felt her blood boil as she laid eyes on the man she wanted to destroy—the man who had taken everything from her. She'd spent months picturing this moment, but it always included his blood dripping down her knife. Instead, the man was perfectly safe, surrounded by people who loved him. In fact, the Chancellor was a star. When Adrien entered the room, everyone cheered and stood.

Hannah reluctantly rose to her feet, but couldn't bring herself to applaud the monster in front of her.

He stood only ten feet away, unsuspecting. Hannah knew that with all of the passion, hate, and rage inside of her, she could take him out right there. She pictured his robes going up in flames.

Adrien started talking, but Hannah couldn't hear a word coming out of his filthy mouth. All she heard was the voice of her dying brother. The students around her sat, but Hannah remained on her feet, her hands tensed at her side.

Dammit, Hannah, control yourself, Ezekiel's urgent voice rang in her ears. *Sit down!*

It took a second to realize that Ezekiel was connecting with her through mental magic. Finally, Hannah sat back down, hoping that nobody had noticed.

I'm sorry, Zeke. It's just seeing him face to face... I knew it would happen one day, but I didn't think it would feel like this, she replied.

Trust me, Ezekiel responded, *I know. I feel it, too. There's nothing I would like more than to end it right here, right now. But if we jump when we're not prepared, we'll hit bottom. Then he will be able to take all of Irth and there will be nothing we can do about it.*

I understand, she thought back. *I'm sorry.*

Don't worry about it. It's not really your fault anyway. You've been using your mental magic all day to fool those around you. Even a simple spell like changing your hair and eye color can wreak havoc on your emotions. Plus, the magic you used during your examination... It's no surprise you're exhausted. Congratulations, by the way. I hear you made quite the impression.

Hannah looked up at Ezekiel. Even through Lord Girard's face, she could see his smile. She gave him a slight nod. *Just doing what you taught me.*

The crowd noise died to a murmur as Adrien paced the stage, smiling over his flock. He took up every bit of the spotlight. The Chancellor owned this place, and he knew it.

"Thank you for such a fine welcome. It is great to see everyone together. We don't do this enough, do we?"

They all laughed together, though Hannah didn't see what was so funny. Adrien's perfect teeth, straightened and whitened through the use of physical magic, shone in the magitech spotlight.

"In a way, it's good that we don't." Adrien chuckled. "We only have a Convocation such as this occasionally to keep it special, holy, to set it apart from the other common days. And today, as we welcome you all to the new term, we also gather together to celebrate the thirtieth anniversary of the Academy's founding."

Hannah snorted, knowing that Adrien would absolutely piss himself if he knew that the true Founder was sitting on the stage just behind him. The nervous boy next to her gave her a strange look, then returned to annotating everything the Chancellor said.

As Adrien prattled, Hannah turned her mind back toward Ezekiel's. *Your former student is full of shit. I can barely take it. How do you sit there so calmly?*

Like this, he said.

At that moment, Adrien turned and pointed toward Ezekiel.

"It is my great pleasure to announce that today the Academy has added another faculty member to our ranks. Lord Girard of Cella, an old and revered Arcadian, has returned home. In his retirement, he has graciously offered his services in teaching a section of the History of Magic." Adrien turned and gestured toward Ezekiel. "I offer you... Lord Girard."

Ezekiel stood and gave them a humble bow as the audience applauded in a more subdued manner. Hannah's eyes were locked on Adrien. The man grinned and nodded like a madman, evidently clueless that it was his old teacher—now nemesis—standing before him. His hubris had blinded him to their infiltration, and that same pride would be the foundation of his downfall.

The fool, Hannah thought. Then she finally realized how Ezekiel maintained his calm. He was enjoying every minute of this act, of pulling one over on Adrien. The old man was feeling the same sense of gratification that Hannah was by realizing that they were one step closer to taking him down.

She smiled as she turned her attention back to the man on the stage.

"It's been thirty-eight years since the founding of Arcadia, and I will tell you, it has gone by in the blink of an eye. When we initiated that first class—which Professor August was a part of," Adrien glanced at the Chair of Physical Arts, "I never expected that our humble little school, which met in half-built homes back then, would amount to anything nearly this grand. In those days, we met out of necessity. Magic was alive, but it was not well."

All eyes followed the Chancellor as he paced the stage. The students and faculty were eating out of his cold, murdering hands.

"Before the Academy was formed, humans—normal folk— tried and tested the magic within them. It was a terrible time; some would say worse than the Age of Madness. Most could not handle the new power coursing through their veins. People were crippled and often killed by magical accidents. The suffering of the commoners was precisely what drove me to develop the Academy. It was clear that not everyone should use the gift; that without proper control, it was a curse."

Adrien paused and flipped a hand to those sitting on the stage with him. "Now, thanks to the excellent work of these fine professors, we are able to control the use of magic. And students like you who graduate from our program will go on to influence all of Arcadia. No, all of Irth."

Adrien paused, and the room broke into applause. Students hooted and hollered and teachers clapped with a certain amount of austerity. The room couldn't agree more with the Chancellor's words.

Adrien held up both hands to quiet the crowd. "I know, I know. It is a good and holy calling. And I thank the Matriarch and the Patriarch every day for blessing me with the task of stewarding magic. Like many things in the world, it isn't easy, but it is right. Now, on this anniversary, I am excited to announce to all of you that the Academy is moving into a new stage.

"For years we have protected people from magic and themselves. We've also brought up a new generation of magicians, of which you are a part. And now, now my friends, I will tell you about the new step in the evolution of magic, in the evolution of Irth."

Adrien paused and let his words float over the room. The reverence that they all held for the Chancellor built rage within Hannah, but she kept it at bay.

"As you all know, magitech is one of the Academy's greatest achievements. Half a century ago when I first started to learn the art of magic from my own teacher, the notion of putting magic into an inanimate object would have seemed like a fairy tale. Thankfully, due to the hard work of our researchers and engineers, we've done just that. And the advances we have made throughout the past decades have been extraordinary.

"We've developed technology that makes life easier. There are new tools for law enforcement, making our Guard stronger and allowing them to maintain peace within the city walls. There are even technologies to help heal the sick. Now, dear friends, it is time for us to dream bigger. In the coming weeks, I will be unveiling a new machine, beyond anything you've ever seen. It is bigger. It is better. And it will allow us to bring peace to the world beyond our walls."

The audience fell silent. Questions obviously ran through their minds.

"Holy shit," one of the boys said behind Hannah. He was right, and she knew it. Adrien's plan was enormous.

The Chancellor continued, "Today marks a new day for Arcadia. We are on the cusp of something extraordinary, of extending our way of life. For forty years, our city has been marked by the walls that surround it. Soon our magitech will lead us beyond these walls. Arcadia will no longer be a city, but it will be a unified, global place for all people, for all walks of life, and for everyone loyal to us. Each of you is part of this mission, and I look forward to pursuing it together for the *next* forty years. May the Matriarch and Patriarch bless our endeavors. Thank you. Good night."

The room exploded, everyone jumping to their feet.

And for the first time, Hannah realized just what it was they were up against.

CHAPTER TWENTY-ONE

Parker breathed like hunted prey as he sprinted down the dark hall, away from the magitech sucking the soul out of that wizard. The sirens bellowing in his ears reminded him of the hell waiting for him when the guards caught up with him.

His plan was risky, but it had worked so far. It only needed to end well.

The hall wound left, then right. Another turn and Parker saw the light at the end of the tunnel.

Freedom! His heart nearly burst. A few more steps, and he'd make it.

Bursting through the open doorway and out into the open air, the light of the sun, which he hadn't seen for weeks, nearly blinded him.

Don't stop now, you bastard, he thought to himself. *Keep running.*

Parker's vision started to come back through his narrowed eyes. He could see a stand of trees separating him from the market square and the Boulevard just beyond. If he made it that far, he could disappear.

He bolted.

Five strides from freedom, Parker's plan came to its end. He looked down at the cuffs latched securely onto his wrists. They hummed, louder and louder with every step. Suddenly, mere feet from escape, the cuffs began to glow. A jolt of energy ran up his arm into his chest. He screamed as the searing pain overwhelmed him, then dropped to the ground, tremors overtaking his body.

The last thing Parker saw before blacking out was the cruel smiles of the guards as they dragged him back into the factory.

Ezekiel smoothed his purple robes, even though he knew full well that his ensemble was only an illusion. He actually wore his own humble white outfit, but to everyone else he looked as if he were the richest man in Irth. Trusting the illusion to hold, he pushed open the door and walked into the classroom.

His classroom.

The students sat dutifully in rows. Everything stopped when he entered; all eyes were on him. It had only been a day since Adrien's speech before the student body and the faculty, but it seemed that the words were still ringing in their ears. These young men and women wanted to be part of the revolution planned by the Chancellor, but to do that, they first needed to run the gauntlet of higher learning.

"Ok, then. Here we are," Ezekiel said with a smile on his face. He realized for the first time that he was quite nervous to teach in front of this efficiently organized group of students. He longed for the informal storytelling culture of the Heights and his mystic friends. He wanted to be in a quiet room; just him, Hannah, and that damned dragon. "History of Magic. Here we go."

All of the students opened books of blank parchment and prepared to transcribe his every word. They knew that if they wanted the highest roles in Arcadia, they needed to pass with flying colors. If not, they'd be relegated to the thankless work of

Hunters or producers of magitech—not much better than common laborers.

The Academy couldn't have a more suitable teacher of magic's history. Not only had he lived an unnaturally long life, he had also spent many years with Lilith, the Oracle. She lived in a cave far to the east, but she had knowledge of the past that spanned hundreds of years—and dozens of worlds.

He thought back to all the things the Oracle had taught him and wondered where to begin. Hungry eyes stared at him from their seats.

"I guess we should start at the beginning," Ezekiel said. "Let's stretch back before the Founder, before the Age of Madness, even before the World's Worst Day Ever. We should begin with the Matriarch herself, and the time when Bethany Anne became the Queen Bitch."

A wall of confusion met him as he surveyed the classroom. The Queen Bitch was talked about in legend. The Prophet preached in Her name, and men and women shared folk tales about Her heroic might in days of old. But it seemed She wasn't usually the focus of a history lecture at the Academy.

"Hmmm. Maybe that is a bit much for one semester together. More recent history, then. Yes, that will do." Ezekiel leaned against a broad wooden table and reconfigured his approach. The Oracle had taught him much about the histories of all realities, but these students were clearly only ready for milk. Meat would have to come later. Instead of turning the clock so far back, Ezekiel opted for a more accessible starting point.

"Of course, you all know about the Age of Magic, right?" Heads nodded in silence. "Ok, good. We start there then."

Ezekiel walked them through the history of their age, starting at the tail end of the Age of Madness. He explained how all hope had been lost; people had turned to desperate acts, and the fear of madness often turned father against son, mother against daughter.

"It was a terrible time, worse than any of you could even imagine." Ezekiel paused to gauge the climate of the room. Most of the students seemed interested, though a few faces looked skeptical, either of the story or of Ezekiel himself. As he began to wind down toward the end of class, he said, "But that time would not last. And that's where we stop for today. Review your notes, and on Thursday, we'll be talking about the coming of the Founder: how he had the power to stop the Age of Madness and worked to usher in the Age of Magic."

A guy in the back row raised his hand. He had been slouched behind his desk for the entire class period and had the most skeptical look on his face of all the students.

"Yes?" Ezekiel asked.

"The Founder? Are you freaking serious?"

"More serious than you can imagine, young man," Ezekiel said with a glimmer in his eyes. "Why do you ask?"

"It's just that I thought we were going to be learning history."

"Ah, skeptics, every one of you then?" Ezekiel asked. Most of the students looked around sheepishly. He looked back up at the boy. "What is your name, son?"

"Morgan," the young man answered. "And I'm not a skeptic; I'm a realist. Those stories about the Founder are for desperate people—those wackos that follow the Prophet—or for the poor. They're just fairy tales, meant to give the weak-minded something to cling to. It's pathetic." All the guys surrounding Morgan were grinning madly. Clearly, he led the pack. "It's all *horseshit.*"

Ezekiel laughed. "Yes, well, maybe it is, but even horseshit exists. And it has some value, I might add—"

The bell rang before Ezekiel could finish, and the students all rushed out of the room. As Morgan passed, Ezekiel gave him a little nod, but the kid ignored him. Clearly, Ezekiel had not made a friend in that one.

After the last student left, Ezekiel gathered his things and followed his students. He ran into Dean Amelia, who waited for him just outside the classroom.

"How'd the first day go?" she asked with a smile.

Ezekiel looked down at the purple robes he was projecting, a habit that he had formed since entering the city. His mental magic was good, but he had to remain sharp to make sure that his disguise remained in place at all times.

"Ah! They're not like me and my friends were so many years ago, when we sat in their places."

She laughed. "They're not the same as I when I was their age. As we get further and further from the past, they seem to believe in it less and less, but I wouldn't let it bother you. Come on, let me buy you a drink. A few of us get together once a week, mostly as an excuse to complain about our students."

"That sounds good," Ezekiel said. "I believe I need one."

Amelia and Ezekiel slid into a booth across from two faculty members he recognized from the Convocation. One was sour-faced and staring intently into his ale. The other grinned from ear to ear, a half-filled glass in front of him, and Ezekiel guessed it wasn't his first.

"August, Nikola, have you met Girard?" Amelia asked as she settled into her seat.

Ezekiel almost said that he had never met either one of them, but August thankfully beat him to the punch.

"Girard? Of course, I know this old bastard!" The smiling man seemed excited. "He and I were first-years together at the Academy. He damn near killed me while learning to make fireballs, if I remember correctly."

Ezekiel laughed as heartily as he could. "I'm still not much better with them, I'm afraid. It's been a long time, August. Have you been in Arcadia since then?"

"No place else would have me. But you don't know Nikola, do you?"

"We've never met," Nikola said without looking up.

As Ezekiel ordered a drink, he realized that the two men played into his deception perfectly, but Ezekiel couldn't help but wonder what August really thought of Lord Girard. Most in Arcadia knew that the old Lord was a bit of a bastard, or at least they knew that he didn't treat his servants very kindly even before they moved out to the country. But was he the kind of person someone like August or Nikola would confide in? That was the question he needed answered.

He decided to play nice and see where it led.

"Very nice to meet you, Nikola. What do you do at the Academy?"

The tall, pale man sipped from his pint glass. Foam from the ale clung to his perfectly manicured mustache. "Magitech. I teach the little bastards how to take our beautiful magic and put it into cheap trinkets—all to make a better world. Or at least that's what I tell myself."

Ezekiel's brow furrowed. He didn't expect to hear such open aggression from the other profs. "And what else?"

The man cocked his head. "What do you mean?"

"Well, what do you teach besides magitech?" Ezekiel asked.

All the faculty members around the table laughed. Ezekiel looked at each one. He had become the fool, and he had no idea why.

He thought about reaching into their minds, but the Dean stepped in, saving him the effort and risk.

"You're pretty old-school, aren't you, Girard? Nowadays, we all focus on one single area."

Ezekiel played up his confusion. "So, you're telling me that you each only teach one thing?"

August grinned ear to ear. "That's about right. Focus is impor-tant, don't you think? It's safer that way, for us and the students. I actually want to specialize even further. Primarily telekinesis, fire, ice, physical alchemy, but we didn't really have the manpower for that. Now that you're on board..."

"Hmm," Ezekiel said. "Are you satisfied focusing so intently on one thing? I've found that studying all the corners of physical magic gives me plenty of room for creativity. It makes me a better magician."

Nikola grinned, but the smile held no warmth. "Maybe, but the Chancellor doesn't want us to be better magicians. He wants us to be better faculty members. Our job is to train workers for the kingdom, and the more that we specialize, the better we're going to be in that one area. Same thing with the students. I've heard the Chancellor say that he wants to start giving the students specialties, too. Divide and conquer, as they say."

Ezekiel shook his head. Nikola was using that phrase in the wrong way, but what Adrien was doing made perfect sense. He kept his own people divided, which made them easier to control.

Practically speaking, he could understand specialization. Not only would it make each of them incredibly good in one area in such a way that they would be equipped to teach the students particularly well, but Ezekiel also knew that it would keep the faculty from becoming too powerful. Adrien hoarded power, and the more he could control, the stronger he would be.

"Well, you're right. It hasn't always been this way. And I guess I can see the Chancellor's point." Ezekiel knew he had to play their game, at least to a certain extent. "But do tell me about magitech. It sounds as if this has become an important part of teaching at the Academy, yes?"

"As a good specialist," Nikola said, "it is my duty to tell you that magitech is the most important part of the Academy." Again, Nikola's words contained a bite. The dour man drained his glass and ordered another.

"I'd like to disagree," August said with a laugh. "But Nikola is right. Our Chancellor places great stock in that particular discipline. He believes that magitech is the future, and I have no reason to doubt him."

"Why is that?" Ezekiel asked.

The Dean stepped into the conversation. "Progress and safety. Magitech lets us shape the world to fit our needs at very low risk. Even the worst magic user can push a button, even those without the gift. Adrien firmly believes that if we want what's best for society, we should focus on magitech."

Ezekiel took a long pull on his pint, placed it down carefully, and said, "But doesn't that take the responsibility out of our hands? If we create technology, but don't teach people how to use it well, use it morally, aren't we culpable?"

Amelia looked down at her cup. "The Chancellor believes that—"

"And what do *you* believe, Amelia?" Ezekiel interrupted.

She sat in silence for a moment. She hadn't expected that question, and Ezekiel knew that she was weighing the difference between her own subjective position and the party line she needed to toe in her role as Dean. Finally, she said, "It is what it is. And what can I do to change it?"

Ezekiel stared at her for a long time before finally speaking. "If something's wrong, you should fight to fix it. Even if it's a fight you can't win. Better to die than fight for the wrong side. But if you ask me, I think there's a tremendous amount you can do, Amelia. And I think you know that, don't you?"

The table fell silent. Ezekiel's questioning had turned from playful banter to something altogether too serious. Amelia stared at Ezekiel, trying to read his words. Nikola stared into his cup. Even August lost some of his smile.

As the silence became too uncomfortable, the portly older man tried to steer it back into more pleasant waters. "So," August said, "what do you all think of the new statue of the Chancellor? I, for one, think it's divine. I was just saying so to him the other day, and..."

As August continued to prattle, Ezekiel tuned him out. His whole focus was on Amelia. He emptied his thoughts and began to fill his mind with hers. His gut told him that she could be trusted, but he had to know for sure.

The risk was too great if he was wrong.

Finally, August and Nikola rose from the table, making some excuse about early morning classes. Soon, only Ezekiel and the Dean were left.

"Did you really mean that," she asked. "About it being better to die than to fight for the wrong side?"

Ezekiel nodded. "Absolutely. And I've known a fair number of people who believed it, enough to prove it true."

Amelia swirled the remaining ale in her glass. "My father used to say the same thing."

"Sounds like a smart man," Ezekiel commented.

"He told me he heard the Founder say it once," she replied, lifting her eyes to look at Ezekiel. "Who are you, really? I've looked into your records. You were a terrible student when you were at the Academy, with no interest in history whatsoever. And by everyone's account, you're not a very nice person either. What brings you back here? Why now? It seems so...out of character."

Ezekiel smiled as he leaned back in his chair. "You certainly don't mince words, Dean."

"I'm just tired of lies," she said. "It feels as if Arcadia is full of them these days. That's not the Academy I knew when I was young."

"And what was the Academy you knew?"

"It was a place of discovery, of passion." She continued to describe it, "A place where you could learn the skills to change the world. That was the kind of person I wanted to be. That was the kind of professor I wanted to be, but now, I don't know what I do. I manage idiot teachers who can't see beyond their own biases so that they can teach unenthusiastic students who care only about their own ambitions." She looked around the tavern before looking back at Ezekiel. "What's the point?"

"But you're the Dean. Surely *you* could do something about it."

She shook her head. "It's like I said. Adrien…" she suddenly paused, afraid to continue. Ezekiel watched her; it was clear she was debating something in her mind. Finally, she spoke. "It's Adrien. He's too powerful, not only in the Academy, but in all of Arcadia. No one asks questions. We all just smile along like August, but Adrien is keeping something from us. Keeping something from *me*. I don't know what it is, but my gut tells me that something here is terribly wrong. Like this internship of his. Why is it so damn secretive? What's he hiding? But it doesn't matter. Even if I knew, I couldn't do anything about it. No one could. And that's what scares me most of all. Only a person who was corrupt would want that much power."

She stopped her rant and looked up. Her eyes were two question marks, and Ezekiel knew what she was really asking. Had she said too much? Was Girard someone she could trust? Or did she just ruin her career with a careless slip of the tongue after too many drinks?

Ezekiel smiled. He leaned in close. "What if I told you that it does matter, more than anything? And what if I told you there was someone who could do something about it? Would you want to meet them?"

Amelia stared Ezekiel in the face. "Hell yes," she replied.

Ezekiel rose to his feet. "Then come with me. No more lies. It's time for the truth."

CHAPTER TWENTY-TWO

When Parker finally opened his eyes, he didn't see much. Darkness covered him. Light crept in from cracks around the door, and when he strained his neck, he could just make out a single window that was boarded up near the top of the room. A chill ran through this body, and the sounds of dripping water surrounded him. The room was wet.

Very wet.

But that wasn't what concerned him. Rather, it was the fact that he had been stripped naked and suspended by chains from the ceiling of whatever hellhole he had been thrown into. Time meant nothing to him; he could have been here for a minute or a year. All he could remember was that he had nearly escaped. The taste of freedom still played on his tongue.

He could feel a burning sore between his shoulders, which reminded him that the guards who had brought him back weren't too friendly. They had used their magitech staffs liberally, and Parker's body paid the price. All the muscles from his wrists to his ankles thumped in rhythm with his heart.

He remembered seeing the Boulevard in the distance right before the forcefield threw him on his ass. Things had gone shitstorm awful in a matter of seconds, and now, he had to figure out his next move, if one existed.

After hanging there for what felt like a day, the door to the room finally creaked open. Light poured in from the hallway beyond and nearly blinded him, but Parker forced himself to look, to try and get any information on where he was. All he saw was a figure silhouetted in the doorway.

Female. Shapely. Powerful.

She quickly shut the door, but carried a magitech lantern which lit the room. As his eyes adjusted, Parker tried to assess his location. Leaning his head back, he saw that he hung from shackles attached to the ceiling impossibly out of reach. The cuffs were common, not fueled with magitech like the shackles the workers were all attached to, the room empty, save for a single wooden chair in the middle.

The woman stared at him for a moment, then moved forward, the clicking of her heels filling his dismal dungeon. Dark hair pulled back, exposing pale, angular features of her face. A finely-pressed suit hugged her curves, and everything about her screamed noblewoman. She was at once beautiful and terrifying, the kind of woman all men wanted—until they had her.

"Parker, Parker, Parker," she hissed. "Not a bad attempt, really. You made it farther than anyone else has. That's quite an accomplishment for some worthless street scum from the Boulevard. But no one gets out of my box."

He snorted. "Sounds like no one's been in your box for a while. You should try it, might loosen you up a bit."

She crossed the room in three steps. Delivering a slap to his face, she laughed. "Quick, for a little shit. Do you kiss your mother with that mouth? Eleanor, right?"

A cold feeling grabbed Parker's spine. "Leave my mother out of this!" he yelled.

"Oh, honey. We haven't met, have we? I'm Alexandra. And the only thing you need to know about me is that I don't leave anything out of *anything*. It's all on the table." She got so close that he could smell the bitterness on her tongue. "I hope that bitch has a sense of humor like yours. It'll make it easier when she's working her life away here with me."

"Kiss my ass," Parker spat.

Alexandra looked down at his naked body hanging from the chains. "Tempting. Really. But I have much better options." She paused, smiling coldly. "Eleanor. Yes, she'd be a nice addition. Hard worker. Way things are going in the Boulevard, and with her doting son hanging like meat in my dungeon, she'll either be working for me soon, or spreading her low-class legs for a few coins and some mead. Which do you prefer?"

Parker felt ready to explode. For a second, he believed could pull the iron chains from the ceiling and choke the woman. But she wanted a response—that was her whole game. And he knew that if he had a chance of getting out of the shitstorm, he would have to be patient.

He remained silent.

"And what about the other one? Hannah, right? Oh, sweet, sweet Hannah. I'd love a night alone with that one. The two of you were close, weren't you?"

Alexandra ran a perfectly manicured nail down between his pecs and slowly scratched a line on his abdomen, pulling away just before getting to his privates. "How close were you, exactly? I hear the Unlawfuls can get a little, you know, kinky. Is it all true?"

Parker pushed up on his toes, trying to take some of the pressure off his wrists. "She got kinky with those pervert Hunters when she blew them to bits, but I doubt that's what you mean."

She made a tsking sound with her tongue as she paced around the room. "Now, Parker, let's play nice, shall we? Tell me where the little Princess Bitch is. I'll even make you a deal. You give me Hannah, and I give you your freedom."

He laughed. Hannah was his best friend. He wouldn't turn on her for anything. "I'd rather stay right here in your wet, filthy box, if you know what I mean," Parker said. "Enough of the good cop shit. Bring in the bruiser, and then you can send me back to the assembly line. You people have put me through so much shit already, you think a few hours at the hands of one of your thugs scares me? I'm from the Boulevard, bitch."

Alexandra smiled. But instead of calling in another interrogator, she slowly removed her jacket, revealing a tight leather corset with nothing else beneath. She carefully folded the coat and placed it over the chair. Parker couldn't help but notice just how stunning she was.

She spun on her heel and walked back toward him. She turned her palms up and tiny bolts of lightning danced around her fingers. Her eyes were black, as dark as hell.

"Parker, you've misunderstood. I *am* the bad cop, as well as the good. I'm, shall we say, *experienced*. With men, magic, manipulation…" She ran her hand across his face. His skin tingled where the magic touched it. "Give me what I want, and I'll give you the night of your life. I'm not shy, after all. But withhold from me.…" She closed her fist and cracked it against his jaw. Her rock-hard strike rattled him in his chains. "And you'll experience a hell that makes living in the Boulevard seem like a dream."

Parker's head rang. His tongue checked to make sure he still had all his teeth as he spat out blood. "I'd rather cut off my own bits, darling." He forced a grin.

Alexandra laughed, and it echoed around the room. "We might just get to that before the night ends."

Without warning, she turned her palms toward him. They glowed blue, wreathed in lightning. Pressing them against his torso, the power burned through his flesh.

She continued to laugh, but it was drowned out by Parker's screams. He screamed loudly enough for Jack and all the other workers to hear him from the factory floor.

This is gonna suck, Hannah thought to herself as she walked into the first class of her life. The classroom scared her more than when she had faced down the lycanthrope, but then Parker had been at her side. His presence made even hustling on the streets easy. But alone, and in this new place, she felt completely out of her element. The Boulevard had nothing on the Academy.

As she entered the room, every eye focused on her.

Guess I'm the new girl.

She reminded herself that to all of them, she wasn't Hannah from the Boulevard, but some rich-ass bitch from beyond the walls of Arcadia. She had mystery, intrigue, and beauty on her side—all she needed to do was own it. At the moment, owning it felt harder than making a dragon out of a lizard.

The room was packed already—apparently, she had missed the memo to show up early. Only one seat remained empty, the one next to the curly-haired boy she had sat next to at the Convocation. His face turned bright red in embarrassment when he realized his situation. She walked toward him.

"This seat taken?" She smiled and tossed her strawberry blond curls over her shoulder. Playing the girly-girl was certainly out of her wheelhouse.

"It's, well, always been like this. I mean…it's yes. It is open." His face turned redder than Ezekiel's eyes when he was tele-porting.

Her smiled widened. "Thanks. I'm Deborah," Hannah said, offering her hand as she took the seat.

He grabbed it with his sweaty palm. "Deborah. I know. I mean, I… We've all heard of you. You're the new professor's daughter. From the other side of Irth."

She could feel the guy swallow, and Hannah felt sorry for him. If he only knew that she was an orphan from the Boulevard who had just had her first hot shower ever, maybe he'd be just a bit more comfortable. "That's right, but I'm afraid I don't know your name."

"Gregory. I mean... Greg, but whatever. Gregory."

Hannah laughed. "Gregory. That's a nice name. Like an ancient knight or something. Can I tell you a secret? I'm scared shitless right now. I don't know anybody, and quite frankly, this place is kind of freaking me out. I'm way behind. In terms of magic, I don't know the difference between my ass and a fireball."

The kid snorted. "Well, that might be a helpful distinction to make."

Hannah laughed, glad she could coax a joke out of him. Before she had a chance to respond, a voice called out from the table behind them. "Don't waste your time with that one, *Deb*. Greggy wouldn't know what to do with a woman if she fell in his lap— even a hick like you."

Hannah looked over her shoulder to find the girl she had run into on the campus lawn. Her comment made the boys at her table laugh. The girl tossed her hair, happy to have scored a point in this weird competition for social dominance.

She thought about turning the girl into a lizard, but then thought better of it. Instead, she decided to play this girl's game. "Spend a lot of time falling in guys' laps? Maybe if you pulled your head out of your ass, you could see where you were going." A scowl that could spoil milk replaced the girl's sneer. She turned in a huff back to her now wide-eyed companions.

Gregory's mouth hung open. "Holy shit! No one talks to Violet like that."

Hannah shrugged. "I don't like it when people talk bad about my friends."

Leaning back, Hannah saw a smile wider than the Arcadian gates spread across Gregory's face. Apparently, he was pleased that the hot new girl called him a friend.

Hannah knew she had just alienated that girl Violet, and probably whatever friends she had, which was the opposite of what Hannah was supposed to be doing here. But she didn't care.

She'd rather make the job ten times harder than work with someone like her.

But at this rate, Hannah would be the most hated person at the school by the week's end.

Score one for standing up to the campus bitch.

She breathed a sigh of relief when the teacher stepped into the room to begin the lesson. Her relief quickly disappeared when she saw who it was.

Charlotte, the woman who had been less than impressed at Hannah's admissions exam, walked briskly to the front of the room. She placed her leather bag on the table at the front and began to speak. The room fell silent.

"Welcome to Magical Basics. My name is Charlotte, and I will be your instructor. Using magic is a serious matter. Anyone not taking it seriously will be dismissed. Am I understood?"

The woman's icy words had a chilling effect on the class. Everyone nodded in unison, not wanting to provide a target for this woman's wrath.

"Good. I'll also remind you that the Dean is currently looking for students to take part in the Chancellor's new internship program. It is an exciting opportunity, and one that is available to students at any level, as long as they exhibit potential. I need to make my recommendations before the end of the term, so focus on your work and you just may succeed."

A low murmur filled the room as everyone began to whisper to each other. Apparently, this program, whatever the hell it was, was a big deal.

Charlotte scanned the room, and her eyes caught Hannah's. "One last thing. Most of you know each other, but we had a late admission this term. Deborah, why don't you stand?"

Hannah felt her cheeks flush, and she rose slowly from her chair.

Charlotte continued. "Deborah is joining us from outside the city. Please treat her with respect. Deborah, I'll remind you that life in the Academy is different from out in the country. I expect you to obey all rules—for however long you *remain* a student here."

Hannah's cheeks turned redder, this time from anger. She understood her new professor's not-so-veiled threat. The whispering began again, and Hannah took her seat.

Hannah overheard a hushed voice somewhere behind her. "I heard her admissions exam was really impressive."

"Yeah, right," another voice jumped in. "More like her daddy was impressive. That's the only reason she's here. But I will say, she's got a nice—"

"There will be none of that, Morgan," Professor Charlotte chastised the student. Hannah turned around and saw the boy who had called to her from the quad. He smiled and waved a hand in her direction. He apparently wasn't done having fun at her expense. She resisted the urge to flip him off again.

"Now," Charlotte directed. "Open your books to page twenty-three, and begin to work the manipulation spell listed there."

The class responded quickly, and before long, the room was filled with a busy hum.

"Manipulation, huh?" Hannah asked Gregory.

"Yeah," he said without lifting his eyes from the text. "It says we need to turn a lump of clay into a vase."

Gregory left for a moment and returned with a ball of clay on a rough wooden tray. He placed it on the lab table in front of them.

He shook his head. "This is supposed to be an easy spell. Most of the other students learned to do stuff like this before coming here, but I've never been able to figure it out." He looked up at Hannah. "Honestly, I'm not sure if I'm even meant to be here. I'm no good at magic, but my father—"

"Your father?" Hannah raised her eyebrows, thinking she might be getting somewhere.

"Yeah," he said sheepishly. "My dad is Elon."

Hannah smiled. "I guess that's supposed to mean something to me. Remember. New girl right here." She pointed to herself. "Assume nothing and speak slowly."

He laughed. "Of course. My dad, Elon, is Arcadia's Chief Engineer. He's one of the best magicians in the city—worked his way to the top—and now he oversees magitech development. He answers to Adrien himself. They let me in because of him, and I know people expect big things of me, but…" He opened his hands in the direction of the clay, "nothing."

Hannah poked the moist lump with a finger. "I'm sure they wouldn't have let you in here if you didn't have potential. What *can* you do?" Hannah was trying to be nice, but she truly was curious. She knew that most of the nobles learned magic at home. The laws of restriction didn't really apply to them. But, she wondered how close their training was to her own."

"Oh, I can do the basics," Gregory said. "You know, move it around a little, heat up its surface. That sort of stuff. But I'm lost when trying anything more complex."

She nodded along and then interjected, "You know that shaping it is really just moving it, right? I'm sure you can figure it out."

"I guess so, but I can't get the damn thing to take shape."

"Show me," Hannah demanded.

Gregory focused on the clay. His eyes flashed black as he twirled his index fingers around each other. The clay rolled, corresponding with his movements. Then he turned his hand over and raised it, palm up. The lump of clay levitated shakily off the table. He made it spin and turn and finally dropped back into place. There was a faint line of sweat on Gregory's brow.

Hannah clapped. "Not bad, Gregory. You've got all the skills, just need to put the pieces together. Here, let me try."

She raised her hands over the clay and started making complex motions with her fingers. Gregory's mouth dropped open as the substance followed Hannah's lead. Within seconds,

Hannah had created a nearly perfect sculpture of Morgan, the douche in the back of the room.

"*Holy shit,* you're good," Gregory shouted, which drew all eyes in their direction—including Morgan's.

It took the boy a second to realize that the clay looked like him. He smiled, flattered at first. But then Hannah closed her fist and made a downward swinging motion. The clay likeness of the boy flattened into a pile of what looked like excrement. Looking back at Morgan, Hannah smiled and blew him a kiss. Several students laughed at Hannah's insult.

First day of class, and so much for the low profile, she thought.

"Quiet," Charlotte shouted over the edge of her book. "Back to work."

Gregory's mouth still hung open. "How the hell did you do that?"

She shrugged. "Not a big deal. I told you. You already had the know-how to do it yourself. It's just a matter of getting your head in the right place. Not to mention, I grew up in the country. Wasn't much to do out there except play with power. I didn't have douche nuggets like Morgan or Violet breathing down my neck. Now, let's see if we can't help you form a vase or whatever the hell we're supposed to be doing."

Over the course of the period, she walked Gregory through the spell the same way Ezekiel had shown her. With her help, he made some progress, and as the class was getting close to its end, he had been able to press the ball of clay into a flat slab with slightly raised edges.

"Good." Hannah suggested, "You're getting the hang of it, but I think you might be trying too hard. Let's do this: try not to think about the task at hand. Let's just chat instead. Allow the magic to come out of the back of your mind. That might help things."

"Um, ok," Gregory agreed, confused by the whole proposition. "What should we talk about?"

"I dunno. Tell me about this internship, or scholarship club, or whatever. Just keeping moving your hands over the clay."

Gregory bit his lip, concentrating.

Hannah jabbed him with her elbow. "Talk. You're still trying too hard with the clay. Let that all go."

He looked up. "Ok. Well, the internship is a program that the Chancellor initiated just this term. He's been recruiting a special team of students who will become, I don't know, like advanced understudies or something. Apparently, he has already taken several upperclassmen from their studies at the Academy, but now he's looking for younger students."

The clay started to change shape as he talked.

"What do you do if you're picked?" she asked.

"Don't know really. You, well, study with him, or something. When the students are identified, they're pulled from normal classes to do advanced stuff, I guess. Violet's older brother was one of Adrien's first interns, but I haven't seen him since. I don't think even Violet has either. Whatever the internship is, it must be keeping them busy."

Hannah furrowed her brow. The way Gregory phrased that, it reminded her of something Eleanor said. Parker was too busy to come home from the factory.

She didn't know what, but Hannah knew that there was something fishy going on—some connection between Adrien's program and Parker's new job. Her gut rarely got things wrong. She committed to finding out more, but for the sake of being above suspicion, she changed the topic.

"So, why in the world do you want to study magic?"

Gregory continued to work the clay as they talked. It was starting to take the rough shape of an animal.

He shrugged. "Seems the right thing to do. I mean, as a noble you don't have many choices."

Hannah couldn't help but giggle at that. She wondered if he would have said that if he knew that he was talking to a poor girl from the Boulevard. "Tell me about it!"

"So, I could have gone into government, or maybe tried to start a business, but you know, I think that the opportunity to do good—make people's lives better—is best achieved through the use of magic. Although at this rate, I won't be able to help anyone."

Hannah wrinkled her nose. She knew that he was right, in theory. Over the course of the last few months, she had seen the sheer power of magic and what it could do in the world. She also knew that if Gregory continued on this path, he wouldn't be making the world better, just life for the nobles, especially Adrien. But the sheep had been blinded by the wolves, and Gregory was just walking the path he'd been taught to follow. Regardless, she knew he was not a bad guy and hoped that maybe little by little she could help him see the error of his perspective.

"Hey, it's coming along," Hannah said pointing at his project. "A goat, right?"

His face darkened. "A cat…"

Hannah laughed, and Gregory's red face came back.

"No biggie. Keep working it."

Hannah smiled, pleased to know that she was accomplishing her mission. She had infiltrated the Academy, made a good connection with Gregory, and gotten some information that would prove useful to their work.

She glanced over her shoulder at Violet.

Now, if I only had kept a low profile.

CHAPTER TWENTY-THREE

Alexandra stood in her interrogation room. A few yards away, Parker, her latest subject, hung naked like a side of meat. Sweat, blood, and dirt covered his body, and she could barely recognize the handsome young man she'd started with. She had tortured him to the edge of death, but she was an expert. She knew precisely how far to go and when to pull back.

"Want me to remove the body?" her assistant asked as he entered the room.

Alexandra smiled, still taking in the young man's broken form and admiring her own work. "He's not dead yet. I still might get something from him."

The assistant raised an eyebrow. "Seriously? You were in here a while. Maybe he doesn't have anything for you."

"He was impressive, that's the truth. But you need to remember that everybody has something. I'll get it out of him yet."

The assistant nodded. "Fair enough. You sure he's still alive? I can't even see him breathing."

"Oh, he's alive. I made sure of that. Give him until morning, and then we'll wake him back up for some more fun and games. I want the other workers to hear his screams. Besides, I haven't even shown the little bastard my best tricks yet. After another round, he'll give me anything I want and a whole lot more."

The assistant turned to leave, and Alexandra followed him out of the dark, dank room.

Once the door slammed shut, Parker's head snapped up and his eyes opened.

"Time," his voice mumbled, blood gurgling in his throat as his eyes tried to pierce the darkness through sheer anger, "to get to work."

The sun had set behind the western wall of the city by the time Hannah walked out of the Old Main building and into the quad. Her first day as a student couldn't have been called uneventful. For years she had wished that she was like them—a noble groomed within an ivory tower—but now she wasn't so sure. While there were plenty of squabbles in the Boulevard, the kids were always on the same side. Even as social groups shifted, they all knew that at the end of the day they were on the same team.

Things were different at the Academy. She thought of Violet, the bitch who had already marked Hannah as a rival, and Morgan, who seemed to view her as nothing more than a target. It was all so superficial, so petty compared to trying to scrounge every day for food or medicine. She realized that such silly squabbles were what the life of luxury bred.

Idle hands created cool kids, and not much else.

Screw them, Hannah thought. She knew that playing nice with people like Violet might give her access—access that she and Ezekiel needed—but Hannah didn't care. Acting like Violet wasn't going to happen.

There was also the Chancellor's scholarship program. Even in those first few hours as a student, she had realized how intense the competition was. The secrecy of the whole thing was disconcerting, not to mention that she trusted nothing that Adrien had a hand in. But she knew that if she could, by luck or providence, make it into his inner circle, she might just have the chance to take the bastard down.

Ezekiel was bent on saving Arcadia, which was fine.

All Hannah cared about was taking the Chancellor's life and hopefully seeing him suffer along the way to a slow painful death.

Hannah walked back toward her room, brooding over the battle to come. But her thoughts of pain and vengeance were interrupted by a voice calling from behind her.

"Deborah, wait up!" Gregory yelled.

She had to remind herself that *she* was Deborah. She turned with a stiff smile. "Why, Gregory, you startled me." Hannah had tried to sound like a noblewoman, but realized she sounded like a freaking idiot-bitch.

He ran his hand through his kinky hair. "Oh, she startles?" Gregory asked with a grin. "After seeing your skills in the classroom today, I thought you could, well, do *anything*."

"I just sounded like a dumbass, didn't I?" Hannah shrugged. "Sorry. New school, new people. I've never done this shit before. And growing up noble in the countryside is nothing like the quarter you were raised in. Don't really know how to act."

Gregory cocked his head to the side. "So don't act. The Patriarch knows we have to act enough day to day. Let's just be us. You be some rich-ass farm girl, and I'll be the nerdy freak who's afraid of his own shadow. Sound good?"

Hannah laughed, and it felt good. "Sounds good. Sun's going down. I better get back to my room."

"First day of classes at the Academy and you want to go home early? Come on. I'll show you around town, then we'll get a drink. Celebrate."

She batted her eyelashes and tried on the thick noble accent

246

again. "Why, Gregory, are you asking the lady to join you for a cocktail?"

He turned red and looked at his feet. "No, I just thought—"

She chuckled a little. "Gregory, I'm just screwing with you. Listen, if we're going to be friends, you're going to have to take zero percent of what I say seriously, at least if it makes you feel uncomfortable. *Especially* if it makes you uncomfortable. We talk differently in— I mean, out in the country." She paused, waiting for him to look up. "And Gregory, cocktail? I gave you a perfect in for a dick joke. Remember, I'm a country girl after all."

He snorted as he laughed. "Yeah, good one. Ok, deal. Let's go."

"I thought there was a curfew, though?"

"Man," he said, "you really are from out of town. Curfew is for those who live south of the Academy and the Noble Quarter. They won't bother us if we stay in the district. I mean, we're freaking magicians. We're not the ones the guards are after."

Speak for yourself, Hannah thought as she started walking down the path.

With Alexandra and her assistant gone, Parker knew that it was now or never. He had precious little time to finish his plan, but what was worse, he had almost no strength. It was a fool's gambit, and he knew it. But there was going to be no escape as long as he wore those magitech cuffs, and the only way he was going to get those off was by seeing the torturer, so he had needed to get caught.

Pain held his only hope for freedom, and he had borne it as best he could.

But Alexandra was good at her job—a little too good, actually. She had beat on him with everything from magic to machines, and smiled like a maniac every step of the way. More than once during her torture, Parker almost gave her something, *anything*, to make the pain stop. But he knew that Hannah trusted him. Arcadia needed him. *She* needed him.

He was finally a part of something bigger than himself. Parker had a mission, and it fueled his will to live.

Every muscle screamed as he pulled his body up, twisting in his chains until his legs were over his head. Iron bit into his wrists, but he pushed away the pain. Once he was upside down, he twisted his legs around the chain and took the pressure off his wrists. His hands were numb, but they were finally free to do some work.

He reached into his mouth and found the thin, sturdy wire he had stolen from his workstation. It had failed to pick the magitech lock, but it would do just fine on a normal chain.

Parker only had one shot, and he knew that if he dropped the tool—or if he moved too slowly—it was game-over for him. He was leaving this room now.

Or never at all.

Still hanging by his feet, he set to work picking the lock on the cuffs. It was hard without being able to see, but he'd cracked harder locks in worse conditions. The shackles were old, and the locking mechanism was simple. With a few turns, the lock clicked, and his right hand was free.

Thank the Matriarch, he sighed before unlocking his left hand.

He held in a scream as he lowered himself to the ground. Rubbing his wrists, he surveyed the room looking for a way out. The window behind him was too well secured, so the only escape lay through the front door.

Checking the door, he found it unlocked. Alexandra and her ilk were confident of their ability to break men down. That confidence now worked to Parker's advantage.

He limped out of the room and down the dark hallway, keeping a lookout for guards. The place where she had scorched his chest burned like the depths of hell, and his jaw hung loose like a broken window shutter.

But none of that mattered. He had one goal: Warn Hannah.

Finding a door at the end of the hall, he dashed through and made his way to the second floor. The place was quiet, and he knew the guards wouldn't be on high alert that time of night. Everyone was either on the floor working the night shift, or locked away in their cells, the doors locked with magitech bars.

He stepped out onto the catwalk over the factory and limped his way across as silently as possible. From up high, he could see more clearly what he and the other slaves had been working on, although it still didn't make sense to him. It looked like a giant boat—at least like the pictures of boats he had seen as a kid, but that didn't add up. Arcadia was landlocked, except for the River Wren, which was far too shallow and narrow to support a ship that large.

He shook his head and continued. There would be time to figure all that out later. For now, he moved steadily toward the broken window that he knew well. He had stared at its cracked frame from his spot on the assembly line for the past few weeks.

I can do this, he thought.

Images of Hannah carried him along. His vision started to blur—apparently, he had lost more blood than he thought—but he kept his eyes locked on the window. His exit. His salvation. The glimpse of the night sky and the thought of his friend were all that kept him moving.

Six feet up an exposed pipe and Parker was out the window. His throat tightened as he felt the breeze on his face. Glancing up at the stars, he thanked the Queen Bitch for Her protection. He peeked over the edge toward the ground below, but his vision was blurry, and the night was dark as hell.

He would have to trust the Matriarch and the Patriarch one more time. Swinging his torso beyond the window, he held his breath and dropped into the darkness.

Years ago, on an expedition toward the foothills of the Frozen North, a lowlander had told Karl what he loved about the rearick: for enough coin and ale, they would do just about any work. As a younger lad, Karl had scoffed at the man and swore he would never be the object of the lowlander's joke. Now, nearly two decades later, here he was, walking around in the dark protecting a building he didn't care about in a city he despised.

The large factory sat in the corner of the town, and Karl was paid to spend his nights walking around it. He had no idea what they made inside and didn't particularly care. What they did was their business. Keeping the building secure from thieves and vandals—that was Karl's.

And business was slow.

Stratton, the head of the factory guard, had given Karl this post and thanked him for his willingness to work for the good of Arcadia. He insisted that there was an important job for the rearick, but that it wasn't time yet. Karl could make the same pay by taking a patrol shift around the factory, which seemed as good a way as any for Karl to spend his time in the city.

Now that he had sobered up, he was beginning to rethink his choice.

As Karl followed the route around the building, he couldn't help but wonder exactly how he had gotten himself into the situation. In his younger days, he had been less of a bodyguard and more of a warrior.

Back then he was hired for real jobs; for true combat. The work paid well, but it also bestowed honor on him. People knew him as honorable both in his words and as a hired fighter who would die for the sake of a worthy cause.

He'd fought the remnant, stopped a horde of raiders from beyond the Dark Forest, and struck the final blow at a tyrant who had briefly taken over Cella in the North.

Now, as his beard showed marks of gray, he was nothing

more than a glorified babysitter, taking money wherever he could find it. But he still longed for something more.

He would give his left arm for a fight he could believe in—and maybe his right too, just as long as it was an honorable fight. A fight for justice.

As he was recounting the series of meaningless choices that led him here, a true cause struck Karl in the head—literally.

"What the bloody hell?" the rearick shouted as the unknown mass landed on top of him, knocking him to the ground.

Karl's instincts took over. He disentangled himself and rolled up onto his feet faster than he had gone down. His hammer extended out before him, ready to strike back at whatever had attacked him.

But instead of an assassin or thief or creature from the dark, Karl looked down at the battered and bloody body of a young man. The boy was naked and staring straight up at Karl.

"I need your help," the young man pleaded. "Please."

"Ya came from in there?" Karl asked, nodding at the factory he was hired to protect.

The kid replied with a desperate jerk of his head. "They'll kill me."

Karl had offered his services hundreds of times, but never to a cause he couldn't at least call acceptable. Seeing the young man's mangled body, Karl was convinced that whatever was going on inside the walls of the factory didn't fit the bill.

Shame swept over him for even taking the work. He knew that nothing good could come from Arcadia, not for the past twenty years. But justification was an easy game when money was on the line.

Maybe the old lowlander was right years ago.

Karl had become *that* rearick—a fighting whore ready to wag his hammer for the highest bidder. He set his mouth; it wasn't too late to change his ways. Injustice ruled inside the walls, and looking into the eyes of the victim on the ground, Karl realized he might have just found the battle worth fighting—or it had found him.

Karl reached down and hauled the man to his feet.

"Let's get ya the bloody hell out of here!" Karl told him as he looked around. "But where to?"

"Queen's Boulevard," the kid barely whispered.

***

As they crossed out of the Academy Quarter and into the Noble Quarter, Hannah didn't notice much of a difference. It struck her as odd, since she had to pass through a freaking toll plaza to make it into Queen's Boulevard, not to mention the wall meant to keep the scum divided from everyone else.

The two students walked in silence for a while. Every now and then, Gregory stopped to tell her about a place from his childhood, or an important historical marker. She pretended to be interested, nodding and smiling, but she didn't give two shits about this place. It wasn't her home; not the real Arcadia she'd known on the Boulevard. But gaining an ally—the Chief Engineer's son, no less—could prove useful. Worth a little disingenuous smiling, at the least.

It's not that she didn't like Gregory. He was sweet; kind in a way none of the other noble-born children seemed to be. It's just that she was itching for a fight, and prancing around the noble district didn't seem like it was worth her time.

"Tell me more about your dad's work," she said, cutting off some story about a historically significant fountain.

"My dad? I told you, he's the Chief Engineer."

Hannah hooked her arm in his, trying to use the womanly wiles she had seldom exploited during her time on the streets in the Boulevard. She forced a giggle. "Yeah. You told me *that*, but what does a Chief Engineer do in Arcadia? Pretend I know literally *nothing* about the city, because that's pretty much the case."

"Right. Well, I don't actually know. He doesn't talk too much about it. In all honesty, I'm not sure he's allowed to. He spends all day either locked in his office at home, or at the factory."

"Working on what?"

Gregory shrugged. "That's the mystery. They don't exactly have 'take your kid to work day' down there. Something's going on, though. Something big. He's been working double-time ever since that crazy-ass girl nearly blew up Queen's Boulevard."

Hannah couldn't stifle her laugh.

"What?" Gregory asked.

"Nothing. I, um, just tried to picture a girl with a crazy ass," she admitted, then added, "I wonder if crazy asses are attractive?"

Gregory shook his head. "You know what I mean."

You bet I do, she thought to herself.

He continued. "Anyway, they're building something big down there. My dad says it will change everything."

"Any ideas?"

"He only calls it *the machine*. Can't help but think that it might have something to do with getting the Unlawfuls in line."

She stopped walking and turned to face him. "You think they need to be in line?"

His face flushed red again. Gregory wasn't like the other students. He'd been raised among the nobles, but somehow hadn't picked up their cruelty. Nevertheless, he was still taught to believe certain things as the Patriarch's honest truth, including a certain view of Unlawfuls.

"That's what everyone says."

Hannah shrugged. "Sorry. I'm definitely not from around here. Where I was from, magic wasn't so restricted. People had a bit more freedom. Apart from how much money we have, what makes them any different from us?"

"Well, we can control it. They can't," he said. "The restriction is for their own good. People used to blow themselves up and shit when Adrien didn't control the users. He's just trying to keep everybody safe."

Hannah had to fight to keep her anger down. She had seen Adrien's vision of keeping people safe.

"How do you know they can't control it? I mean, do you really think it's fair that someone like Violet can use magic just because her parents are rich, but some poor father trying to provide for his family can't, only because he was born on a dirty street? And no offense, being born a noble doesn't automatically mean you can control it. *You* of all people should know that."

Gregory's face flushed, and he looked down at his shoes. Hannah cursed herself. That was a low blow, and she knew it. Now she had probably offended the only friend she had here.

"Look, I'm sorry. I shouldn't have said that. That was a pretty nice clay goat you made."

"Cat. It was a cat." Gregory smiled. "It's ok. You were right anyway. I know I'm not a great magic user. And people like Violet *are* jerks, but the law is the law, right? I'm sure Adrien has a good reason for it."

"Oh, there's a reason for it, but it's not a good one."

He gave her a strange look. "What do you mean?"

She cursed herself again. All the magical power in the world apparently couldn't help her keep her damned mouth shut. Before she was forced to make up some lie about what she really meant, a crowd of people caught her eye.

They were quickly moving down the street, all dressed in coarse white robes.

"Holy shit," Gregory said. He pushed Hannah back off the street and stood in front of her as the angry crowd passed. She thought it was sweet that this rich kid was trying to protect her. Sweet, but stupid.

"Who the hell were they?" Hannah asked, this time with unfeigned confusion. There had been no one like that in Arcadia last time she was in the city.

Gregory kept his wide eyes locked onto them as they moved past. His face had paled. "They're disciples of the Prophet. I've heard rumors that they have been patrolling the streets, trying to find Unlawfuls. I didn't expect to see them up here, though. Damn, did you see how angry they looked? And those clubs they were carrying! That was scary shit."

Hannah grabbed her new friend by the shoulders and forced him to face her. "Gregory, what do you mean they're searching for Unlawfuls? What would they do if they found one?" she asked, terrified that she already knew the answer.

"Punishment," he said. More color drained from his face.

She turned back toward the mob, and for a brief second, she caught a glimpse of what they were heading toward. Two figures limped across the street into an alley. The disciples let out a roar and followed.

CHAPTER TWENTY-FOUR

Parker did all he could to keep up with the rearick's quick short strides. About a foot taller than the guy, Parker limped at full speed as they wove through the noble district. He caught that the rearick's name was Karl, and clearly, he was some kind of badass. Parker pushed those questions out of his head.

After escaping the factory, Karl led Parker straight to his house. The darkness was thick on the Boulevard, and almost no one was out.

Relief turned to fear when Parker entered his house and found that his mother was nowhere to be found. It wasn't like her to take risks like being out after curfew, and Parker couldn't help but feel like something terrible was afoot.

His fear was alleviated when a neighbor came and told him that she had taken a job keeping house for some nobleman. The neighbor passed along the address, and Parker and his stout new friend were on their way to the rich part of the city—the lion's den.

"I've gotcha, kid. Hold it together," the rearick said through huffs.

Parker wanted to respond, to assure the rearick that he was

fine, but most of his energy was focused on staying conscious. His chest burned like a mother, and his arms and shoulders ached. It felt like they had walked to the Heights and back, even though it had only been a few blocks.

They tried to stick to the shadows, but as they moved into the noble district, their cover became less effective. He had no choice but to proceed.

As they came around a corner, Parker and Karl were stopped in their tracks by a large crowd.

They were dressed in the Prophet's colors, and each of them held a solid wooden club.

Parker locked eyes with a woman around his own age. She stood in front of them all and was giving some sort of motivational speech about the virtues of the Prophet and the return of the Matriarch and Patriarch.

Shit burger, he thought.

Jez, his childhood friend who had nearly taken him out just before he went to work in the factory, locked eyes with him.

A grin spread across her face just before she screamed. "Unlawfuls!"

"We gotta go," Parker whispered. "Run!"

The rearick responded, nearly picking Parker up and heading for the nearest alley. Limping as fast as he could, Parker looked for cover, or some building to escape into. He knew the Boulevard like the back of his hand, but in the Noble District, they were running blind.

"Let me go, rearick. Save yourself," Parker ground out.

His new companion gripped him tighter. "That is not the way, lowlander. I've promised to protect ya, and I'm gonna do that. Or die tryin'."

Turning another corner, the rearick shouted as he looked around. "*Scheisse*! Dead end."

A solid wall stood before them, and the religious zealots were on them before they could turn to find another exit. The angry mob blocked their way out. The rearick leaned Parker against the wall and unslung his hammer. "Stay back, lad," Karl grunted as he swung his weapon forward. "My hammer has grown hungry fer heretics, and it looks like she will be satisfied this night."

Jez stood at the front of the group, a crude club in her hand. A half-dozen others held pitchforks, sticks, and knives. She pointed at Parker. "Seems like our work is half-done for us. The Unlawful is already on his last legs." Her eyes turned to the rearick. "Step aside, foreigner, and let us do our duty. The gods have called us to cleanse this land of the unworthy. Would you really try and stand in between that criminal and the gods' justice?"

The rearick's knuckles got white as he gripped his hammer. "Honestly, I don't even know the lad, but if ya try to lay a hand on him, me and me hammer will send ya to meet yer gods with haste. Get the *fuck* outta here *now*!"

Jez laughed. "We have been blessed, little one. The gods are with us! No weapon of man can stand against us. The Unlawfuls must die!"

As Jez spoke, she raised her club into the air. Just as she was about to attack, a confident voice cut through the alley. It was coming from behind the disciples. "You're looking for Unlawfuls? Well, it's your lucky night, you ugly-assed douche nuggets."

The swarm of disciples split down the center, and through the middle of them, Parker saw the woman. She was strong, dressed in noble garb, had strawberry-blond hair, and her eyes glowing red like fire.

Even in her disguise, Parker could pick out his friend anywhere.

He smiled, knowing the hell that Hannah was about to unleash on the unholy disciples.

Karl had spent most of his life with a weapon in his hands. He had seen his fair share of bloodshed, but to call what he witnessed tonight anything but a slaughter would have been underselling it.

Karl didn't recognize the pretty noble who stared down this group of unholy zealots, but the red in her eyes was a sight he had become very familiar with. And he was ready for the display of power that came with it.

The leader of the disciples jumped into action immediately. "It's her!" she yelled. "It's the bitch from the Boulevard. Get her!"

A dozen or so religious fanatics charged Hannah with their homemade weapons, but the woman was more right than she knew—no weapon of man could stand against the power of the gods.

Hannah turned her hands and raised them high, like she was instructing a class of students to rise from their desks. As she did, a large chunk of stone broke loose from the ground in front of her. Hannah sent the missile hurtling into the disciples.

It crushed two of them beyond recognition.

But the disciples were undeterred. Karl knew the look of murder in someone's eyes—there would be no reasoning with them.

So he decided to let his hammer do the talking.

With a yell, he lowered his shoulder and rushed into the crowd.

A young man turned to face him, raising a hoe like it was a spear. Karl's hammer splintered the primitive weapon before splintering the man's ribcage.

He let his momentum carry him forward, swinging his weapon wildly but also with perfect precision. Anyone foolish enough to stand against him didn't remain standing for long.

Despite the chaos of the fight, Karl never lost sight of the noble woman. It wasn't until he saw the blade in her hand, his blade, that he realized her true identity. Hannah threw his old knife, and he watched it sink into a woman's stomach. Before the disciple hit the ground, Hannah twisted her wrist and the knife flew back into her hands to be used again.

Karl smiled. He hadn't had this much fun in years.

———————

Hannah looked around the alley as the haze cleared from her eyes. In front of her, standing amidst a dozen broken bodies, was an old rearick, beaming from cheek to cheek.

"Ah, lass!" He said giving her a nod. "Is this some cruel joke? At this rate, I'll never pay back the debt I owe ya." He chuckled. "Ya gotta stop saving me life."

She smiled. "Over my dead body, Karl. Now, what the hell were you doing picking a fight with this bunch of choir boys and girls?"

Karl shrugged. "I guess they didn't like my charming personality. Or my taste in friends."

He turned and looked down the alley, and Hannah followed his gaze. There, trying to lean against the wall, was her best friend.

"Parker!" she yelled. Abandoning any thought of Karl, the disciples, or even her mission, Hannah ran to his side. His right eye was swollen shut, and there were bleeding sores all over his body.

"Hey," Parker muttered. "Nice outfit." He tried to smile, but his face barely moved.

"What the bloody hell happened to you?" Hannah demanded as she leaned over him, gently hugging his body.

Parker closed his eyes. "Occupational hazard. I'll fill you in when I feel better—in about a year, maybe two." He tried to stand up straight, but collapsed into a coughing fit. Hannah saw blood on his hands.

She glanced over her shoulder at the rearick. "Karl, we have to get him back to the Boulevard, now. I have a friend there, Miranda, she'll be able to help him"

Parker coughed, blood mixed with saliva spilling out onto his lips. He weakly shook his head. "Can't. Miranda is dead... She..." His words trailed off into the night.

"What? Miranda? *How?*"

Parker's eyes are barely open. "Murdered by the disciples. They hung her up—a spectacle."

Anger and rage rushed through Hannah's body, and she could feel the power inside her start to take over again. Miranda had been a friend since her birth, nearly a second mother, and now she was gone. Hannah wished the disciples were still alive so she could kill them all over again.

She looked down at her friend. "Well, we need to get you off the street and inside. If we don't get you to someone fast, you'll die."

Gregory ran down the alley, his chest burning from the exertion. One minute he was walking around town with the prettiest girl who had ever spoken to him hanging on his arm. The next minute she was chasing a group of religious nuts.

The change in his fortune was so startling that he stood frozen in place.

Once his thoughts caught up with him, he ran after her, praying she wasn't hurt.

As he sprinted around the corner, he nearly stumbled over a dead body. It was one of the disciples with a large spear of ice sticking out of his back.

Gregory had never seen a dead body before, certainly not one that had been killed like this. He fought the urge to vomit. As he looked up, he realized there wasn't just one dead but a dozen dead men and women, in varying states of destruction. Half were smoldering, smoke rising from their burned flesh. The other half looked like they had been trampled by wild horses.

And there in the midst of it was Deborah, the sweet nobleman's daughter from the country, completely covered in blood.

Once again, his thoughts ran away from him.

It took him a minute to realize that the girl standing in front of him was no longer Deborah. Gone were her strawberry blonde curls; they had been replaced with long strands of straight hair the color of dark leather. Gone was any sense of flightiness or playfulness on her face. Instead, her face was grave, like a soldier after battle.

"Deb... Deborah?" Gregory finally squeaked out.

She turned to look at him, but before she could speak, an angry rearick jumped in front of her. He lifted a hammer above his head, and Gregory saw his life pass before his eyes.

"Karl, wait. He's with me."

The rearick hesitated, then lowered the weapon to let Gregory pass.

"Deborah...what the hell is going on?" Gregory asked as he stepped forward. He looked down and saw that she was kneeling over a man who was clearly dying.

The man looked up at her and said, "Who the hell is Deborah?"

She looked back and forth between them, then said. "It's a long story. I'll tell you all about it later, but for now, we need to get you to a healer."

"We should go now, Hannah," the rearick said. He had moved to stand watch at the entrance to the alley. She nodded toward the rearick, then looked back at Gregory.

"Deb, I—"

"My name's not Deborah, it's Hannah. And I'm not the daughter of a nobleman who's visiting the city for the first time. I've lived here my whole life—in the Boulevard."

Understanding slowly came to Gregory as her words sunk in.

"You're...you're *her*, aren't you? You're the Unlawful that everyone's been talking about." He looked down at her bloodstained gown. "You killed all these people."

"That's right, Gregory, and I'd do it again. Because this," she pointed to the man on the ground, "is Adrien's idea of safe. And good or bad, rich or poor, powerful or weak, it's time we stood up to him. I know you have questions, and I'll answer everything later, I swear, but for now I need your help. My friend Parker is dying. You said you wanted to do good? To help people? Well, now's your chance. Help me get him somewhere *safe*."

Gregory stared into her eyes, which were no longer blue, but chestnut brown. All his life, he had heard about the danger Unlawfuls posed. Heard people say that they were no better than animals. And looking around him at the dead bodies, Gregory couldn't help but wonder if people were right. But looking into this girl's eyes—Hannah's eyes—Gregory knew in his heart, beyond any doubt, that she was good.

And he knew that she was a person worth taking the time to listen to.

He gritted his teeth and nodded. "Tell me what you need."

CHAPTER TWENTY-FIVE

One of the things that being chancellor afforded Adrien was time to work. Not on class development or administrative duties, but on pure research. Ever since the old fool had taught him his first spell, Adrien had been convinced that there was more power out there, if only he had the time to reach out and grab it. It was how he first discovered his ability to make magitech.

Sheets of parchment were laid out on the table in front of him, and he pulled on his hair as he paced the room and thought of possibilities. Ezekiel was more powerful than when he left, and Adrien needed to be equally powerful if he was going to succeed. Magitech would be his answer.

"Sir," Doyle shouted, snapping Adrien out of his fixated state.

Adrien turned around. "What the hell, Doyle? Can't you see that I am working!"

The assistant flinched at the rebuke and dropped his eyes to the floor. Interrupting Adrien was a risky task. He was damned if he did, and damned if he didn't. "My apologies, sir, but I have news for you."

Adrien glanced down at the parchments, trying to mark his spot so as not to lose it. "This better be damn good."

The man nodded. "Better than good, Chancellor. We have the kid. The little bitch's friend. He was caught trying to escape the factory. Alexandra has been questioning him for hours. It is only a matter of time before he breaks."

Adrien smiled. He knew full well what Alexandra was capable of. "Where is he now?"

"The factory, sir."

Adrien brushed past Doyle without a word. The prisoner might be the key to finding the girl. And she would lead them straight to Ezekiel.

***

Ezekiel nodded to the guard as he crossed into the Boulevard. The bored-looking man grunted back. Ezekiel had altered his appearance again. No longer looking like the nobleman from the North, Ezekiel's mental magic allowed him to look like any other dweller of the slums. Amelia, in a flash of red eyes, had been changed to match.

The Dean of Students kept looking down at her dirty and frayed dress. She'd pulled her long hair out where she could see it, and in place of her luxurious strands was a dry, filthy mane, complete with split ends. "But how did you—"

Ezekiel raised a hand. "Not here. Not now. I will make it all clear in due time."

Weaving through the Boulevard, they kept their heads down. Although they looked like they belonged among the masses, they were still strangers there, and the residents of the Boulevard knew their own. However, enough people were moving about that no one gave them more than a second glance.

He held open the door to a darkened tavern. The name **Lloyd's** hung over the door on a crooked sign. "After you, my lady," Ezekiel said with a grin.

Amelia stepped into the depressing, dark, and damp establishment. A few drunken heads turned to look at the new arrivals and then returned to their brews. He led her to a table in the back, just out of sight of the front door. Signaling to the bartender with two fingers raised in the air, they were soon sipping a bitter ale that tasted like it was made with dishwater and crusty old hops.

Ezekiel sipped on his. "Tastes like the old days." He looked up and noticed Amelia staring, her mouth slightly open. "I know, the beggar's look is unbecoming to a rich man, isn't it," he said.

Amelia looked back down at herself. He had given her a pot belly, which made her giggle as she tried to poke at it. "How the hell did you do this, Girard?"

"You've heard of mental magic?"

She nodded. "Of course. The mystics practice it, but I never knew it could do this," she said, waving her hand over herself. "How did you learn it? I thought that Adrien kept a close eye on those who studied at the temple."

Ezekiel looked over one shoulder and then the other, making certain that the coast was clear. "Not as close of an eye as he thinks."

Amelia shook her head. "That's not an answer."

"Do you trust me?" Ezekiel asked, a grin spreading across his face.

Ezekiel asked Amelia the question, but he was asking himself whether he trusted her. He had not known the Dean long, but he had come to appreciate her direct demeanor.

She was honest, gutsy, and obviously held her students' well-being in high regard. That was a start, but he couldn't be sure if it was enough to go on. Unfortunately, time wasn't on his side, so he decided to roll the dice and tell her the truth.

If Amelia proved untrustworthy, then he would have to take... other measures.

The woman snorted. "Trust you? Hell no! *Double* hell no. Look at what you're capable of! You might not even be Lord Girard..."

Ezekiel cocked his head and grinned slightly.

"*Shit*. Are you kidding me?" Suddenly, her peasant's face filled with fear. Her eyes darted around the bar, looking for a way out, looking for help.

Ezekiel held his hands up in front of her. "Easy. I come in peace. Just give me a chance to explain."

He watched her settle back. "You have three minutes, and then I'm leaving. Go."

"You asked me earlier how I learned the mystics' magic. The answer might surprise you. *I* taught *them* mental magic years and years ago. Just like I taught the druids their arts. And, believe it or not, I took in your boss—the Chancellor—when he was only a child and taught him as well."

Her mouth dropped farther open. "*You* are the Founder?" She shook her head. "Bullshit. Prove it."

"I think I already have, Amelia. And you know it. The Prophet, that man speaking on the corners of Arcadia, has been preaching my return. And he's been right. Well, half-right. I've come back, but it's not the Unlawfuls I'm coming to destroy. It's Adrien and those loyal to him who have earned my wrath.

"I left Arcadia in the hands of a man I trusted, and he has squandered both my trust and my city. The natural ear doesn't hear it, Amelia, but Arcadia is groaning under his oppression. The city has waited patiently to be restored, and the wait is over."

She shook her head, placing a hand over her mouth. "Why are you telling me this?"

"Because I need you," Ezekiel explained. "Like I said, *this* is the right fight, but it's one I can't win—not on my own, at least. With the help of some people like you..."

Amelia lifted her glass. "I'm going to need a few more of these." She drained it, then slammed it back down onto the table.

"Be my guest," Ezekiel said as he waved to the bartender for more.

If walking through Queen's Boulevard was repugnant for Adrien, the factory was completely disorienting. He had created this place, and yet he hated it all the same.

Seeing the workers chained to their stations sent chills up his spine. Adrien's power extended to every corner of Arcadia, and this was a testimony to his strength. But it was dirty, and the lack of dignity within the place made him realize just how much he'd sacrificed for the sake of his dreams.

But...it was *worth* it. His vision was greater than the life of every soul on the floor of the factory. He would kill them all—and more—if it meant he could achieve his goal.

Heart racing, Adrien wound through the labyrinth-like hallways toward the interrogation room. There was a good chance that Alexandra had gotten all the information he needed out of that boy, Parker. He was just some street rat after all. He hoped that she had saved just a little fun for him.

Standing outside of the door, he straightened his robe and then pushed into the dark, damp room. A single beam cast its light on a naked, bloody body. His eyes narrowed as Adrien took in the obese man who hung from his wrists, weeping like a school child.

"What the hell is this?" he asked.

Alexandra turned, a whip in her right hand. A crazed smile painted her face. "Ah, Chancellor. So good of you to join us. This is Jack. He worked on the line next to Parker."

"Who the hell cares? Where is the boy? Where is Parker?"

"You haven't heard?" Her smile faded as she realized the meeting might go sideways. "The little bastard got away."

"That's impossible." Adrien's words were as hard as granite.

She laughed, trying to set the man at ease. "Impossible? Adrien, do not be naïve, darling. Nothing is impossible. His escape was an unfortunate oversight. We'll find him again, just relax."

In three long strides, Adrien crossed the room. His large hand reached out and grabbed her by the throat. "Speak to me like that again, and I'll tear you apart."

"I talk as I wish, *Chancellor*." Her face held no fear, and something between resentment and desire dripped from her lips.

Without warning, Adrien snapped an open hand across her face, knocking her to the ground. A drop of blood rose on her lips. She wiped it off and then sucked the blood off her fingertip.

"Charming," she purred, "but I don't think we have time for foreplay."

Adrien snarled. "You *bitch*. Parker was our ticket to the girl, and you lost him. You'll pay for this with your life."

Alexandra pushed herself to her feet. She tucked back a loose strand of hair as if she had not a care in the world.

"At least allow me to buy it back, for old times' sake," she said, a cruel smile back on her lips. "You only need to ask nicely. I know exactly how to find the girl."

The door of the noble mansion nearly fell off its hinges as Hannah kicked it open. Karl and Gregory supported Parker, but by now he was barely able to stand. He hung on the edge of life and death.

Hannah led them into the dining room. She swiped dishes and an arrangement of flowers off the formal dining room table. Their clatter filled the room. "Here. Bring him here."

They carried him over and eased Parker's body onto the hardwood surface. For a beat, they all looked at one another—each waiting for the other to do something. Time stood still. Hanna knew it was her move, but she didn't quite know what to do. "Gregory, hot water. Go!"

The boy nodded and sprinted from the room.

As he left, another person took his place. It was Eleanor. Her confusion immediately turned to fear as she recognized the beaten form of her son lying on the table. She screamed as if the world were ending.

"Parker! My baby." The woman kept crying, and Hannah knew how she felt. But she blocked out Eleanor's words. Hannah needed to focus.

She looked up at Karl. He nodded. "I've got this, lass. Ya just do what ya need to."

Hannah didn't watch, but the screaming got quieter as Karl led Eleanor down the hall.

Parker's eyes opened, only a sliver. "Hey... I knew you'd..."

"Shhh. Quiet. You need your strength."

He smiled, but only barely. "I knew you'd come back. Never doubted for a second. I saw things, Hannah. Things you wouldn't... I'm glad for this, before I..."

Hannah shook her head. She had seen too much death. Too much destruction. "Shut the hell up, Parker. You're getting off this table."

Her eyes flamed red as she tried to focus on Ezekiel. She still wasn't very good at this kind of communication, especially over long distances—and Ezekiel could be halfway around Irth for all she knew. At one point she thought that she was close to him, but she couldn't hold it. She was too worried about what would happen if she failed.

The door opened again, and Hannah could feel Gregory standing next to her. He reached down and placed a finger on Parker's jugular. Shaking his head, he said, "It's weak."

"What do you know? What the bloody hell do you know?" Hannah snapped at the young noble.

Gregory gave a resigned nod. "I know enough. The body is a machine. I might not know how to shape clay with magic, but I know how machines work. He's broken, Hannah. Let's make him as comfortable as possible. Help him leave well. Assist him toward—"

"There is no *toward* anywhere." Hannah's voice lifted in anger at the situation, in fear of losing him. "No Matriarch or Patriarch. No other side. There is here, and there is now, and I *need* him." She turned her eyes toward Parker. "I *need* you," she both pleaded and demanded. "You will not leave me!"

CHAPTER TWENTY-SIX

Over the course of an hour, Ezekiel told Amelia the entire story, leaving out very few details. He talked about the Oracle, Lilith, and how they ended the Age of Madness together. He described the founding of Arcadia and his early attempts to share magic with the world. He skipped his forty-year absence—that was a story for another time—and focused instead on Hannah, the girl he had put so much hope in.

He placed three empty ale glasses in the middle of the table. Placing his finger on one at a time, he said, "Imagine this is physical magic. Mental magic. And nature magic." Her eyes followed his finger as it bounced from glass to glass. "Each of them is different, but they all come from the same source—the Etheric realm. It is the font of all magical power, and it dwells inside of all of us.

"Each group of magic users—the druids, the mystics, and physical users like you—developed their magic in distinctly different ways, ways that fit their natures. It makes sense that the druids and the mystics each nurture power in their own ways. The mystics, people of transcendence, connected to the mind in ways most could never fathom, and for the druids, people of the woods and wild, nature magic just made sense for them."

"And Arcadians?" she asked.

"Think about our history. When I first came to his land, the Mad were running wild. The people in this valley, they were all hustlers, really, like Hannah and Parker." Ezekiel laughed. "Just trying to survive. Trying to make it day by day. Physical magic was fast, simple, and effective. It was precisely what they needed to crawl back from the darkness. And things developed along those lines."

Amelia nodded. "Makes sense. But you know them all?"

Ezekiel shrugged. "I'm not really from the Arcadian Valley, even if I was born here. Where I was raised, I had the freedom to develop my power in a variety of ways. When I first came back, I originally tried to teach all of what I knew, but I found that most people grabbed onto what they were most comfortable with. The mystics and the druids had already started to differentiate themselves from the Arcadians before I left, but I never expected things to become so divided. I imagined the different communities working together, learning from one another and benefiting each other, but that is obviously not what came to pass."

"You can blame Adrien for that," she said. "He always taught us not to trust the mystics, and most Arcadians don't even believe the druids exist. They've become legend—like the Founder."

Ezekiel smiled, showing off a mouth full of yellow teeth, a part of his illusion. "I can assure you that they, and I, are real."

She laughed and looked at herself again. "I'd say so. But what about the girl, Hannah?"

"I'm glad you asked." He stacked the ale glasses inside of each other. Holding them up, he said, "As far as I can tell, this is Hannah. She can do all three."

"Like you."

"No. Better than me. I can manage all three *kinds* of magic—each separately. I can combine them to work together, you know, cast a fireball and make the wind whip your hair around at the same time, but she's different. She combines all of them into one form. A new art has been *awakened*."

He told the Dean about how Hannah had transformed the lizard from a newt into a dragon, and then given him wings.

"Bloody hell," she whispered. "Transmogrification?"

"I've never seen anything like it before, and I have seen quite a lot." Ezekiel stared at the stack of glasses. "Hannah is the key. With her gifts, she could radically change the city. Hell, she could change the world."

Amelia was nervous, but then again, so was Ezekiel.

Neither of them knew they could trust the other. She wondered for a moment if he was some sort of spy for Adrien, sent to test her allegiance. Because right now she wanted to spill her guts, tell him everything she knew about the Scholars' Program, but she didn't trust that he was safe.

But she had gone so far already, she might as well take the shot. If even half of what he said was true, it would be worth it. "There's something you need to know about Adrien."

Ezekiel nodded, but held a hand up as she began to speak. "There's something you need to know about him as well, but let's wait for my colleague to get here. Then we can place all the cards on the table. I just told you my whole story. What about yours? Seems only fair that you reciprocate. How did you become the Dean?"

Amelia glanced over her shoulder, wondering if she should be afraid of Ezekiel's colleague. She pictured Adrien himself walking through the door. Realizing she had come this far, she started her story. "I shouldn't even be here."

"At Lloyd's? Eh, the place isn't so bad."

Amelia smiled. "No. In the Academy. I wasn't born a noble. My family lived outside the walls—farmers. We certainly weren't wealthy, but my father was a shrewd man, so we made ends meet in the lean years." She paused, looking at the bottom of her glass.

He prodded her. "And then?"

She shrugged. "Don't remember much. I was so little. I only remember a few images of the night it happened, like a dream you have between waking and sleeping. It was nighttime, and my mother was getting me ready for bed. My eyes were burning because I cried when I got in trouble for not finishing dinner. Funny what you *do* remember." She paused and looked down at the table. When she looked back up, her eyes were teary. "I do remember the racket. There were screams that sounded like a mix of men and beasts. My father grabbed me, threw me over his shoulder and ran for the pig pen. I saw their terrible faces as they ran toward the house."

"The remnant?" Ezekiel asked in a hush.

She nodded. "Yeah. My dad pushed me in with the pigs. Told me not to move. Said the pigs were magical, that they would keep me safe." A smile slipped through the tears, and she laughed. "Now I know it was the pig shit."

"The pigs covered your scent," he said.

"That's right. My dad was really bloody smart. He ran back for my mother and sister, and that was the last I saw any of them." She wiped a tear off her cheek and cleared her throat. She wanted to look strong in front of him, but memory and alcohol proved stronger than her will. "The next day, I was found by the guards who came to investigate the slaughter. They brought me in, and that's how I ended up in Reston's house."

"Reston? That name's familiar."

"Would be if you're really the Founder. He's been here since the beginning. Since before the city walls.

Ezekiel laughed. "I'll be damned. You're talking about little Resty. He was just up to my knees when I left. *He* became a noble?"

She nodded.

Ezekiel took a long drink and pictured the boy he used to know. Resty could be a brat, but he was just so full of life. They all were back in those days; survivors of a dark time who were still able to dream of a better future. Zeke thought about Resty, muddy from playing in the unpaved streets.

He remembered Genevieve and Alton, young and in love and about to have their first child—an act of braveness that could have only been devised in hope. *I wonder what happened to them*, he thought. *Their kids probably have children of their own by now.* He remembered Eve and her beautiful gardens, and the way she'd smile when spring came.

But he also remembered Adrien and Saul. Fierce friends. *They were supposed to be the future*, Ezekiel thought.

"Didn't see that coming," he said, shaking away his nostalgia and returning to the matter at hand. "But then again, I didn't really see the whole noble versus poor thing coming either. I'm powerful, not perfect."

Amelia drank again and finished her third pint. "There are good people in the noble district. They're not all what you think."

"You don't know what I think," Ezekiel said.

She smiled. "You've said enough. And you don't get to be the Dean of the Academy with sand between your ears. Resty and his wife treated me like their own. They're the only parents I really know. I'm where I am now because of them."

Ezekiel nodded and then glanced over Amelia's shoulder. "We'll have to continue later. My friend has arrived."

Amelia turned and saw an enormous brute of a man pushing through the room. On his chest, he wore the badge of the Guard. Amelia choked on her drink. Her fears were right, it was all a setup. How could she have been so naïve?

Amelia raised her hands, ready to fight if she had to, but Ezekiel placed his hand on hers. "Relax. My friend might look ugly, but she's really quite nice."

"She?" Amelia asked. She looked the brute up and down as the man pulled up a chair.

The man smiled. "Never judge a book by its cover, sweetheart."

Ezekiel laughed as Amelia looked back and forth between the two of them, confusion plainly written on her face.

"Like I said, this is not a fight I can win on my own. Luckily for us, my dear friend Julianne is better at the mystic arts than I am. I'll fill you in on her story in a bit, but first, I need you to tell me your suspicions about Adrien. What is he up to?"

Amelia took another long drink, then started to speak, but before she could get two words out, a sharp pain stabbed Ezekiel's brain. He dropped his glass and it spilled across the table, causing the women to jump.

Amelia and Julianne looked at him concerned. Julianne put her hand on his shoulder. She was trying to tell him something, but he couldn't hear her voice.

All he could hear was the sound of screaming in his head.

The pain and the screams were Hannah's.

Gregory winced as Hannah began to scream. She was coming apart, but only because she knew she couldn't stop the inevitable. Her best friend would soon be gone. And she didn't have the power to save him. It was like William all over again.

"Damn it, Ezekiel. Where the fuck *are* you?" she cried.

Gregory took a step backward and tripped over his own feet, a terrified look on his face. Hannah thought for a second that the boy was afraid of her, but a loud screech filled the room and Hannah knew its source.

The gust from Sal's wings blew through Hannah's hair as the dragon swooped down from the landing. He landed not-so gracefully on the edge of the table. His tongue lashed out and licked the side of Parker's face, then Sal looked up at Hannah; she could almost read the sadness on his scaly face. It reminded

Hannah of the first day she had met Sal, back when he was nothing more than a common lizard.

And it struck her.

"I made you," she said at the creature. Looking back at Parker, she exhaled. "I can do this." She looked around the room and shouted, "Everyone out!"

Gregory, without taking his eyes off the dragon, scampered from the room.

Hannah cleared everything out of her head—the fear, the anger, the agony of watching Parker drift away from the world. She reached for perfect stillness, but she knew she couldn't stay there. She had learned, that day that Sal was made as well as the day that she had destroyed the Hunters in her old house on the Boulevard, that her most powerful acts weren't done like the magic of Hadley and the other mystics. Her greatest power didn't come from repose, but from passion.

She performed miracles amid chaos.

Once her head cleared, she brought it all back. She pictured her brother, dead in her arms. She imagined the bits of her father's body strewn around the house. She remembered Miranda, the loving alchemist from her neighborhood, now dead at the hands of zealots. She imagined all the pain and hurt that she had experienced in her years in the Boulevard, held down by the corrupt systems waging war on the lower class. Finally, she pictured life—daily life—in a world where Parker no longer existed.

Power boiled under her skin and threatened to blow her up from the inside out, but when she locked eyes with Sal, she knew she could contain it. It was like the dragon was encouraging her, giving her the will to go on.

Laying her hands on Parker's chest, she forced every ounce of passion through her hands and into his body.

Her eyes glowed red like the flames of Hades. She said a silent prayer to the Matriarch, then screamed as all the magic left her in a single wave.

Her knees turned to mud, and she crashed to the ground. Karl and Gregory ran back into the room. Gregory stood at her side, trying to help her gain her feet. Karl's wide eyes were locked on the table, on Parker. She could see the fear in the rearick's face, and she knew what it meant.

Shit, she thought. *He's gone.*

One large tear rolled down Hannah's cheek. Her ears were ringing; she could hear nothing around her.

Until a single voice broke through. "What the hell are you doing on the floor?"

She looked up. Parker was staring down at her from the table. His face was full of color, even if it held the scars of his torture, and he was beaming.

"Parker!" she yelled as she worked to get back on her feet with Gregory's assistance. She threw her arms around him, knocking him back down onto the table.

"Don't take this the wrong way," Parker wheezed, "but you feel *really* heavy right now."

Hannah stood up, her eyes wet with joy. "You're alive."

"Of course I am. Parker the Pitiable always bounces back. Plus, I had to. I knew you'd be utterly useless without me."

Hannah landed a right hook on his shoulder. "Bastard."

Laughing, Parker said, "You saved my life just so you could go back to torturing me? Can I take back that whole death thing? And... Could you repeat that part about needing me again? I liked that."

"Did you hear the bastard part?" Hannah asked with a wicked grin.

He swung his legs over the edge of the table and slowly sat up. Every inch of his body ached, but he knew he was fine. She had saved him, and Parker realized just how powerful his friend had become.

He stretched his newly-healed neck. "Next time, go a bit easier, ok? You almost overcooked me."

"There had better not be a next time, you douche nugget."

Parker smiled, then pulled her back for another hug. He whispered in her ear, "Don't leave me again, ok? It was hell here without you."

She leaned back, but didn't let go. Their eyes were inches apart. Hannah glanced down at his lips and then back up into his eyes.

The sound of a throat clearing loudly broke the spell between them. Hannah straightened and turned to the doorway. Ezekiel was there, standing with arms crossed. He had two women with him.

"Damn college students," he said. "Can't leave 'em alone for a minute!"

Adrien leaned in, inches from Alexandra's face. Even though she had been in the depths of the factory for days, she smelled amazing. She always did. "My best men have been searching for her for weeks, and they've found nothing. What makes you so confident?"

"Darling," she lifted a hand to his chin. "Your best men are a bunch of bitches. I'm the only one with the balls to do what's necessary to find your little bitch. However, my methods...aren't very popular. When I'm done with them, I doubt your precious citizens like me as much as you do."

Adrien smiled a wicked grin. "As if they aren't scared enough. Jed's disciples have stirred up enough terror in the Boulevard and the market to keep them in line. A few more casualties could be justified. In fact, kill whoever you need to, just as long as you bring me the girl."

She returned the smile. Alexandra had worked for him for nearly three years, and there was no one in Arcadia whose skills he trusted more than hers. She could make a mute mystic dedicated to his vow of silence sing the Arcadian anthem faster than he could take a piss. Her methods were unorthodox, but orthodoxy had never gotten him very far.

"Do what you need to do," he confirmed. "You're off your leash."

"As long as you'll put me back on my leash in due time, Adrien." She raised an eyebrow as she drew a long, crooked knife. "But first, I should finish this business."

She turned back to the big man hanging from the chains in the middle of the room.

"Should have given me more, Jack."

The man turned his heavy eyes toward her. They begged for mercy. "No," he whispered. "Please."

"Say hello to the Queen Bitch for me," she said as she sliced him from ear to ear.

Blood splattered on her maniacal face. Flecks of red covered her. Turning back to Adrien, she ran her tongue down the smooth side of the knife. "Yummy. I can feel the power, just as She did."

Adrien shook his head. The woman in front of him was insane. And more than that, she was a monster. But she was *his* monster. She would spill a river of blood without a second thought.

"Get it done," he said. He turned and left the room, thinking about the fun he'd have once the bitch, Hannah, was in his hands.

CHAPTER TWENTY-SEVEN

Everyone was assembled in the great room of Lord Girard's house. Hannah and Eleanor, the two women who meant the world to him, flanked Parker. Karl sat across the room, his mighty hammer, still red from the blood of the disciples, laying across his knees. Gregory stood in the doorway, his face as pale as milk. Hannah wasn't sure what he made of all of this, but he hadn't fled yet, so that was a plus.

Sal was curled in a ball in the middle of the room, apparently uninterested in what the humans were discussing.

Ezekiel took a moment to introduce Amelia, the Dean of Students from the Academy and Julianne, who had transformed back into her mystic form within the safety of the mansion.

Other introductions were made, but Ezekiel kept them brief.

He stood and looked around the room, then launched into his speech. "I don't know most of you—not well, at least. Many of the relationships in this room were forged in fire, blood, and lies. In reality, we're more strangers than friends, but we share one thing in common—a love for justice. And that's a tie that binds us stronger than any family.

"And beyond that, I believe that we have all been brought here for a glorious purpose. Though it might not look like much, we have been given the power to take this city back from those who rule it with fear and cruelty. We have a chance to make the world better.

"Adrien is a wicked man. Many of you suspected this, though, he hides his villainy well. If we are honest with one another, I believe the truth will come to light. I will begin with my story."

Ezekiel spoke slowly, but was as concise as possible. He walked them through how he had first met Adrien as a young man filled with potential. Then he explained what he observed upon his return. He ended by relating his recent meeting with Adrien on the streets of the city: how he saw evil in his old student's eyes and heard him confess to a plan to extend his power beyond Arcadia.

Ezekiel sat as he finished his story. "Something foul is brewing, and it will soon be served, but we cannot stop it if we don't know what it is. I'm powerful, but I am not omniscient. That is as far as my knowledge goes."

They all fell silent for a moment, each wondering who should go next. Finally, Parker spoke up. "For the past several weeks, I've been on the inside of the factory. It's where the men are going; scores of them from the Boulevard. We went voluntarily, but the moment we set foot in there, they chained us to our workstations and kept us working as slaves."

"How'd you get out?" Gregory asked from the edge of the room.

Parker glanced at him, acknowledging the boy he didn't know, but who had helped save his life. "It's a long story, but it ends with me bleeding to death in an alley. Before I left, I had a nice long conversation with Alexandra, Adrien's torturer. She was very interested in Hannah. It seems the Chancellor would like to have a word with you," he said, looking at Hannah. "But I don't imagine it would be a nice one."

Hannah looked down at her hands and cracked her knuckles. "Perfect. I have some words I'd like to have with him, too."

"What were they building in there, lad?" Karl drummed his fingers along the side of his hammer as he waited for Parker to continue.

"I have no idea, but whatever it is, it's huge. Like a giant boat or something, but that's not the weird part. When I was trying to escape, I stumbled across a large room. In the middle was a giant glowing contraption. No freaking clue what the thing was, but I could barely look right at it, the blue was so bright. And they had a magician attached to it. He was tired, like a damned mule that'd been driven for a week straight."

Amelia stepped in. "What did the magician look like?"

Parker shrugged. "He was young, although he didn't look it. Nice, noble clothes. He had long black hair that hung back in a ponytail."

The Dean's face darkened. "That was Rian. One of my best students. I had offered his name to Adrien weeks ago to be a part of the Scholars Program." She paused. "Damn him. I knew that the program had something to do with developing magitech, but it sounds more like they're being used to *fuel* it. He's robbing them of all of their energy." She paused a moment in thought. "It will kill him."

"That's crazy," Eleanor said. "I've never heard of magitech that big before. And why would the Chancellor do that? There must be some misunderstanding."

"There's no misunderstanding, ma'am." Karl cleared his throat before speaking. "I can't speak for yer Chancellor's intentions, but I know that factory has been payin' a fortune fer as many amphoralds as the mines can produce. We can't rip 'em out of the ground fast enough. They're hungry, although for what, I don't know. But I do know they've bought enough gems to power a whole freakin' city fer a thousand years."

"They don't want to power a city, Karl, they want to destroy one," Julianne, said. "Arcadia is preparing for war. When I was on the inside I caught wind of some things. The Guard knew that the Governor and the Chancellor were preparing for an attack, but no one knew on whom or how. But there was plenty of talk about a secret weapon that would make them unstoppable."

The room fell quiet as the pieces started to fall into place. Adrien's plan was secret no more, even if it was still lacking in detail.

"But what kind of weapon could require that much energy?" Ezekiel asked.

A throat cleared, and everyone turned to look at Gregory, who had been standing in the corner since this all began. His face shifted from pale to beet red, and he fidgeted awkwardly. He second-guessed what he was about to do, then looked at Hannah and pushed the fear away.

"I know what it is. I know what Adrien is building."

Adrien walked above the factory floor on the catwalk. The din of his worker bees rose to meet him. The men working below looked ragged, but there was no rest in sight. The machine needed to be finished, and to do so would take sacrifice from the men of Arcadia.

The catwalk terminated at a metal door with a Capitol Guard standing next to it. He stood upright, clicking his heels as the Chancellor approached.

"Sir," he barked, eyes straight ahead.

"At ease," Adrien replied. "Nice work here."

"A pleasure, sir," he replied as he turned the knob and pushed the door open.

Adrien stepped through onto another catwalk, much like the one he had just left. Open before him stood a room like the last, only bigger and quieter. There were a handful of men moving about on the floor with tools in hand. In the middle of the massive space, a machine of extraordinary dimensions glowed like a full moon.

Elon, the Chief Engineer, stood in the middle of the floor in the shadow of the great machine. His eyes were sunken and dark-rimmed from living on three hours of sleep a night and one meal a day, if he was lucky. His own family hadn't seen him for weeks, but it was worth it if he could get the job done. He knew the consequences of failure and the rewards of success.

When he saw Adrien approaching, he straightened his cloak and swallowed hard. The Chancellor seldom came to the factory himself; he preferred to send Doyle to do his dirty work.

"Sir, this is, well, a surprise."

A sneer spread across Adrien's face. "Hopefully not a bad surprise, Elon. I thought it was time I came to see how things are going. Maybe offer a little encouragement. You know, leadership and all."

Elon forced a smile. "Yes, of course. And I appreciate it. We are moving right along—"

Adrien interrupted. "But it could always be faster, right?"

Sweat beaded on Elon's brow. Clueless about how to respond, he blurted out, "I… I don't think so, sir. We're running on all cylinders and burning out the workers left and right. Not to mention, we need more magicians to fuel the amphoralds."

Adrien leaned in. Elon could smell hate on his breath. "Is that right?"

"Nothing like this has ever been done before, sir. With all due respect, we have the best of Arcadia working this project. It will be done, and soon. More importantly, it will be the greatest technological feat since before the Age of Madness—hell, maybe ever. You will not regret the care we're putting into it."

Adrien lowered his voice and inched closer to Elon's face. They were nearly nose to nose. "Had a nice talk with your son, Gregory. Smart boy. Must make you proud."

Elon looked down. "He does, sir."

"I mean the kid is shit with physical magic, but his aptitude for technology is off the charts—not that that should surprise us, with his bloodline and all. Maybe he could help speed things up." As Adrien said this, he looked down at the young man chained to the machine. The man had a day to live, maybe only hours.

Elon swallowed hard. "That won't be necessary, sir"

Adrien smiled. "That's really your choice. Pick up the pace, or Gregory and the rest of your spawn will pay the penalty for your failure. I'm running out of engineers, but I will replace you if I must. So get your damned head out of your ass and get this thing done. There isn't much time."

Elon nodded, knowing that the man wasn't bluffing. "As you say, sir. I am yours to command."

Gregory moved out of the doorway and took a chair in the circle. What he was about to do would change his entire life, and that of his family.

"I know exactly what it is. I just didn't think it was possible." His hands shook. "My father, he's Arcadia's Chief Engineer. He's been working on some all-consuming project for months. I mean, we almost never see him, and when he was home, he just holed up in his office.

"One day, after he had been called away for an emergency meeting, I got curious, so I snuck into his office and looked at the plans laid out on the table." Gregory shook his head. "I thought it was just theoretical. You know, a work of his imagination. Never thought he could…" He trailed off.

Ezekiel spoke, his voice both calm and urgent at once. There was a certain resonance that could convince a whore to go holy. "What was it, son?"

Gregory's eyes scanned the room. "You're right, it's a weapon, but not what you think. It has the power to blast entire cities back into the Dark Ages. To wreak more havoc than the world has ever seen."

Karl's eyes narrowed. "Aye, but a weapon like that would be massive. How could they move such a weapon beyond the walls of the city?"

The blood drained from Gregory's face. "That's the thing. The weapon is more than some kind of cannon. They're building an airship. A mighty, flying fortress that will be able to rain down the fires of hell on anyone, anywhere. It's a flying apocalypse."

As Gregory finished, a silence filled the room. Everyone knew what they were up against now. Adrien was a powerful sorcerer, with the wealth and resources of an entire city behind him. On top of that, he had a weapon like something made of legends at his disposal.

"Then it's settled." Her voice was no more than a whisper, but everyone turned to Hannah as if she were speaking through a microphone. "We have to stop him."

"I admire yer spirit, lass, but weren't ya listening to the rich kid?" Karl meant well, but his voice was harsh all the same. "It's a task that's beyond us."

"It's a task precisely *for* us. I was listening, Karl, but I didn't learn anything new. Adrien is a bastard. Airship or no, we can't leave this city in his hands. I've already lost my family to this maniac. Tonight I almost lost a friend. I don't care who we must fight or what weapons they have. Adrien will die. And I will kill him, or die trying. The question is, are any of you going to help me?"

Ezekiel smiled, admiring how much the young woman in front of him had grown. He looked around the room. No one spoke, but they didn't need to. It was clear from the determination on their faces that they would follow her to the end.

Ezekiel said a silent prayer to the Matriarch.

He thought about Lilith, and the real reason the Oracle had sent him back to Arcadia.

Adrien was evil, but he was just one hurdle on a much longer and darker path, fraught with dangers he could scarcely imagine. But even so, hope welled up inside of him. He had Hannah. And she now had her team.

Ezekiel only wished he had more time.

EPILOGUE

Alexandra's face was still covered in the blood from Jack's jugular, but she didn't care. She didn't even notice. The only thing that mattered was finding the girl, and fast.

The crowd split for her as she passed, making a path through the market toward the Boulevard. Toward her prey.

One look at her, and the henchman working the gate looked the other way, letting her step right into the quarter.

She headed straight for the seediest bar in the slums, Lloyd's. The place was packed. What men hadn't joined the ranks at the factory were getting their fill of cheap liquor before curfew set in for the night. It was a mangy group, and all eyes fastened on her as she entered. The drunks lining the bar sobered up at the sight of the gorgeous woman drenched in dried blood.

"I'm looking for the Unlawful named Hannah. Anyone with information should speak now."

And just like that, all eyes dropped to the bar.

Alexandra walked up to the man on the end closest to her. She raised her voice. "Anyone?"

Lloyd's had never been quieter.

She raised one hand in the air and stroked her fingers. Her eyes turned black, and one by one her fingernails grew in length.

Then, with one quick motion, she grabbed the man in front of her by his long, tangled tuft of hair, pulled back his head, and plucked his eye from its socket.

A collective gasp filled the bar as he clapped a hand over the place his eye had been only a second a before.

Blood seeped between his fingers. He fell off his stool and stumbled out of the bar, screaming.

She held the eye in her hand, examining it like it was a rare stone before dropping it on the dirty ground. Then she stepped forward and glanced at the next man along the bar. "I'll say it again. I'm looking for the Unlawful named Hannah. I have all night, and I just *love* the color red."

As she reached for the next man's head, a voice rang out from across the room.

It was the bartender. "There were some strangers in here tonight. They might be the lead you're looking for."

Alexandra smiled. Lightning began to crackle along the palm of her hand. "Tell me everything."

FINIS

REARICK

(Artwork by Eric Quigley)

REMNANT

(Artwork by Eric Quigley)

I finished my draft of *Reawakening* the day after *Restriction* came out. My wife and I had just left a baby shower for our soon to be first child, and we talked the whole way home about how much love and support we felt from our friends and family...then I checked to see how my new book was doing and I nearly hit the floor. The support and positive feedback from readers like you was overwhelming, more than I had yet to experience as an author—and it was only the second day.

Now, almost a week later, as we put the finishing touches on *Reawakening*, *Restriction* already has more reviews than any book I've ever written. It's mind blowing, and I have you all to thank.

And I'm doing my best to put those reviews to work. Even though book two was almost finished when your reviews came in (sorry, we were trying to move fast!), we've started shaping book three (*Rebellion*) around your feedback.

Hannah's team has come together, and now it's time for her to start taking the fight to Adrien. *Rebellion* has more humor, more explanations on how magic fits with the rest of the Kurtherian Gambit Universe, more well-earned ass kicking, and way more

Sal. It's been my favorite book so far (although I say that about whatever project we're working on).

I hope you'll like it, but leave us a review for *Reawakening*, and we'll try our best to follow course. In my mind, Hannah and friends are as much your characters now as they are mine.

Peace,

Lee

PS

As I'm writing this, my cat has completely passed out on my lap, which means I won't be moving off the couch anytime soon. That works for me. I've got plenty more of Hannah's story left to tell. The plan is to have four books out by the time the baby comes in May, which is an intense schedule for me as I juggle work and other responsibilities with my part-time writing. Maybe I'll get a break when we have the baby...that's how it works, right? Babies give you more time to write?

Oh shit. My wife is shaking her head no. So I better write like the devil now.

Later

PPS

One of these days I'll learn how to get all of my thoughts down on the first go. If you want to chat, we'd love to hear from you over on the Age of Magic Facebook page (I'm very interested to see fan theories about where The Rise of Magic is going or how you all think it connects back to previous arcs). Or you can find me on Twitter @lebarbant. I spend most of my free time there, looking at and posting cat photos.

Want a free book from Chris and Lee? Sign up for their newsletter and get a copy of The Devil's Due:
https://www.subscribepage.com/chris_and_lee

When I signed my name on the dotted line to join the Kurtherian Gambit Universe, I knew it was going to be a wild ride. I'd seen Michael's success in the original series, and I heard of his voracious fans—but I wasn't ready for the support and engagement I have received from the family!

In all honesty, I thoroughly expected that the overwhelming response from TKG readers would be troubling. I mean, hell, we're shoving the storyline 300 years (or so) into the future, we're introducing brand new characters with brand new stories, and we're playing with the ideas that those pesky little nanocytes and the Etheric power could *actually* change humans into magicians and fuel magical devices—not to mention altering human physical characteristics.

When we kicked around the idea, the three of us thought... this is badass.

And then I realized, "The fans are going to freaking eat us alive!"

Over the past week, a LOT of feedback has come to us through Amazon reviews, Facebook, and email. I've been over the moon by the fact that you readers are, for the most part, totally into this new age in the TKG—and hungry for more. Thank you, thank you, thank you for giving Hannah, Ezekiel, and the rest of the Arcadian crew a shot.

Now... there's also a bunch of folks who are skeptical about this future fantasy world, the seeming disconnection from weres and vamps, and a ton of unanswered questions of how we got here! If you were looking for instant answers, sorry for that. BUT there are answers to your questions. We promise we didn't ruin the end of Bethany Anne or Michael's stories (no way Michael would have let us do that). And if you stick around and watch the Age of Magic develop, you'll learn more and more about how it connects with each book and have some ass-kicking fun along the way.

There is one more group... For those of you who have no idea about this Kurtherian Gambit Universe... welcome! We tried to do what we could to have the books be able to stand on their own, and thankfully, we've heard that they can. If you loved our work, you should really check out the other TKG stories. They provide the awesome backdrop to everything we're doing in the Age of Magic.

Thanks again, everybody! Time to finish writing Book three.

Cheers,

Chris

PS

My twelve-year-old daughter Simone started a novel this weekend. She's had her share of false starts. Since she's 6,000 words in, I think this one just might take. She said she wants to write in the TKG someday... Be warned!

Want a free book from Chris and Lee? Sign up for their newsletter and get a copy of The Devil's Due:
https://www.subscribepage.com/chris_and_lee

AUTHOR NOTES - MICHAEL ANDERLE
WRITTEN 03/24/17

Wow, it is one week since I wrote the last Author Notes for Restriction, and now I am doing it again for Reawakening.

The acceptance of this new series has been pretty over-whelming from both a sales (but more importantly) an emotional standpoint. You see, I had no idea when working with Chris and Lee whether or not anything we did was going to resonate with the fans, you know?

When you listen to the guys talk about their experience after the first few days of the book being on sale (their podcast is here: https://itunes.apple.com/us/podcast/part-time-writers-podcast/id1092617862) you realize a couple of things…

One: They keep their expectations low, so they don't stress out too much. This was good because I was stressing out enough for the *three* of us.

Two: They have been amazed at the fans interactions. Every-thing from engaging on Facebook, to reviews, to contacting them and listening in on the podcast (link above). The guys (well, let's be honest, mostly Chris as Lee is a total Twitter twerp and doesn't join in on Facebook much at all) are so danged down to earth it's like you are working with some buddies on the weekend.

I have been allowed this opportunity to grow the TKG universe through the support of the fans, and all of us couldn't do what we do without you.

Now, what's happened in a week?

Well, let's see. The following Authors now have opportunities to write in the Age of Magic: Justin Sloan (new series, not a Reclaiming Honor spinoff), Amy Hopkins, Candy Crum, Brandon Barr and the latest is PT Hylton.

It will be fascinating to see how this group plays together as we build this time and area in Irth's history.

Please, if you get a chance, welcome these authors into the Kurtherian Gambit universe. For some of them, access to you, the TKG Fans, is going to change their lives in amazing ways!

Ad Aeternitatem,
  Michael

CONNECT WITH THE AUTHORS

Receive updates from Oz by registering your holo/ email address here:
ellleighclarke.com

Facebook:
http://www.facebook.com/ellleighclarke/

Michael Anderle Social

Website:
http://kurtherianbooks.com/

Email List:
http://kurtherianbooks.com/email-list/

Facebook Here:
https://www.facebook.com/TheKurtherianGambitBooks/

Made in the USA
Monee, IL
13 May 2022